THE LOVE OF WOMEN

Denise Neuhaus was born near Woodbridge in Suffolk and raised in Houston, Texas. She has degrees in Economics, French and Creative Writing. She has worked as a freelance journalist and has contributed short stories to magazines and anthologies, including *First Fictions: Introduction 11*, published by Faber and Faber. She now lives in London.

The Love of Women

DENISE NEUHAUS

faber and faber

LONDON · BOSTON

First published in 1993
by Faber and Faber Limited
3 Queen Square London WC1N 3AU

Phototypeset by Intype, London
Printed in Great Britain by Clays Ltd, St Ives plc

A CIP record for this book is available from the British Library

ISBN 0–571–16953–8

2 4 6 8 10 9 7 5 3 1

For my sisters
With love and thanks to Louise

I finished writing, pushed my chair back, and surveyed the disorder of my desk. Mounds of papers lay undisturbed against the wall, entrenched as a squatters' camp: scribbled notes, memos, photocopies, files. Day after day I cleared a path to an ashtray overflowing with smouldering cigarettes, yellow-tinged and lined with the faded pink of my lipstick.

My report was now finished, two weeks overdue. I didn't care. I was a marketing consultant and I hated it. I picked up my report and walked slowly down the hall, past other offices, where industrious heads bent over neat desks. I had been one of those once.

I was supposed to be happy. I had a real apartment, with a separate bedroom and a kitchen with a sink. I was well-paid, single, professional. But I had to drag myself out of bed every day. I came home every night thinking, *What I need is a drink.*

I walked up the stairs to my boss's office and stopped to chat with Elaine, his secretary. She glanced at me and turned some pages on her desk upside down. I looked past her into the office. The door was closed, but through the glass I could see some sort of meeting going on inside.

'Think they're likely to go on much longer?' I leaned against the filing cabinet and flipped the pages of my report.

I usually spoke with the secretaries in a familiar and bored tone meant to imply, *Isn't-this-place-a-grind?* and *Wouldn't-you-rather-be-somewhere-else?* It was an attempt at female comradeship, disguising a plea: don't hate me; I'm really just like you. But they smelled my hypocrisy immediately. They knew they terrified me.

Secretaries could arrange and cancel meetings that would make the difference to a promotion. They could deliver messages late, put typing at the bottom of the pile, make well-placed observations of minor and major mistakes. I had never had to work with people who could control my life to that extent.

'Could,' Elaine said, in a not particularly friendly way, and turned back to her word processor.

I looked past her again. Inside, my boss was sitting in his leather chair. I could only see the side of his face, his balding temples, his aviator glasses. The glasses were a new addition which I attributed, along with some sporty new suits, to a mid-life crisis.

Surrounding his desk were three men. Personnel, the least senior one, was taking notes. The two from Admin were looking through files. They were all turned slightly away and didn't notice me.

I couldn't imagine what they were doing there. Normally my boss couldn't spare a minute for any of them. He was a high-flyer, bringing home bonuses twice his salary. He had complete contempt for administrators.

He had hired me, I found out afterwards, against Personnel's wishes. My boss had liked that I had 'proven entrepreneurial drive', that I had run my own business, an art gallery and café. But of course the others were right, they knew I would never fit in.

I had sold the gallery, rashly I now saw. I had thought what I needed was a corporate hierarchy. I was tired of being responsible; I wanted to follow orders. I wanted to be able to open a file called 'Firm Policy' which would tell me what to do. I wanted a pension plan and medical insurance, a regular pay cheque.

I had begun determined and optimistic; now I made stupid, unthinking errors. I realized that I was not cut out for salaried employment, but it was too large a mistake to admit.

I watched as my boss reached for his cigarettes and shook one out. He held it, looking for his lighter, opening and closing the drawers of his desk. Finally he found it and, holding it up to his cigarette, struck the flint several times. A flame appeared and I saw his hand was shaking. Then I knew what this meeting was about, and why Elaine had turned those papers over so quickly. The meeting was about me. I was going to be fired.

They didn't fire people easily in that firm, especially not women. There were so few, and they were afraid of law-suits. They liked to amass evidence. Suddenly, I saw with clarity the past months fuse together: they had been build-ing a file on me, probably at the instigation of Personnel, who had spies.

I turned abruptly around and went downstairs to my office. I began going through my desk. I was completely calm; my inertia had suddenly lifted. I glanced at each file and fed it to the shredder. I pulled out packs of cigarettes, my good pen, a box of tissues, my calculator and my pocket dictionary. I felt almost light-headed with decisiveness.

A few minutes later, the telephone rang. I went upstairs, I went into his office, I was fired.

Not that quickly, of course. He hemmed and hawed. He asked me if I would go out to lunch with him. This I declined. I didn't want to be pumped full of rare steak and burgundy when I was fired. I wanted to be lean and hungry. He asked me how my report was going. Finally, he said, 'Look here, Kris, just how well are you getting on here?'

I didn't answer.

3

'I mean, you don't seem very happy. You don't seem to be giving it your all.'

'No,' I said.

He looked relieved at this agreement. He took off his aviators and rubbed his eyes. 'I've been wondering just how much you really want to stay here.'

I decided I wanted to make him suffer a little more, so I did not reply. He offered me a cigarette and we sat smoking for a minute.

'Do you want me to resign?' I said.

'No, no. I want to know what we in the firm can do for you to make your . . . To help you . . .'

I could have forced him to give me another month or two. I could have told him I was having a crisis, personal problems, whatever. I could have said I needed the money, which was true. But I didn't want to drag it out. 'Look, Harry, let's just call it quits. I don't want to work here any more. You don't have to fire me. I quit. Today.'

I caught an uptown train home, something I'd never done on a weekday afternoon. I watched the unfamiliar stream of diverse, normal life: tired women with heavy shopping, idle young men, old people, students, the homeless collecting newspapers. I was no longer part of the morning and evening tribe of blue and grey suits.

I walked down 35th, and slowly up the stairs to my apartment.

I made a pitcher of dry martinis, without olives or lemon. I drank the entire thing, nearly a half-bottle of gin, and ate a box of crackers and a wedge of very old Brie. I was twenty-nine years old, divorced, with an MBA and a first-class honours degree from the University of London, few savings, no job, no ambitions and no prospects. For someone who started out with such a bang, I had suddenly come to a screeching halt. At about 11.30, I fell on to my bed still in my suit, in a drunken stupor, and didn't wake for ten hours.

I opened my eyes, looked at the ceiling and decided to go home. *Home*, I thought, dejectedly, I suppose I'll go *home* – as if to say, I suppose I'll go on welfare; I suppose I'll get married. I had nowhere else to go, and I needed time to recuperate, rebuild my strength. The people I had sub-let from were due back in three weeks and I knew I was in no shape to find both a job and an apartment that quickly.

I hung up my suit and brushed the fuzz from my teeth.

I looked in the mirror. I had been unemployed for less than twenty-four hours and already I looked like a bag lady. You're homeless, I told my mirror. You've lived in too many places, made too many changes, lost touch with too many people, burnt too many bridges. Going home is what you do when you don't have any money and all your plans have collapsed.

I made a cup of coffee and called my mother in Houston.

Mother worked as a receptionist in a clinic for a group of doctors. She answered the phone in her efficient, sing-song, office voice: 'Clearview Clinic.'

She had started working when my father left her, during my first year at college. I thought of her as a kind of refuge from the fifties: once an unthinking, passive housewife, and still somewhat pathetic, unwilling to take any responsibility for her life.

But when I saw her at work, she was a different person. During my last visit, two years before, I had met her for lunch. This was just after my divorce. She was a whirlwind of activity, a small, plump, middle-aged woman with neat, short hair, a practical suit and a brisk manner. If she hadn't been my mother, I would have thought her pleasant, independent, competent, overworked.

5

'Hello, Mother, Krystal here.' That was my name until I turned seventeen, graduated from high school, went to college, and changed it – legally – to Kristina. Krystal always made me think of country-western stars, the Grand Ole Opry, white cowgirl boots and mechanical bulls, Cadillacs with long horns on the grill.

'Hello, dear,' she said in a surprised voice. This was a bad sign. When she sounded surprised, it was because she didn't want to be bothered.

'Are you busy?'

'Well, no,' she said uncertainly, meaning yes. 'Not *really*.'

'Well, say so if you are.'

'No, I have a *few* minutes.'

'All right, well, I thought I might come down for a couple of days or a week to visit. I have some time off, and I want to get out of New York.'

'Oh.'

'Well, if it's a problem, just say so. If you're busy, I understand. I don't want to be in your way.'

'Oh, no, I'm not too busy,' she said in her hesitant, abstracted way, very polite, as if she couldn't imagine how she could possibly put me up. I nearly said, oh, forget it. I wondered how many children had parents who actually resisted visits, particularly when they were few and far between. 'It's fine. If this is a particularly good time for you.'

'Look, Mother, if it isn't a good time for *you*, just say so.'

'It's fine for me, as long as it's fine for you.'

No, I just called for the hell of it. 'Yes, Mother. All right; I'll book a flight for tomorrow night. I'll call you back with the details.' I paused, then added, 'Do you think you can pick me up at the airport?'

'At the airport?'

'Yes.' *You know, where the planes land.* 'Unless, of course,

6

you can't; I could take a cab.' There were no buses to Clearview, and she knew a taxi would be ludicrously expensive.

'Of course I'll pick you up,' said Mother doubtfully.

'Don't worry, I won't arrive till the evening.'

After we hung up, I called a travel agent. It was $300 round-trip or $210 one-way. I looked at my bank statement: $1,000. Where had all my money gone? I booked a one-way ticket for the following evening.

I had only clothes to pack. I cleaned up the apartment, paid a couple of bills, went to the bank. The next afternoon I locked the door, left the keys with the super, and caught a Cary bus to La Guardia.

It takes less than three hours to fly from New York to Houston but it feels like flying to a different continent. No matter how hot it is in New York (this was May), no matter how swollen your feet get in flight, or how stuffy the plane, nothing prepares you for the wall of heat upon disembarking. It was so humid, I could hardly breathe.

Mother was waiting at the gate. She seemed to have both shrunk and widened. My mother was becoming a box. She was wearing working clothes: navy skirt, tailored striped shirt. She held a straw bag with a bamboo handle that was too big for her. As I approached, my steps slowed: surprise and an involuntary reflex I recognized a little shamefully as distaste made me draw back. In only two years her eyes had become dim and watery, her hair grey, her skin puffy and sagging. My mother had aged, and not very gracefully. I now saw her as she would be in the years to come, more and more like this, a little old lady, dwindling next to her big handbag.

I gave her a brief peck on the cheek. 'Hello, Mother.' I took out my ticket and baggage claim.

'It's so nice to see you,' she said uncertainly.

'Yes, well, thanks for having me. I simply had to get out of New York. I thought I would relax a little, sew a few things.'

This was to stave off explanations for a while. It was absolutely plausible that I would take a week off work to sew. Mother and I were fanatical seamstresses, although very different in method. Mother followed the instructions on the pattern envelope to the letter. I altered, and mixed the pieces of several patterns and fabrics to create new designs; I found this very therapeutic. After Tomas and I broke up, while I was trying to think of something to do with myself, I bought an enormous amount of fabric and sat down for a month and sewed.

We got my baggage. Outside it was sweltering, even though it was nearly 8 o'clock in the evening and the sky was dusky and edged with rose. The car was like a sauna and we had to open all the doors and windows to let it air before getting in.

As we drove off, I remarked on the heat. Mother replied with the vague, slightly surprised tone that irritated me so much, 'Oh. Yes, I suppose it *is* warm.'

I sighed and asked her about her job. It was, she said, fine. She worried about her future from time to time, of course. If anything ever happened to this job, nobody else would hire her at her age. She was grateful to have it . . .

As usual this sort of talk made me aggressive. 'Well,' I interrupted, 'I've just quit mine.'

She stared at the road ahead, clearly alarmed at the prospect of my having dropped in on her permanently.

'I may go back to New York,' I reassured her. 'I haven't decided yet.' She didn't know how little money I had, so she did not question this. She was probably afraid to ask more.

We drove through a myriad network of freeways, very fast and at never more than a few feet from another car. I thought of Houston as an unplanned sprawl of buildings, with no downtown to walk and shop in. There were only malls and freeways, on which people drove eighty miles an hour.

I stared out the window. I had forgotten how much of this city existed in the air, suspended at freeway-level: forests of signs hovered from the tops of towering poles; an aged grand piano sagged on the roof of its home; a pick-up truck leaned precariously from an elevated platform; a grizzly holding a rifle stared out of a glass showcase above a sign, TEXAS GUN SUPPLY; a church steeple grazed the freeway edge. I began to have doubts about having come. I had forgotten how much I detested the place. It was so *ugly*.

I waited somewhat resentfully for Mother to ask me why I quit my job, but, of course, she wasn't going to. I felt that she had never shown anything but a passing interest in my life.

She said, 'I've made up the other room for you.' Mother still lived in the cramped two-bedroom tract house my father had dumped us in when I was in high school. The house was the only settlement she had got out of the divorce. She should have got half of everything but, typically, Mother had a bad lawyer, and my father had a good one.

The drive took nearly two hours. As we left the city, clusters of dingy green road signs and swarms of abruptly merging lanes gave way to a ribbon of freeway rolling through long stretches of scrub prairie. Cheap new buildings sprouted at irregular intervals alongside the remains of old ones: dilapidated and newly built shopping malls, abandoned houses, video rental stores, truck stops, windowless warehouses, massive furniture outlets, country-western clothing discount centres. We drove on and on, south, towards the Gulf, past relentless freeway construction, bulldozers, banks of gravel and dirt, and these sights repeated themselves, littering the dull landscape. It was all depressingly familiar, yet strange and new and alarming: it had grown, like mould, as if I had opened the refrigerator one day and suddenly realized all this haphazard, aimless life had been spreading while I had been busy elsewhere.

After an hour or so, sub-divisions began to appear, grids of streets, new houses and construction sites, signs announcing NEW MID-PRICED HOMES, freshly paved exits with unfamiliar names. We passed these clean, comfortable neighbourhoods and drove off the freeway at our old and decrepit exit, for Mother's was one of the first suburbs built, and then through a pair of brick walls that said CL AR on one side and V EW on the other.

The exit took us over the railroad track and past sights of heart-sinking familiarity: the ageing Clearview shopping centre, an enormous water tower the colour of lichen, a field of scattered oil rigs, the local water-treatment plant.

The houses looked even smaller and shabbier than I remembered: low-roofed, of crumbling brick, built on stilts to withstand the regular flooding. In Mother's next-door neighbour's yard was a dismantled sail-boat rusting on to a trailer. We pulled into the gravel drive. Mother's garage door was lowered half-way at an angle, as if it were stuck (it was). Just inside the angled door I could see a rusted washer and drier on a strip of blackened carpet, a lawn-mower and various tools lying about.

We got out. Garbage cans lay in the ditch. The lawn needed mowing and the shutters painting. The screen across the front door was ripped.

We went in and I put my bags into my old bedroom. It all seemed worse than before: the dark blue wallpaper, in a design of sailing ships, now peeling; the scratched end-table wedged between twin beds; the yellow, plastic-framed photographs of my sister Alicia and of me at our high-school graduations.

I washed my hands in the bathroom and then joined Mother in the kitchen, where she was making a salad.

I looked in the fridge for the ubiquitous supermarket white wine and poured us each a glass. Mother was never without a full stock of cheap Chablis. When we sat down to our salad, I asked her if she had plans for the weekend. 'I thought we might go fabric shopping,' I suggested.

'Fine . . . The only thing I have to do is go to my women's group Saturday night.'

'Oh, do you still do that?' This group consisted of divorced women about Mother's age, most of whom had been deceived and defrauded by their husbands and were very bitter about it. I had gone with her to one of their meetings the last time I visited. As far as I could see, the group's purpose was to drink as much as possible and rant about men.

'Well, yes, although it's changed, of course.'

I laughed. 'You mean, you've mellowed.'

'Well, I suppose you could say that,' said Mother defensively.

'May I come?'

'If you would like to.'

'Yes, I would.' I wanted to see these embittered women again, now tempered by time. I thought of them as a generation of casualties. They had dropped out of college to get married, moved to the suburbs, raised their children according to Dr Spock, and probably agreed with their husbands that women's liberation was something for ugly spinsters and hardened lesbians. Then their husbands ran off with younger women, leaving them without a penny. By that time Betty Friedan and Simone de Beauvoir had been sufficiently diffused and refashioned; suburban feminism was born.

They loved me, of course. I was in the process of getting a

11

divorce, for one thing, a state close to their hearts. For another, I was educated, had financial independence, no children, my own business, had lived abroad. I was the new woman. They fawned over me and over Mother, as if she were about to receive a medal for having produced me.

Now, sitting across from her at the kitchen table, I reflected that she probably hadn't the faintest idea what to say to me. I thought of my life as outside her own, full of the unexpected. This latest event was beyond her interpretation. She was probably wondering what I was doing here.

I wondered myself. I had done this, like so much in my life, on impulse. I poured a second glass of wine. *I just need a bit of time*, I told myself in a brisk voice. *An address to receive mail, a phone, a word processor to type up a c.v.* I would be out of here in a matter of weeks.

2

I woke up conscious of several things. My back hurt, the
bed sagged in the middle, there were small blue sailing
ships on the walls. A musty smell pervaded the room and
my mind, familiar and unwanted, suggesting old furniture,
unwashed linen, undisturbed corners, mouldy tiles, defec-
tive plumbing, my childhood.

I listened for a moment. The house was silent.

I put on my dressing gown and slippers, padded out to
the kitchen. The only noise was the fluttering of the air
conditioning. Outside it was already brilliantly sunny.
Despite the tacky, cheap surroundings, the early morning
stillness and serenity calmed me, as if assuring me that
anything was still possible.

The chocolate-brown wall-to-wall shag compressed
under my feet. It felt matted, impregnated with dirt, almost
organic. I recalled how it would fluff up a bit if vacuumed
vigorously, but not for long. It camouflaged anything on the
floor. I had forgotten this last time and, crossing the room,
felt the hideous quivering of a large cockroach skate across
my bare foot. As a child luxury meant to me white carpet,
hardwood floors, cleanliness, going barefoot indoors. I
dreamed of a life without shaking out my clothes before
dressing, inspecting the toilet before using it, smelling
omnipresent insecticide, storing every bit of food in airtight
containers. I wanted airy rooms, bowls of fruit. I wanted to
open a cupboard and not see tracks of cockroach droppings.

I put coffee and a filter in the machine and added water. I
took a dishcloth, went outside and wiped the dew off one of

Mother's plastic garden chairs. I sat down and lit a cigarette. The grass was deep and green and glistening; the temperature was just beginning to rise. A neighbourhood cat appeared from behind the magnolia and made its way gingerly through the stalks of grass, ignoring me, but alert, ready to streak away at my slightest movement.

I smoked my cigarette, delaying the moment I would open the patio door, pour coffee and hear my mother call out from her bed, as she always did during my visits. *Do I smell coffee?*

I pushed my hair back, already limp from the humidity, remembering how I had washed my face three times a day as a teenager and my hair nightly. I still made an effort to keep fresh and groomed during my visits and I always ended up wilted and sweaty. It made me think of the English in tropical colonies, not letting themselves go. I knew I would iron my shirts, bathe and make myself up carefully, brush my hair back, and within seconds the insidious heat would seep through and reduce me to despair.

Why did I never remember this until I was here?

I thought about taking a walk; regular walks made me feel better about everything. I smoked less, drank less coffee, had more energy. Then I had a vision of walking through streets and streets of cheap houses up to a shopping centre of Pizza Hut, Wendy's Burgers, Safeway, Colleen's Gift Shop, Nails by Arlene and Video-to-Go. I reached into my pocket for another cigarette.

I knew that very soon I would go in, Mother would get up, and we would drink two or three cups of coffee over a breakfast of toasted white bread, margarine and jam. We would get dressed and go fabric shopping. We would have lunch somewhere, or at home. Then we would change and go to her women's group. Beyond that, I could not see.

For the first time in my life I didn't know what was going to happen next.

My father began the process of leaving my mother when I was sixteen, and from then on I knew what would happen. Not the specifics, of course. I didn't know he would eventually live in a two-storey, six-bedroom, white-columned, mock plantation house in a lakeside 'recreational community' with a wife my age and two young children. I didn't know my mother would be a medical receptionist living from pay cheque to pay cheque in a crumbling tract house. But I knew well enough.

Alicia and I loved their break-up; we'd never had such freedom. My father came home less and less, each time following the same routine. He would walk in and dump two or three or four days' laundry on the living-room floor. Mother would follow him around the house.

If you would just talk to me, we could work out our problems. He always went into the bathroom, ignoring her. He would lock the bathroom door and she would stand outside, shouting over the spraying water. *Why are you doing this to me? Just tell me what I've done. Talk to me, honey. Whatever it is, I'm sorry! Please forgive me!*

We would steal Mother's car keys from her purse and sneak out. We knew from experience it would take at least another two hours for our father to shave, shower, primp and pack clean clothes. We did not want to watch this: it sickened us.

In the car, we giggled and imitated Mother in an histrionic voice: *Please forgive me!* We knew of course that we did not enter into the picture. Mother did not care that my father hardly ever noticed us, except when we disturbed him. He had never shown more than an erratic interest in the house, mowing the lawn or painting when the mood struck; and in the family, taking us places only if it suited him.

When we got back, our father's car would have disappeared, and Mother would be washing clothes. She would look up at us, vague and distracted, forgetful, taking refuge in the lies she had led her life by: *Oh, hello girls. I'm just doing the wash. Your father's had to go out.* We would flee to our room, rolling our eyes at each other; we felt no pity, only disgust.

One night we came in and she was sitting on the sofa. Stacks of clothes and books were piled on the chairs and on one end of the sofa, leaving only one place to sit, next to her. She looked up at us, her hands folded in her lap. *He won't even sit next to me.* She looked at us with something like triumph, as if she had finally proven something. *I put something on every chair so that he would have to sit here, but he wouldn't even sit down. He just stood. He wouldn't sit next to me.*

I had a driver's licence by then; Alicia was fourteen.

Sometimes we drove down to a yacht marina in Seagate and walked on the pier, smoking and looking at the boats. Alicia was still a beginner at smoking and got nicotine on her fingers and lips. This irritated me enormously, seeing the yellowish-brown stains. She would press her lips together, to hide them from me.

We talked; I, about later, after high school. I knew, of course, already. I knew for me it would be college, Europe, a glamorous job, an interesting man, travel, independence, all far away from this life. I didn't know how I would do it, but I knew.

Alicia never saw beyond the small world of her immediate surroundings. She collected porcelain cats, with smiling or mischievous faces and iridescent ribbons around their necks, lined up on an old wooden shelf on the wall. Her half of the room was crowded with possessions: old records in a wooden fruit crate – Rita Coolidge, Judy Collins, Leonard Cohen; a mirror draped with scarves and beads; a chipped Blue Willow platter filled with cheap chains and rings; a lace tablecloth over her bedspread. My side was functional, empty but for clothes: I was in transit.

Alicia did not talk about herself; I talked and she replied. I tried out ideas on her, practised different selves. I wanted to do everything, thought I could do anything.

Alicia had no opinions about what I should or could do, and if I pressed her she would shrug her shoulders and mutter, *I don't know, I guess so.* My dreams were so far beyond her expectations, she could not imagine them.

Occasionally her dullness irritated me and I would demand to know her plans, her goals. *Don't you want to do anything? Don't you want to be something? Don't you want to get out of here?* She would look up in alarm, trapped, knowing she was about to fail some test.

Out of where?

Here. A wave of the hand. *The house, Clearview. Houston.*

I don't think I'd like travelling.

You want to spend the rest of your life here?

I don't know. Intransigent, stubborn; yet wilful, since I knew that deep down she understood my urgency, but refused to acknowledge it. She said sometimes, *I don't know why you hate it so much.*

And once, when she said, *I don't want to do what you do,* I thought: she will rebel in the most stupid way, against anything I do. She would only resist challenge, oppose change. I knew I would do what I set out to and she would never do anything.

She was prettier than I, but hers was a beauty which would fade quickly after eighteen or nineteen. She did not

17

have my good bones, my thick, mahogany hair. She was short, and would have weight problems later. She was not as good at school as I, not because she was less intelligent, but because she lacked my discipline. She only did well at what she enjoyed – art – and was even languid about that, drawing animals and trees in a juvenile, comic-strip fashion. It was the only thing she could do, and so she was tagged; it became a family axiom. I was good at school. And Alicia? My mother would roll her eyes in despair, surrender to forces beyond her control. *Well,* she would say with bitter irony at the worthlessness of such a child, *she can draw.*

It would not have surprised me to be told that Alicia would end up in a rotting apartment complex called Chateau Estates, five miles from Mother's, trying to keep off drugs, working various crummy jobs; when I came home from New York, Mother told me she was working the graveyard shift as a taxi dispatcher.

I would have taken almost any ticket out, although by the time I was a senior in high school I knew it would be college. Before then, I wanted to go to New York and be a model. I was tall, thin and large-boned. I knew I was not *beautiful*: I knew my limitations. I analysed my angular face and short forehead, and saw that my eyes were good, my mouth sensual, my hair glossy. I knew I had to make the most of what I had.

At twelve, I began reading magazines passionately: *Seventeen, Mademoiselle, Vogue, Cosmopolitan, Glamour.* My best friend Madeline and I went to her house after school – her mother worked and we wanted privacy – where we carried our elaborate beauty rituals. We steamed our faces, and applied oatmeal and cucumber and honey masks; washed out hair with egg and beer and avocado and rolled it in pink foam rollers. We gave ourselves pedicures and rubbed our feet with pumice stones. We even dyed our hair once, with washable jet-black dye, and shampooed it out before 5 o'clock, when Madeline's mother came home.

I liked Madeline's house. Her parents had new furniture, from Sears, and everything matched. They had a set of green ashtrays shaped like leaves, in descending size, each nesting inside the next. On one wall were two flags crossed, Confederate and US, surrounded by photographs of someone in her family who had died in the civil war. There was a wooden sign which said THE SOUTH WILL RISE AGAIN.

Madeline's parents drank and smoked, even though they were Baptists, and pretended not to when their preacher came to visit. They threw card parties and danced in the evenings to Nat King Cole and Frank Sinatra. Her father would pinch her mother suddenly and she would squeal and slap his hand. Madeline used bad language in front of them and her mother would shout at her in a kind of off-hand indignation that provoked Madeline further. Once, her mother picked up the fly-swatter and chased her around the house, whacking the air. I loved their unpredictability, their inconsistency. My parents considered them vulgar.

Madeline was short, petite, blonde, blue-eyed: everything I was not. She started her periods early, wore a bra first, went steady first. There was not a time that boys were not after her.

We lived in the city then, in a new sub-division, two streets away from Madeline's family. Madeline and I had known each other since first grade; we did everything together. We went on vacation with each other's families, we walked to elementary school together, and, later, took the bus to junior high together. We smoked Madeline's parents' cigarettes in the safety of her nicotine-tainted house. We became lovers.

We didn't know what lovers were then; we were thirteen. We hid the passion of our kisses and caresses behind the fantasy that one of us was a boy and the other a girl, and that this game, in which we took turns, was merely practice for what would come later. We did not know that we loved.

Trapped as children are by cliché, I was more often the boy, as I was large and flat-chested. I tired of this, but when I protested Madeline persuaded me to carry on, as I was so good at 'being a boy'. This meant, good at initiating sexual play, creating new, teasing, erotic games. It was true: I loved her body. I never ceased to delight in it.

But times were changing. We turned fourteen and the importance of competition for boys made us both feel we were indulging in embarrassing, juvenile play. The possibility of not having a steady boyfriend – and the engraved ID bracelet they all gave the chosen girl to wear – produced in me shame and fear. Madeline had her choice of four or five boys, and I was left with her cast-offs, boys with braces on their teeth and sweaty hands, who settled for me with a sigh, suspecting this would always be their lot in life.

Elementary school had been simple; we were all from the same neighbourhood. There were two bad girls, who were stupid, drew on themselves with ballpoint pen and always got caught smoking and passing notes in class. There were the one or two beautiful, precious, well-groomed girls, who we hated for being stuck up. And there was Madeline and me, never the good ones, but never very bad; we could, our teachers probably said, go either way.

Junior high was full of distinctions: large, and integrated, and rich and poor, as well as black, white and Mexican. There were gangs, girls who wore heavy chains to sling in a fight, whose boyfriends were tough and carried knives. There was a group of black boys who were hip, into soul and jazz, wore Afros and called themselves 'The Soul Patrol'.

Both black and white hated Mexicans, and would defend one another against them, shouting obscenities in the street Spanish we all picked up. We feared their unfamiliar, pungent odour, their slick black hair, combed with kerosene to kill lice, their prodigious families, their Catholicism. And they in turn went out of their way to beat up anybody who appeared overly studious or ambitious, whether white or black, for their English was already marked and inferior and their destiny predictable.

And though blacks and whites mixed, our association was uneasy. The first day of school, two white kids held a black kid down and cut part of his ear off.

The girls from 'upper-middle-class' neighbourhoods belonged to country clubs and took tennis lessons; we called them 'the jets'. They wore narrow shoes trimmed with small chains, pleated skirts with matching belts and cardigans. They wore sleek pageboys and pink frosted lipstick. They would become cheer-leaders in high school and in college marry football players, for whom we had supreme contempt.

Madeline's and my neighbourhood was 'middle-class' because all the houses were brick and had garages. I was anxious about these labels; they had strict meanings. 'Lower middle-class' meant car-ports of corrugated fibreglass, wooden houses with concrete steps up to a tiny porch, air conditioners stuck into windows instead of central air conditioning. 'Lower middle-class' meant one step from the unthinkable slope descending to poor white neighbourhoods, mixed neighbourhoods, black neighbourhoods.

In school, I followed Madeline, but with caution, knowing that down her path I would only suffer. She courted danger in a way I knew I would never get away with. She relayed 'nigger' jokes her father had told her to other white kids, yet in the toilet she would share cigarettes, her comb, her make-up with black girls. She was never subservient or, like me, fearful, liberal, condescending; they liked her. She was the perfect hypocrite: she knew the safest, clearest line would be eternally drawn between her and them. I, on the other hand, felt only chance divide us.

I did not know where I belonged, which way I would turn, what to defy or value; I hovered in the middle, biding my time, waiting for a sign, wondering where my path lay.

The strictest division separated boys' and girls' activities. Girls took Home Economics and would scream with indignation if a boy came into the sewing room or the kitchen. Girls took dance; boys took track. Girls acted in the junior high-school play. The boys built the sets in woodworking class, which was taught by the football coach.

We were taught biology together, but only cell division, not reproduction. We were also taught evolution, sandwiched between obligatory warnings the teacher read out from a card that it was unproven, only a theory, that there were many opposing views.

Sex education was forced upon the school by female puberty. The girls were led into a room one day to watch a film called *It's Fun to be a Girl*; and although most of the girls were menstruating by then, we filed out afterwards in weighty silence: sex education was explosive, embarrassing, bringing forth furious letters from outraged parents.

That year the play was a melodrama, with a black-caped villain, dashing hero, beautiful heroine, and the heroine's impoverished, virtuous parents.

I got the leading role, the villain.

I had tried out, as everybody did, for the heroine. But delicate femininity would never be my gift; my height and strong voice won out. Madeline didn't get the heroine's role either: her femininity was too blatant and sexual. It went to a slight, pretty girl called Jenny whom I had hardly ever noticed, but was well-chosen and looked suitably vulnerable and desirable on stage. It was only after my initial disappointment that I realized I had the best part.

One black girl auditioned. She got to be a tree: one of several girls wearing sheets dyed brown, and holding branches to create a forest in which I appeared alone, an entire scene to myself, to plot my evil doings with only the audience as witness. No Mexicans tried out.

Our director was an enthusiastic and well-to-do matron, a substitute teacher and Girl Scout leader, and the mother of freckled, gangly Cynthia who got the worst role – the minuscule part of the hero, who was lifeless, ridiculous, wholesome and had only one good line: *Take that, you scoundrel!* ('Well, she had to give her *something*,' Madeline said to me cynically.)

Cynthia's mother had been an actress and model before her marriage, which seemed incongruous to me for a woman who went in for civic activities and Chanel suits. It worried me that such a past could lead to the predictable ending of husband, children, Girl Scouts, the junior high play.

Now I took a different bus after school, to an expensive neighbourhood called Woodland Park. Woodland Park was 'upper middle-class'; it had sprawling ranch-style houses on rolling lawns, dotted with tall pines, long, winding driveways. Behind Cynthia's house was a stone terrace, covered by a white colonial-style roof, furnished with white wicker chairs and glass-topped, wrought-iron tables. Above, mahogany ceiling fans revolved in silence. Cynthia's black maid brought out Coca-Cola and cookies on a tray while we rehearsed.

I still hung around with Madeline in my free time.

Madeline and I wore heavy eyeliner and white lipstick, black fishnet stockings and dangling earrings, although it was against school rules. We pierced our ears without telling our parents and were not allowed to see each other for a week. They made us let the punctures heal.

We rolled our skirts up by the waistband on the bus to shorten them as much as possible, and then pulled them down for gym class when the girls' coach measured us for the requisite three inches above mid-knee. We liked older boys with leather jackets from the nearby high school who drove motor-cycles and vans with tape-decks.

I began to lead a double life. I memorized my lines for the play in the evenings. I made Alicia sit on her bed with the script while I recited line after line, over and over, standing in the middle of the room, waving an imaginary cape as I threatened to foreclose Jenny's parents' mortgage and banish them to the poor-house if she did not marry me. I seized an imaginary Jenny and made as if to kiss her. We had practised what Cynthia's mother called a 'stage kiss', in which I buried my head in Jenny's neck.

I froze in this position, soon to be pushed away, waiting for Alicia to read out in her flat, uninflected voice, *Oh! Release me! Oh! What shall become of me?* I then cackled and replied as though my life depended on it, *You shall become mine yet, my pretty little bird.* Acting came easily to me.

We had a dress rehearsal. I was made up with what I learned with delight was called *pancake*, and it was indeed like pancake batter. Thick black eyeliner was drawn around my eyes, and a moustache attached with glue that smelled like spearmint. My hair was stuffed into a flesh-coloured cap and a wig pinned tightly over my head. I was slightly jealous that Jenny got to wear false eyelashes, but I got a top hat, black suit and, of course, my floor-length black cape.

24

I never missed a line; I never hesitated. From the moment I set foot on stage, I bellowed my lines towards the last row of the empty auditorium; I gloated with evil intentions. But the night of the play, I surprised even myself with the comic viciousness of my performance and my command over the audience. I inhabited, breathed, my web of deceit; I felt myself reach out and compel each person to believe in me.

At the end of the performance I bowed over and over, washed in applause, and was not surprised when Cynthia's mother brought an enormous bouquet on stage for me, for I had worked the hardest, had been in every scene, had memorized twice as many lines as the others. And I knew I had exceeded everyone's expectations. I whipped off my top hat, whirled my cape and kissed my director's hand in mock gallantry to further applause and laughter. But the best part was imagining the parents in the audience whispering, *Isn't that the girl that hangs around with the tough crowd?*

In eighth grade, we discovered drugs. Everybody did them, and those who didn't were hopeless, straight, queer. We smoke marijuana in boys' vans before school. We laughed at the anti-drug posters and films. We couldn't believe that our teachers were so stupid as to think that a film of Sonny and Cher in their fringes and beads telling us not to take drugs would have any effect. They were the sixties: flower-power, hippies, Donovan. They were *old*.

Madeline and I bought two hits of LSD and took them one night at her house when her parents were out, but after an hour nothing happened and we raided the liquor cabinet instead. We cursed the guy who had sold us the two orange dots stuck on paper and swore we'd get some real stuff next time. But I was secretly relieved.

We listened to Frank Zappa, Alice Cooper, the Stones,

Led Zeppelin, Grand Funk Railroad, Black Sabbath, Iron Butterfly. We pinned black-light posters over our bedroom walls. We wore faded bell bottoms low on our hips, T-shirts with peace symbols, men's clothes: suit vests, baggy shirts with the sleeves rolled up. We tied beaded strips of leather around our necks and wrists. We walked on the street singing 'Volunteers of Amerika!'

I managed to stay in with the hip crowd and still avoid heavy drugs. I refused to be straight, but I wasn't about to risk overdose and addiction, wreck my skin, ruin my future modelling career for the sake of getting high. I persuaded my mother to enrol me in a modelling course at a department store in the local mall.

Madeline started going out with Garth, the hippest, best-looking, richest kid in the high school. He had a downy black moustache and one pierced ear. His mother was a local television newscaster and his father an oil-man. He had a van streaked with orange flames across the sides and fitted out with quadraphonic stereo. The inside was covered, both floor and walls, with shag carpet and filled with cushions. He was a junkie.

Garth's parents gave him all the money he could ever need, but it was not enough to support his habit; he became the main dealer in the high school. It was the only reason he did not drop out, as he was old enough at seventeen to do so.

When I wasn't going to my modelling course, I rode around with Madeline and Garth and other kids, smoking joints and drinking beer. They kept me like a mascot, a kind of joke; I was the straight one. At home, I secretly practised deportment, did sit-ups, plucked the bridge of eyebrow above my nose, steamed my face, scrubbed my blackheads with a cornmeal paste.

As a hanger-on, I had to pay my way with Madeline's gang, and did so by being the one to buy syringes at the drug store. I looked the least likely of all the kids to take drugs, and relatively young for my age. Madeline looked like a cross between Jean Harlow and Marianne Faithfull. She bleached her already blonde hair nearly white, wore thigh-high black leather boots, hot pants, and a fringed leather jacket on which she had hammered silver stars in the shape of a fist with the middle finger extended.

Garth would park out of sight and I would be sent in, wearing short sleeves to demonstrate my unmarked arms. I would pick up two or three chocolate bars and a *Seventeen* magazine and go to the counter.

'And a dozen twenty cc. syringes,' I would say nonchalantly to a suspicious clerk.

'And what do you need these for?'

'Oh, my brother's a diabetic,' I would say as if by rote, impatient, uninterested, opening a chocolate bar.

In the van, I became an expert in tying people off and mainlining them. Most did it themselves, but some were cowardly, or got a kick out of me doing it, or simply had run out of veins and couldn't reach a fresh one. It was an achievement to have had all the veins in your arms collapse and have to use your feet, hands, the backs of your knees.

They called me Nurse Krystal. I cooked the powder, pulled it into the syringe, tapped it to clear the air bubbles out, tested the bulge of vein, slipped the needle in, pulled off the tie.

I always passed the chocolate bars on to whoever was not too stoned to want one. I never ate chocolate: I didn't want my skin to break out.

One day I came home from my modelling course and my

mother said, without looking at me, 'I want you to start going through your things. We're moving.'

'*What?* Moving?'

'The house is for sale.' She was standing at the kitchen counter, chopping onions for chilli. I hated her chilli. It was bland and thick and hardened in your stomach, like concrete setting. 'Your father is looking for another house.' She scraped the onions into the electric skillet and added a mound of ground beef from a white Styrafoam plate streaked with blood. She began breaking the meat up with a wooden spoon.

I was shocked, angry, dismayed, amazed. My parents had never done anything so unexpected before. We had never moved before; I could not remember when we had not lived in this house. And the last thing I wanted to do was leave Madeline, my friends, my life.

'Where?'

'Your father has decided to look in Clearview.' Her voice was without expression.

I stared at her in shock: Clearview was in the middle of nowhere, a poorish sub-division far away from the city, on the way to the beach. It was flanked by swamp, built on a cleared and filled site off the freeway, the only sub-division in a stretch of hokey little towns: Seagate, El Puerto, Beauvue, Juanita, Harmony. Its houses were brick and attached with garages, but they were jerry-built, shabby.

We sometimes stopped in Harmony, the exit after Clearview, for gas on the way to the beach. Harmony was hardly a town, just a dip in the freeway, by a canal leading down to the Gulf. Across from the gas station and restaurant stood Harmony Bait and Tackle, with its muddy parking lot and strings of blinking Christmas-tree lights. Along the decrepit pier, rusted fishing boats pulled up at an ancient gas pump. Entire families squatted on the canal, next to buckets of bait and Styrafoam ice-boxes of beer, fishing. A beach house with boarded windows, painted garish pink and covered with plastic sea-shells and fishing nets, sagged on its posts: Maybelle's, reputedly run by an ex-madam from New Orleans and now a bring-your-own-bottle night club.

We stopped in Harmony because the gas station was close to the freeway exit. Outside the restaurant was a sign: EAT AND GET GAS. A gap-toothed redneck in a dirty T-shirt would come out to our car, wiping his face with an oily bandanna, and say, 'How'r ya'll today?'

Alicia and I would scream with laughter afterwards, imitating him.

How'r ya'll today?

Why we're just right down fine. How'r ya'll?

Not too good. Got kicked by a cow this mornin' right in the hay-ed.

Now my mother was telling me we were going to move to Clearview.

'You're joking!'

She looked at me indignantly, as if she could not understand my objections. 'I am not. And you're going to like it. You're going to go to South Bay High. You ought to be glad your father and I think enough about you to move for your sake.'

I had no idea what she was talking about. My father had never given any of us enough thought to do anything for our sake. For Alicia my father felt the merest contempt; I inspired in him mild, patronizing amusement. My modelling course, the play, my good grades at school: he smiled pityingly at these childish tricks. I bored him. He once glanced in passing at a composition I was writing on the Renaissance. The encyclopedia volume *R-S* lay open in front of me. I had written at the top of the page, *The Renaissance was a time of great change in the history of man.* He stopped

29

and commented, 'My, my, what a big subject for such a little mind.' I always laughed at his jokes; I thought it was sophisticated to take cruelty in my stride.

After stopping in Harmony, my mother would glare towards the back seat at our antics with artificial disapproval. *Now stop: that isn't nice.* My father would turn his head, a narrow slice of attention, and expel air, expressing something infinitesimal – disapproval or amusement, we did not know; it did not matter much to him what we did.

'Your father and I are sick of the kind of company you keep and all this riding around you do with those kids at school. You are going to go to school with *decent* people. You needn't look like that; you think you're too smart for your own good. You think we don't know what goes on, but we're not stupid. And you are not to see that Madeline again.'

I stared at her and then walked away, towards my room. I knew by that it was some trouble Madeline had got into.

'Do you hear me?' she shouted down the hall. 'Not ever again.'

My father came home and we had one of our silent dinners, my father annoyed, as I had dared to disrupt the equilibrium of his life; my mother snippy and disgusted; Alicia, morose and guilty over nothing; and me, bored, impatient, suspicious. I kept a reserved, expressionless face, which enraged Mother. Alicia played with her food, and Mother snapped at her, which made Alicia hang her head lower and cry, always willing to take blame as her due.

It was not until I went to school the next day that I heard what had happened. Garth was barrelling down a residential street, thirty miles an hour over the speed limit, and hit a kid on a bicycle; both he and Madeline were stoned, and the van was filled with plastic bags of cut heroin, syringes, speed-soaked cottons, burnt spoons, blackened pipes, rolling papers. The kid wasn't dead, but he was in intensive care.

We moved to Clearview two weeks later, to a smaller, supposedly temporary, house. I never saw Madeline or Garth again, and I never found out whether the kid lived or not.

It never occurred to me that I would end up in London. During my one and a half years in Clearview, I lived for Paris; I dreamed of the left bank, cafés, walks along the Seine, the Louvre.

I took my first French class primarily because of the teacher, Mme Smith, which she pronounced *Smeet*, who had long, expressive hands, exquisite eyes, thick blonde bangs, and little round wire-rimmed glasses. I thought her the perfect combination of elegance and intellect. She seemed completely out of place, here at South Bay High solely for me. Indeed, she was there only because of her (American) husband (why would anybody marry an *American*, I wondered); she hated living in Houston, and could find no other job than to teach her own beautiful language to belligerent, embarrassed, indifferent fifteen-year-olds an hour's drive down the freeway.

She loved me. I threw myself into French, imagined myself to be the illustrated Dior-suited model in the slides, Mme DuPont. *Bonsoir Madame*, I whispered to myself in the halls; *Bonsoir Monsieur, Bonsoir Mademoiselle*. I rolled my r's, puckered my lips, lovingly memorized irregular verb conjugations.

Mme Smith told me about Simone de Beauvoir; I read *The Second Sex*, and did not understand a single word, but imagined myself to be a writer, independent, living in an elegant left-bank apartment with a balcony, and in love with a great European intellectual.

Coming from the city and joining school in the middle of the term, I supposed myself to be the object of much attention and curiosity. In fact, I needed to believe this in order to perfect my reserved indifference to the other students. I would not cultivate any friendships; I could not bear being rejected by country hicks; I decided to undergo this interlude with nothing less than icy dignity.

I sewed cheap cotton dresses for school. I had outgrown ragged jeans, and anyway, South Bay dress codes were more conservative and more strictly enforced. My mother gave me a paltry allowance, which I eked out by using the same patterns over and over in different fabrics. I usually rejected these dresses soon after making them and cast them off to Alicia.

We seemed suddenly to have so little money, and my father was gone a lot. We did not move from our house, as my mother had promised. I was ashamed of this life, and of my clothes, of not having a real leather handbag. But I refused to get an after-school job like the other kids: sacking groceries at Safeway, cleaning shrimp at some restaurant on the waterfront. I was in the honours programme and would never sacrifice my grades.

I tried to cultivate pride in my poverty; I imagined myself to be a starving artist or intellectual, although I could not envisage any ideal worth living in poverty for, nor could I imagine anything romantic about poverty unless it were in a garret overlooking Notre Dame. I clung to my French, to my college entrance exams, my plans to get out, get out, get out.

I would come from school, gloomy, and sequester myself in my room. Sometimes my mother would accost me in the hall. Never had I been interested in or informed of my father's whereabouts, but Mother now greeted me with, *Your father's playing tennis tonight*, or, *Your father's had car trouble and is going to stay in town tonight*.

I saw through this. I remembered Madeline once saying, *Your father's really good-looking*. I had made a face at her, surprised and revolted she could look at him in that way. I hated the idea of any physical contact with him, his perfectly manicured nails, his coiffed hair, which he combed with something greasy from a tube and dried with Mother's hair-drier. I thought his primping was a joke, and disgusting. But Madeline did make me think, perhaps women found him attractive.

It did not surprise me to discover that the move to Clearview was merely part of my father's plan to hide money, and thereby minimize the amount my mother would get in the divorce. The incident with Madeline had been a convenient pretext. He had feigned outrage, insisted to my mother they move at once. In fact, he had already picked out the Clearview house. It was far enough away that he could make excuses to stay in town. And it was cheap; he stashed the remainder of the money from the sale of the old house in a bank account in his own name.

When he left, there was $10 in their joint bank account. My mother sold her wedding silver to feed us until she found a job. Which she did, filing in an office of some kind, for $3 an hour. I never forgot that: *$3 an hour, minimum wage, my mother*. I imagined myself wading through papers in a filing cabinet day after day, watching the clock, thinking, *Now I have earned $3, now $6, now $9*. It would never happen to me.

I passed my college entrance exams, graduated and left at seventeen, bound for university on grants and a scholarship, far away from Houston, with no idea of looking back, remembering Mme Smith's last words, words of a woman who has lost something of her own, knows she will never have it back, and can only warn a younger woman with a measure of vicarious hope, 'Please, please, my dear Krystal, don't get married too quickly. And don't give up your French.'

3

'That would look nice on you,' said Mother.

We sat on adjacent stools, at the pattern counter, our feet encircled by packages. Heaped on the counter in front of us were the tattered spring/summer catalogues, and the pristine fall/winter ones. I had sat exactly like this so often as a teenager, looking through pattern books with Mother. Now it felt strange, as though it were odd that I should return to find these same catalogues – *Vogue, McCall's, Butterick* – the very ones that I sewed from in Europe, New Mexico, New York.

Mother spoke, and placed a hand abruptly between the pages of my catalogue; I turned back. Much to my surprise, she was right. It was a designer dress, with French cuffs, oversized buttons, an enormous collar that folded across the bodice, not at all something she would wear. Mother wore double-breasted suits, tailored shirts, gathered skirts, pastel blouses tied at the neck in a bow.

She had always advised me as a teenager to wear the clothes she herself would wear had she been my age: A-line skirts, shirt dresses. They had to be – her favourite words – *appropriate* and *practical*.

She would flip through the catalogues ruthlessly; these were among the few times I saw her decisive and self-assured. She could inspect, analyse and dismiss in microseconds, all accompanied by a running commentary: *Not wool, I'd have to dry-clean it; I don't want anything that has to be cut on the bias; Good Lord, all those button-holes; I've done smocking once and I'll never do it again.*

I sewed what Mother told me to sew. But I lingered over the patterns I could not, greedy and absorbed. They told me how women should look, how I wanted to look. They were my portal into another world, imports from Paris, Milan, New York. I thought of myself as living at the end of a long, disused railroad, a mining town in the wild west; the presence of these catalogues was a miracle.

I still loved pattern books. It took me hours to get through a stack. I loved every style bouncing back flamboyant and unapologetic from the past. As soon as sixties polka-dots came back, I made a *Vogue* sack dress, red with enormous fuzzy black dots. I wore forties suits in college, straight skirts and snug jackets with shawl collars; a few years later I made a fifties taffeta cocktail dress, deep green, ruched and strapless.

I never complained, as some women did, about the manipulation of designers, or the recycling of ideas nobody would have been caught dead wearing the week before. I made a black silk sheath with a transparent lace over-dress tightly buttoned at the cuffs and neck. Five years later, it was back in fashion and I made it again, having abandoned the old one in London.

Now I looked at a designer dress in the pattern book in front of me. Mother returned to her own catalogue, and, as if embarrassed by her comment, chattered as she flipped pages. *Where on earth would anybody wear that? Look at the hem on that skirt. Can you believe pedal-pushers are back?*

We had already been to three fabric stores downtown and had stopped at the local mall on the way home. I had bought crisp, gold linen for walking shorts, and pale grey silk flecked with gold for a blouse. The clerk had commented in a pleasant way on the fabric, and I had looked up, surprised. I was no longer used to such indiscriminate friendliness. I had not replied: I looked at my pattern and fabric, wrapped myself in the serenity of grey and gold, saw myself quiet, cool and untroubled.

But now I wanted to turn Mother's attention back and ask her, *Why did you say that would look good on me? Why now?* And I could not. She would only look embarrassed or annoyed and say with her habitual defensiveness, *Well, I only thought you might like it.*

She reached the end of 'Dresses', and, skipping the Designer, Bridal and Children's sections, ran her finger down the tabs to 'Co-ordinates'. She slipped her hand in and pushed the two inches of heavy glossy paper over with a slam.

I realized she had come to the end of the last of five or six catalogues while I was still on the first.

She turned two or three pages, and then said, 'Should we go home and have lunch?'

'Oh, sure, of course. If you're ready.' I realized I was staring at her and at the space just beyond, where a girl behind the counter was pulling open a pattern drawer.

It struck me as dangerous that I suddenly found my mother's view of me worthy of interest. This strange desire to shake her and demand to know what she saw when she saw me, what she thought about me, seemed as much a sign of weakening character as my dry martinis and slobbishness had in New York. I wondered where my old self had gone, my certainty.

During my last visit, out of the clear blue, my mother had asked me, shyly, with a sideways glance, 'What made you decide to take French?'

I was so surprised, I did not answer for a moment. I knew this question really meant, *Why did you turn out like this?*

I did not know the answer to Mother's question. Why was I like this? Where did I get this driving ambition to study, to go abroad, to speak French? My parents had never been abroad. Mother had dropped out of college to marry my father, who was studying on the GI Bill. It took him ten years to scrape to the finish. They had never pushed me or Alicia to study. School was a place where parents parked their children in order to work, to clean the house, to see other adults in peace and quiet. We never discussed where I would get money for college, where I would live, what I would study. My mother seemed to think Alicia and I would forever remain children; there was no need to discuss the future.

I knew she would probably never ask me such an intimate question again. We had not talked about my divorce, or my years in London and New Mexico in anything but the vaguest terms.

I could think of no answer. I realized that even if I had known what to say, she would treat the offering of any particle of my inner self with her usual indifference. I said, 'I don't know.'

When I opened the letter that was to send me to France, I knew I would find whatever it was I wanted there. I had been accepted as an exchange student. It wasn't Paris, but I was too excited to quibble with such a detail. I sat down on my dorm bed and saw my entire life change, open.

According to the letter, all my credits would be transferred back when I returned to finish my degree. But I knew I would never come back.

The letter was no surprise; it had never occurred to me that I would not be accepted. My grade point in my major – art history – was nearly a perfect 4. My French was already extremely good, due to many hours in the language lab. I had two irreproachable references, one from the most famous professor in the department, a specialist in Greek vases. And I had aced my interview, which I remembered now with some awe, thinking of my young, brash, powerful self.

I had walked into a room with six older, important people from the exchange programme, the university and the French department. I did not once falter or hesitate. I was poised and calm, answering each question with a thoughtful dignity that bespoke modesty, good manners, maturity: exactly the kind of student a university would send abroad.

This posture was entirely premeditated. Yet I knew nothing about interview techniques, had received no advice. I had never even had a job. Where did I acquire this shrewdness? It never occurred to me to be nervous; I knew what I wanted from these people and I knew exactly what I had to do to get it.

I moved back home from the dorm to save money. I got a job at the local college, in the anthropology department, running errands for the faculty, looking up references to obscure Mongolian language groups, photocopying journal articles on Maori and Hopi customs. It was the perfect summer job: close enough to Mother's that I could ride my bike, not too strenuous, and it necessitated long hours in the library, where I could hide and read French novels. Also, I did not have to type, something I had carefully avoided taking in high school.

In the events I sewed: a soft cotton skirt and blouse for travelling, which could be packed and shaken out without wrinkling too much, a plum wool skirt for the winters which I could wear with black pullovers. I would look French, I decided: I envisioned, with surprising accuracy, busloads of American students in backpacks and jeans and sneakers milling about in front of the Tour Eiffel, while I, in a tight skirt, baggy pullover, Isadora Duncan scarf and black beret sat at a café reading *Le Monde*.

I selected and reselected my clothes, spread out across the

39

living room in neat, folded piles, along with my open suit-case and Mother's bathroom scales. I read the Michelin Guide to Paris, where I would be spending my first week. I studied the Métro map. I looked at my passport and one-year student's visa. Alicia and my mother ignored me.

I flew to New York and on to Paris, accompanied by nine other girls from my university and chaperoned by a French civilization professor. We saw Chartres, Versailles, Notre Dame, the Louvre. We stayed in a hotel near La Bastille, where we slept little. When we were not out, we stayed up in our rooms, comparing our backgrounds, our plans. I thought of myself as utterly different from these girls, who would return home, graduate, marry. Several were already engaged..

We were then put on different trains and sent off to our different towns and cities. I spent the journey trying to look as though I had spent a lifetime on trains, and hoped nobody would talk to me. I showed the first taxi in the rank the card I was given, and was dropped off outside a large house surrounded by iron gates. It was a girls' boarding house, run by lay nuns, with two dozen other girls of various nationalities.

It was the beginning of September and I was nearly nine-teen. I had slept with two people: Madeline and my Medi-eval to Early Renaissance teaching assistant, a young male graduate student, who had been hurried and nervous, a major disappointment. By Christmas I would have slept with three more: the girl I was about to meet, her boyfriend, and Tomas, whom I would marry.

We were all assembled for our 'orientation', during which we received keys to the gates and doors of the house and to our individual rooms, and were obliged to swear allegiance to the curfews, hot water limits, meal times, and visitors' hours, which were strictly held in the television room, where we were then sitting.

The Italian girls gathered in a semi-circle to one side, giggling; a few Germans and Swedes listened conscientiously; one lone Japanese girl sat polite and miserable, obviously failed by her French. There were several Americans, three of whom were studious, overweight, wearing brand-new jeans and starched cotton shirts, probably education majors, whom I resolved to avoid. A pimply intellectual type with stringy hair avoided everybody's eye, pretending she was not American, but I knew, as I had seen her registration form.

Then Meredith walked in. She was hot and sweaty, and was wearing an enormous backpack. She was short, with an athletic body, compact and full, but trim. Her streaked blonde hair was coming apart from its braid. She had a little snub nose, lightly freckled. She was carrying a ten-speed bicycle, the cross-bar suspended on her right shoulder.

The lay nuns looked up in alarm at this interruption, and then with shock at the sight of the bicycle.

They firmly indicated that the bike had to go outside, at which Meredith let out a vitriolic and very impressive burst of French, although with a clear American accent.

She had spent the summer biking from Bordeaux, clear across France, *en faisant du camping*. She had not yet had her bike stolen and was damned if she was going to let it sit outside on this busy road just asking to be lifted into the back of somebody's truck. It was expensive, French, a *Motobécane*.

The head lay nun sighed and said, '*Eh bien, laissez-la en derrière de la maison*,' and I knew I wanted to sleep with this girl.

We walked to campus in the mornings. Along our road, Mediterranean blue signs directed cars to the *Centre*, a long

41

boulevard lined with shops at the end of which was a monument, a small obelisk on which was inscribed MORTS POUR LA PATRIE.

Meredith and I would walk along the boulevard, then down a narrow stone street which opened out on to a *place*, on which there was a market every morning. They sold live caged chickens and crates of long black radishes, enormous oranges and tomatoes, thick white asparagus. From caravans, aproned families wrapped up red, black, white and pink larded sausages; brown, coarsely chopped pâtés; round cheeses, skinned rabbits, roasted chickens, quails' eggs.

After a while, people began to know us, saying, *Ah, les deux belles Américaines*. We stopped for our espresso after class in the same café, La Rotonde, bought our baguettes and croissants at the same bakery, our notebooks in the same bookshop, our shampoo and soap and make-up in the local Monoprix.

The first time Meredith and I slept together, nothing happened. We were too drunk.

We had made a habit of sitting up together late in bed, talking far into the night and drinking hot cocoa and Grand Marnier. We were allowed to keep electric hot-plates in our rooms. We cooked ratatouille and drank cheap red *vin de table*. We stored long-life milk, vegetables and cheese and sausage in a net shopping bag on the ledge outside the window, shaded by the shutters.

Meredith was from a little place in Wisconsin, called Sheboygan. We told competing stories of the ordeals of our respective home towns. We wore identical old-fashioned, long, white cotton nightgowns that buttoned at the throat and wrists, bought at a retro shop in Les Halles. We hitch-hiked to Paris nearly every weekend.

We avoided Americans. We peppered our conversation

with French, pretending our English was languishing from disuse. Meredith found a French boyfriend, Didiet, and his friend, Roger. Before I met Tomas, I went around with them. Didiet was an obsessive wind-surfer and always driving down to the Côte d'Azure. Roger was at university for a good time; his father owned a vineyard and his future was written in stone.

It was after a party with Didiet and Roger that we first slept together. It was an Arab party, full of Moroccans and Algerians and Libyans who had been told that Western girls would sleep with them if they said they were medical students. 'What is *your* name?' they would ask, very earnest. 'What are *you* studying? Me, I am studying to be a doctor.' They would smile. 'You want to come back to my room?'

There were platters of North African food, vegetables and grains, passed around and eaten by hand, wrapped in lettuce leaves, and, amazingly, a massive amount of alcohol. We got very drunk.

Meredith and I stumbled out of Didiet's car at the gates of our house minutes before curfew. We managed to get to my room, take off our clothes, and fall to bed in each other's arms.

We kissed in the dark, once. Then Meredith rushed to the WC down the hall and I could hear the splatter of vomit, and then water running. When she returned, I knew she had brushed her teeth and used mouthwash. I was trying to hold my eyes open and still, knowing that I would be next to run down the hall if I closed my eyes or moved them. The bed gyrated, the room tilted wildly, and as she got back under the covers I cursed my condition, but could not move. I tried to put my arm around her again, without moving my head, but she would not budge. Seconds later, she was snoring peacefully, and then I too slipped into oblivion.

Meredith, I thought sometimes, *that bitch*. Histrionic, possessive, melodramatic. Our parting came towards the end of the year; I left with Tomas, and she, determined to make a point, married Didiet.

But we did have fun: mornings of giggly sex in my bed in our unbuttoned nightgowns, nights drinking Entre-deux-Mers and eating messy picnics of baguettes, Brie, *saucisson*.

I loved to run my hand over her smooth hips, which were rounded, not bony and square like mine; I could press against one thigh, embracing her breasts for what seemed like hours. We lay on our sides, entangled, drawing out soft, caressing kisses, the enveloping of lips. I pressed my entire face against her shoulders, arms, thighs, slowly, so as to feel each moment suspended, brushing skin against skin in amazed, perpetual delight. My art history teaching assistant was nothing like this.

Here was the crux of the problem: I wanted a man, an interesting man, an artist or intellectual, preferably with money. But I couldn't keep away from girls. I knew men were nasty, bristled, hard, egotistical; they did not understand the value of hesitation, of guessing, of waiting. The slow tracing of a finger, the discovery of delight in some ordinary curve of skin: these things did not happen between men and women.

Sleeping with men was something you did, it was *normal*, expected. Sleeping with each other was fun, a temporary indulgence. Sleeping with another girl, you knew what she wanted: sex, friendship, intimacy. With a man, you got what girls didn't provide: romance, marriage, money, children. Real life.

4

I dressed carefully for Mother's women's group, in grey linen trousers, a cream shirt, sandals and silver earrings. I had washed my hair and pulled it back. I sat on the edge of Mother's sofa with my feet together, like a well-dressed woman in a dirty train station.

Mother came out of her bedroom in running shoes and a red tracksuit with a family of black cats appliquéd across the chest. She looked at me with some annoyance and said, 'You don't have to dress up.'

I didn't reply. I never left the house without thinking of where I was going, whom I might meet, how I should appear. It did not bother me much that she did not know this. It never occurred to me that she should know me, as mothers perhaps know their daughters. I could not remember her ever holding me in her arms, or a time when I had wanted to touch her, turn to her. And she never understood that I created clothes much as I created myself. She sewed only for economy; she might as well have worn ready-made clothes manufactured by anonymous hands for some imaginary, collective woman.

We were going to somebody's called Janet, who lived on the other side of the freeway, near the college.

I had always thought of the college as a sort of community centre for bored housewives to pursue outside interests and high-school drop-outs to take remedial English. It had been a rural high school before South Bay was built, and then remained empty for years until renovated to serve as an extension service for the small towns between

Houston and the Gulf. Mother told me it had since expanded. When I worked there, it was a two-storey building of grim red brick, and still retained its jutting flagpole and an atmosphere of green lockers, sour teachers and small-town kids reciting the Pledge of Allegiance.

I had just spent a year at a state university, with forty thousand students, eight main libraries, and its own newspaper. I thought of this college as one step above a vocational school – it did not offer carpentry and shorthand, but it could hardly be a university; it was not ivy-covered and sprawling, with lecture halls for two or three hundred, research institutes, lectures by Russian dissidents, protests against defence contracts, film societies, teaching assistants, gossip about tenure and grants.

We drove into one of the new sub-divisions, called University Place. It looked how the neighbourhood of my childhood must have looked to my parents twenty years before: clean streets of fresh brick houses with double garages, new and immaculate. The grass looked as though it had been laid down and cut to fit, like upholstery. Trees had been planted in the right places, pristine flower beds freshly dug. It all promised normalcy, safety, goodness.

I found myself wondering, as I always did when driving through new suburban neighbourhoods. *Why do people buy these houses?* They seemed to me an insidious trick, a grand deception, built to entice and then crumble and collapse. With time, they would become Clearview houses.

Of course, people bought them not because they were idiots, but because they lived here, and had jobs and families here. People weren't stupid or horrible because they had bad taste (worse than bad taste: no taste). I knew this, although I felt inside my heart the sharp edge of contempt, unsoftened by time. I ignored it; I would never live here and I did not particularly care why other people did.

Then a memory sparked. 'Is Naomi still going to your group?'

'Oh, no,' Mother said. She seemed not at all surprised that I should ask. 'Not any more. She's living with someone now.'

I thought of Naomi with a wistful smile. I had met her during my freshman year, during Mother's divorce; I was home for Easter break. She was in her mid-thirties, half-Navajo, tall, large-boned, and played college basketball. I fell in love with her the minute I laid eyes on her.

She was exactly the kind of woman I wished I could be and wanted to attract. She was serious, dark and tall. She didn't need to make a thing out of being gay: she was never 'out', but she never concealed it; she was supremely confident, beyond classification. She drank straight whisky and smoked long, leisurely cigarettes. She seemed to me very wise and worldly, although she never talked about herself. She acted as though everything I had to say was interesting and important. I recalled this later with some embarrassment, realizing that she had been very kind to me.

She was some kind of administrator at one of the medical schools downtown, and had met Mother through her job. Naomi's lover, Rose, taught at the college, which was why they lived in Clearview. Rose was unremarkable – small, grey, efficient, and at least fifteen years older. They kept a motor-boat, which they took out on weekends to fish, and two cats.

We went to their house one evening. What struck me, as Mother and I sat in their living room and drank cocktails, was that their house was so *boring*. It could have belonged to anybody, not to two professional gay women. I could hardly believe they lived in Clearview, and at least expected something special: original prints or Navajo rugs, wooden floors, or pale, Danish furniture. What they had was a marginally larger house than Mother's, although cleaner, a pine-panelled living room with colonial-style furniture and a glass cabinet which lit up on the inside when Naomi opened it to take glasses out.

'They have so much in common,' said Mother on the way home, rationalizing the relationship. She was a burgeoning feminist then, during her divorce, and I looked at her, interested in her reaction. 'They really get on well together. If I could find a woman I got on so well with, I'd much rather do that than live with another man.'

I stared at her. Was my mother turning gay?

'They really enjoy their boat,' she rattled on. 'Of course,' she continued, turning a corner, 'it's purely platonic.'

I smiled to myself. Mother was just beginning to get out in the real world. She was ready to accept homosexuals, but couldn't bring herself to believe that her friends were among them. A couple of years later, Naomi dumped Rose for another woman and Rose had a breakdown. By then Mother couldn't deny it any more.

My mother had a kind of unconscious radar. During my last visit, I saw Naomi again. It was the day I stopped by Mother's office. Naomi was there and invited us both over for a drink. She was living alone in the house; the woman after Rose had come and gone. I kept trying to get Naomi alone, to ask her if she wanted to meet again, but Mother wouldn't let me out of her sight for a second. But did she know? I could not ask.

On the other hand, would Naomi have been interested in me? I had not considered at the time that she might turn me down. Now I saw myself through her eyes: once an indiscreet, flirtatious college girl interested in clothes, sex, being different; now a divorcee looking for a bit of adventure. She of course was interested in a relationship. Like most serious

48

gay women, she was probably highly suspicious of women like me.

Perhaps, at that time, I *had* recognized all this (I was not stupid, I could not have been completely unperceptive), but thought of myself as worthy of interest to her because of what I thought I had become (sophisticated, educated) – because I was on my way somewhere (graduate school), and, of course, because I was attractive.

When I was a freshman, I had thought of Naomi as an ambition, a goal, a model I would eventually grow towards. Newly divorced, I thought of her as akin to me, an equal, an intelligent, dynamic, mature woman. It occurred to me now, driving to Janet's with Mother, that I had thought of myself as having become a version of Naomi: strong, secure, independent. Except, of course, that I hadn't. I had got married.

'How is she?'

'Oh, fine. They seem very happy. I think she's finally in a *solid* relationship.' It was one of my mother's favourite convictions that homosexuality was fine for those who *really* wanted it; promiscuity was what she disapproved of.

We came to Janet's street, which was sectioned off from the rest of University Place by a sign which read UNIVERSITY PLACE CONDOMINIUMS. It consisted of identical pink-brick townhouses with narrow, tall windows, a balcony and tiny patch of lawn in front, a small fenced patio in back, and a single-car garage separating each house. At the entrance a crescent of hedges partitioned off a maintenance lodge and a small complex of laundry, recreation and meeting rooms. I could imagine the developer's marketing brochure: *The perfect residence for the busy professional.*

Inside, the design was urban and modern: exposed roof beams and skylights, an open fireplace. I thought, nastily, *The perfect residence for the busy professional who wants to pretend this isn't a suburb.*

Somebody handed me a glass of white wine. We joined a group of women who were standing nearby. Mother introduced me; I smiled politely at each. One nodded brusquely and then ignored me, as if to say, *You may be young and attractive, but I am not impressed or interested.* I wondered whether this was out of loyalty or pity for my mother. One of the other women looked curious; another, surprised. These were the stock responses I got from Mother's friends; I looked nothing like her.

I slipped away and sat down on a leather sofa to observe the crowd. Mother was right; it had changed. No longer abused and rejected housewives, this group had gone back to college, found jobs, thrown away their hair-rollers and high heels. There were a few younger ones, too. They all wore professional clothes, or youngish casual clothes, jeans and khaki, loose pullovers, T-shirts. One corpulent woman completely in black wore the studiously self-assured expression of an overweight feminist who refuses to diet.

From where I sat I could eavesdrop on three conversations. It was obvious that to talk about men was considered bad taste; the talk was about jobs, politics, art exhibits, and a few accepted feminine topics: cooking, if it were gourmet; children, if they were interesting; clothes, if work-related. Insecurity was out. Turning grey was *okay*.

Janet turned out to have protruding lips, sloping shoulders and a stomach she could have rested a tray on. She stood near with a group of three or four women. She was holding a wine glass in one hand, her elbow wedged into her hip, saying, 'Oh, I'm just so tired of these *angry* women.'

'Oh, so am *I*,' replied the woman next to her.

I felt weary, and, looking around at the younger women, wondered what they did here, where they worked. I suppose it was cheaper and safer than living in the city. And there must be jobs. Everywhere were new businesses, office buildings, restaurants, apartment complexes, houses, shops. The new sub-divisions with landscaped grounds and bright, appropriate names like Brook Grove and Elm Forest had surrounded and engulfed Harmony and Seagate, which, like Clearview, flooded often and smelled of rotting wood and fishing boats.

It occurred to me that if I had stayed here or come back to live, I could have been one of these women. After all, I had been to these parties before, the sort of every-fourth-Friday white wine parties of a group of women and their friends, which expanded at times and then lulled, retaining a core of the dedicated four or five. I thought, matter-of-factly and without regret, *This kind of friendship has never been part of my life.* How odd that it was now a part of my mother's. My mother had been part of that circuit of housewives who drank coffee in each other's kitchens, complaining about their children and gossiping about who dyed her hair and whose marriage was in trouble. Such women were friends only because they lived on the same street and their children went to the same school. They shared nothing, apart from the weekly bridge parties I remembered with such distaste: the folding card tables, the sectioned platters of nuts and olives, the pink heart-shaped soaps put out in the bathroom.

Now Mother was standing in her tracksuit, a statement of all she had since rejected, sipping a glass of cheap wine and discussing – what? With me she talked about fabrics and patterns; perhaps with her friends she discussed funding cuts in social programmes, battered wives, AIDS, the sorry state of the Democratic Party. I realized I did not know.

The woman sitting next to me caught my eye, and asked, 'So, what do you do?' She was about my age and had an intelligent, plain face. She looked as bored as I.

The question made me stop for a moment. What did I do? *Nothing*, I thought. She was looking at me and I realized that she did not really care what I did; I merely had to explain my presence here. I said, 'I'm visiting my mother.' I pointed. 'The one in the red tracksuit.'

She nodded morosely, as though I had just told her I had inoperable cancer. She had long, straight hair, no make-up. She wore jeans and a T-shirt. She said enviously, 'So you don't live here.'

I realized then she was not from here and cheered up a little. 'No,' I said, thinking, *But I don't live anywhere else either*. I said quickly, 'Why are you here?'

'I'm teaching at the college. I'm only here on a one-year contract.'

'The local one?' I tried to sound neutral, without much success.

'Oh, you don't have to be polite; I know it's a joke.'

'Where are you from?'

'Washington.' Then she added, gloomily, as if from habit, 'State.'

'Oh, then you must hate it here,' I thought of green forests, a rocky coastline, glacial lakes, drifts of powdery snow.

'It's not what I expected.' I could tell she had been a different person in Washington State. She had probably thought she was sure of who she was until coming here, and been astonished how shaky that certainty actually was, how easily depression can settle in, diminish, erode. I liked her. She did not seem to notice my sympathy. She seemed to want nothing, expect nothing, except my company, as though we were in a waiting room. She looked away, not rudely, but companionably, knowing I too had nowhere else to go.

She said, 'I'd like to move into the city and commute here, but I've signed a lease.'

52

I thought, *We are the kind of people who become friends out of need.* If I lived here, my friends would consist of the temporary, the unhappy, the dissatisfied. *But I am not here for a year,* I reminded myself. *I can afford to be kind to this woman.* Our glasses were empty; I offered to go fill them.

I worked my way to the wine and food table and was pouring when an unmistakably local voice said, 'Did you go to South Bay High?'

I turned and saw an emaciated girl in her twenties with a pointed face and stringy brown hair. I suddenly found the question highly offensive. Did I look like I was from here? I threw her a malevolent glance and turned back to the bottle of wine. 'Unfortunately.' I immediately regretted saying this, and giving her the opportunity to respond.

'Yeah, I feel the same way.' She giggled. I thought, *There is nothing about which you could feel the same as I.*

'I was a year behind you. My name's Charlene. You're Krystal, aren't you?' She spoke as though she knew I had changed my name and now used my old one to mock me. This was impossible, but I still wanted to slap her impertinent face.

Behind her, the Washington State woman was making her way towards me. She leaned past Charlene and said, 'We're going out for some late night Tex-Mex. Want to come?'

I smiled with gratitude, but then felt irritation overcome me: Mother would resent my desertion. I grabbed my bag and looked around for her. I would do what I always did in these situations: escape quickly.

'I'm going out with some women, Mother, for a drink.'

'Oh.' She pressed her lips together grimly, a familiar grimace I chose to misinterpret as concern.

'Don't worry. I'll get a ride home.'

An hour later I was on my third Marguerita at a Mexican

53

place off the freeway. Plastic fruit hung from a net-covered ceiling; nearby, a fountain with plastic birds attached gurgled. Three tables had been pushed together, and were now pasted with oily paper on which were strewn ravaged platters of nachos, red plastic baskets picked clean but for the last grains of fried tortillas, mashed quarters of dark green limes, salt shakers, candles melting over blue and red ceramic sombreros.

Our group had joined a party of five women from the college. I had immediately noticed one as the most interesting to talk with and stood near the chair across from her. She was about forty, with short black hair, streaked with grey, large earrings, definitely gay. Washington State said, 'This is Kris,' to the table.

I sat down. I realized after a few minutes of listening to the conversation that the group we had joined was all gay and had just come from some women's studies class. The interesting one said across the table, 'Are you here visiting?'

'Yes,' I said, pleased that she could tell I was not local.

I knew this kind of woman well. She would be very 'out', the type to wear a pink triangle. She was dark, part Hispanic, I suspected. She would be very into Latin American literature. She would automatically consider me straight until enlightened. She would be the type to condemn, lecture, at least scold somebody like me. We could possibly be friends, the combative, debating sort who could never quite forgive the other: she would disapprove of the cowardice of my appearance; I would find her doctrinaire. Although she was attractive, I would never want to sleep with her.

I looked around the table as another tray of Margueritas arrived. Was all this really so bad? I briefly imagined myself as part of a group of friends, living and working here.

I realized the tequila was affecting me when I could not quite remember why I hated Clearview so much. But then longing filled me as I thought of everything that made life here fade in comparison: the red and green vegetables of French markets, soft, warm baguettes hastily wrapped in a square of white paper; the streets and houses of London and their round blue plaques that informed passers-by that Dickens or Kandinsky or Liszt once lived in that house; coming up from the dingy tube to a stand of brilliant flowers; crowded bookshops; the perfume of Indian tea in shiny mahogany teapots; my adobe house in New Mexico, the mountains and trees, the vast, living desert. I wanted beauty and texture: I could never, never live here.

I picked up my fresh Marguerita and then noticed a girl to my left, squeezed in at the corner. I noticed first her eyes, because they were large and intense, and because they were looking at me. She turned quickly away.

Her hair was braided and tied with a black ribbon. It was too dark to determine the colour. I guessed she was in her late twenties. She was not beautiful – in fact, apart from her eyes, she was rather unattractive. I could tell her skin was not particularly good, and she fidgeted nervously with her cigarette, glancing at it and then tapping it unnecessarily against the ashtray, a habit I had always disliked.

How can I explain this sudden attraction? She wore an oversized black T-shirt that slid off either shoulder. She leaned forward, one elbow on the table, holding the cigarette, curving her shoulders, bending over in a vulnerable and young way. I wanted to hold those shoulders.

She had looked at me with something like humility, as if thinking, *This woman would never talk to somebody like me.* Her glance made me remember, as I did occasionally, how I must look to other, usually younger, women: well-dressed and well-mannered, the polished, educated and elegant woman I had worked so hard at imitating. She glanced again at me, as if daring herself to do so. Without warning, I found myself imagining I was kissing her.

I looked at her in little snippets; each time, we caught each other. Finally, out of embarrassment, we smiled.

She got up to go to the toilet. I watched her walk away, her tight black Levis belted over that loose T-shirt. When she came back and sat down, I leaned over and asked her if she was also at the college.

She was, she said self-deprecatingly, only part-time. I asked her what she was studying. Oh, nothing, really, she said, now actually blushing; but she thought about doing women's studies. She had dropped out of high school and had to take all these courses to make up for it – she stopped abruptly.

I assured her in a rather patronizing way that I thought that an admirable and difficult thing to do. 'I am always trying to get my sister to go; I know it's not easy.' This was not true, but it was something to say.

She put out her cigarette nervously and said she had a class the next day, and ought to leave. She had her room-mate's car – she said this self-consciously, as though she were afraid of being too obvious.

I looked at my watch – it was midnight. She took this as a sign of hesitation, took the plunge and asked me if I wanted to drop by. Well, I said, I *could* use a cup of tea. This was true; there was no way I could go to bed without sobering up.

I went to call my mother.

I started feeding her lies like quarters in the pay phone. I was somewhere, I said. I didn't know where. But I'd probably be pretty late. One of the women here had offered me her sofa if we drank too much to drive far. So she shouldn't worry if I didn't show up.

We drove in silence to a street alarmingly close to my

mother's. The house was in unbelievably bad shape. It was the Clearview version of a Spanish hacienda, a design of white brick and decorative twisted ironwork. The brick on one side of the house was crumbling. The front lawn was at least three feet deep.

We parked and went through the back door into the kitchen, which was empty except for a very dirty red vinyl folding table and two folding chairs. The counter top was bare. On the sink was a white plastic bottle streaked with congealed green liquid. Next to the tap, two fat cockroaches waved their antennae but did not bother to move. The cabinets, Swiss chalet peaked and decorated with heart-shaped cut-outs, looked coated with a patina of greasy, accumulated grime. I walked across the floor, which was its original green fleur-de-lis in the corners, along a greyish path where the pattern had worn smooth. She opened an unlined cupboard, empty but for three cups and two smaller cockroaches, which fled upwards into a crack in the ceiling.

She took out two of the cups. From another cupboard she took a saucepan. She filled it with water and put it on the stove. I knew I could not put my mouth on that cup. I had to wash it. Inside the sink was a wadded-up net dishcloth, nearly black.

I spoke with difficulty. 'I'd like to rinse my cup out, if you don't mind.' She did not answer. I washed it with the green dish-soap under running water, with my hand. I shook the water from it and set it down on the counter. She put in a teabag and added the warm, rather than boiling, water without comment.

I wondered briefly what I was doing with this woman when I should have been with the professional, short-haired, interesting one. I would never end up with the Naomis of the world. I looked at her shoulders and the back

57

of her neck, where delicate wisps from her braid had pulled away, and pushed the thought back.

We took the tea through to the living rom, which was furnished with a sofa, a single chair and a television. I felt the same matted shag carpet as at Mother's beneath my feet, but there were no lights on and fortunately I did not have to see it. Behind closed doors in the hallway were two other bedrooms: her roommates, she explained. 'I can't afford this house by myself. It's my parents' but I have to pay the bills. They're living in Australia.'

She turned on a single lamp in her bedroom. On one wall was a poster of Virginia Woolf in profile. 'Do you like Virginia Woolf?' I asked politely.

She glanced up at the poster. 'Oh, is that her name? I bought it because she is so beautiful. Who is she?'

I turned away, and said with some effort, 'She's a writer.' I looked around. Near the open closet, a large woven basket overflowed with crumpled clothing; an old iron, more clothes and a sewing box were piled on an upright ironing board.

Bookshelves, erected from cinder blocks and plywood, leaned against one wall. I recognized a book I had once used on how to write term papers; there was also an English grammar book, a geometry textbook and at least a dozen murder mysteries.

Against another wall was an old walnut dresser, cluttered with hair ribbons, a comb and brush, bottles and jars. Above the dresser hung a mirror, speckled with age. Alongside was her bed: a mattress, unmade and partially covered with a patchwork quilt. Above the mattress was a sheet tacked over the window as a curtain.

She watched me with apprehension; I kept my face neutral.

We sat down on the mattress facing one another and held

our mugs of tea. I cannot explain why I did not get up and leave, except to say that I was so overcome with wanting her that I forcibly eliminated from my mind everything around us. I did not look at the sheets, which I suspected were far from clean. I did not look at her fingernails, or suggest we take a bath together. I did not want to see the bathroom.

We talked for a moment, wondering who would move first. My heart was beating wildly, my stomach contracted and the tea tasted bitter. A roommate came in; a door opened and closed. I put my tea down. She touched my hand, which I realized with some surprise was shaking. We held each other and then lay down on the bed. I unbraided her hair.

Time slipped away and I was only conscious of feeling, of remembering, the intensity of *pleasure*, at once violent and sublime: skin over the curve of shoulder, dimpled in the crook of elbow, stretched over solid bone; the tenderness of another woman; the strength of my desire to touch and see; the same, yet so different.

We were at it for three hours.

5

The light the next morning was dazzling, and things looked clearer and uglier, the way they do when you haven't slept much. I felt sweaty, dirty, drugged with lust. And guilty. I did not remember this girl's name.

I walked home, backtracking in my memory for landmarks we had passed the night before. I remembered the playground next to the elementary school and the Congregational Church, a red-brick, white-columned suburban copy of a country church. Outside was a sign announcing the hours of a Bible study group. I knew Clearview shopping centre was about a half-mile away.

I knew I would see her again, sleep with her again, and that I would probably regret it. I had nothing in common with this girl. I felt my need for her like a fever, and knew that I would not stop myself until it cooled.

I had woken about 7, from habit, looked at her asleep and felt lust creep up me yet again. I kissed her awake.

I left before I had to meet her roommates.

Mother was up, drinking coffee in her robe and reading the Sunday paper. I knew I looked ridiculous and was sure she realized that I had spent the night with someone, or at least passed out, drunk and ugly, on somebody's sofa.

'Hello,' she said, polite and neutral, meaning, *You're an adult, and I'm not going to ask what you've been doing.* I felt her smugness: here I was, normally so fastidious, now unbrushed, unwashed, hung-over; the same knowing look she had when I told her I was getting a divorce.

'Is that coffee?'

'Yes, I'll pour you a cup. I'm only on my second.'

I sat down at the table with her and sipped my coffee. I wanted to strip my clothes off and shower immediately, but I felt glued to my chair. 'I really overdid it last night. I've got a helluva hang-over.'

'Oh, well,' she said jovially. 'Coffee works wonders.' She pointedly was not going to ask me where I had been. 'Nancy called this morning and asked me over.' Nancy was one of my mother's friends from our old neighbourhood. 'She'd love you to come too, if you'd like to.'

I knew this was my cue. 'Oh, thanks, Mother, but I really don't feel up to it. I think I'll take two aspirin and read a book or something.'

'Of course.'

She got up to dress. I sat at the kitchen table, drank more coffee and looked at the comics. I always avoided reading the local papers. I read the *New York Times*, and in London the *Herald Tribune*. Even in New Mexico I had had the local grocery order the *Times* in.

Mother walked around with her coffee cup, disappearing into her room, reappearing half-dressed, talking about the group, looking for her brush.

'We went to a Tex-Mex place,' I volunteered. 'I drank so many Margueritas I can't even remember where it was.'

'Oh, that's nice' – said with the crisp, exact politeness that I had heard throughout childhood, and which meant, *I am not interested.* 'I love Tex-Mex.'

I rolled my eyes at the empty chair across from me, as I used to do with Alicia. *Oh, that's nice, dear.*

As teenagers, Alicia or I would joke to one another, *Hey Mom, I've just been raped by a black junkie;* the other would respond, *That's nice, dear.* I had always accepted my mother's remoteness, always thought of her as being completely wrapped up in my father; now I detected something more to it, something sinister, like jealousy or resentment. I thought, *Mother does not like having other women around.*

I watched her disappear into her room again and remembered, *I should call Alicia.* When Mother returned, she was dressed. She picked her bag up and, jangling her keys, called out to me as she closed the door that she wouldn't be back until late afternoon. I swallowed the last of my coffee. The car started, rolled down the driveway, changed gear and drove away.

I took off my clothes and stood for a long time under a hot shower, exhausted, numbed, weak in the knees. When I got out I fried two eggs in margarine and laid them on a bed of white toast. I ate quickly, drank a glass of orange juice, then crawled into bed and slept until 2 o'clock.

When I woke up, I knew I needed to sweat out my hangover and decided to mow the lawn. Besides, it would put things right between Mother and me: she hated mowing the lawn. I put coffee and water into the coffee-maker and let it filter as I put on shorts, shirt and shoes.

I stood in the kitchen and drank two cups of hot black coffee as quickly as I could bear. I opened the dishwasher before remembering that we had been washing our dishes by hand; the dishwasher was broken and Mother had not yet had it fixed. I looked in: it had not been used in ages, probably months; a faint stench of brown corrosion, hardened minerals, decayed food drifted upwards. I closed it quickly.

I pushed open the back door to the garage. On the grease-stained carpet in front of the washing machine Mother had dumped a load of dirty clothes. A box of detergent sat open on top of the drier; balanced on the edge was an enormous, shiny cockroach. I moved slowly away, towards the lawn-mower, without taking my eyes off the roach, wondering if I really wanted to go through with this.

Old tools hung on the walls: my father's, probably untouched since he had left. A ladder lay on the rafters, covered in cobwebs. I was afraid of disturbing anything; the very air felt inert and abandoned, the walls and shelves and corners teeming with colonies of minute life; I gingerly tilted the lawn-mower to push it under the jammed garage door. There was no way I was going to scramble under it myself. I turned back and the cockroach was gone. I went through the house and out the front door.

I mowed the lawn steadily, sweating, walking up and down in blissful mindlessness, leaving ribbons of dark wet grass behind me, deviating from my precisely overlapping rows only to circle the magnolia. My head cleared, and I felt purged of the tequila.

I put the lawn-mower away, showered again and took out my fabric and patterns. As I waited for Mother to return, I trimmed my pattern pieces and pressed my silk with a cool iron. I knew that when she came home she would tell me about Nancy and then we would make dinner, discuss my fabric, find out what was on television. I would cut out my shorts and blouse while we watched a movie and things would go on between us as if last night had never happened.

The next day I awoke feeling energetic and decided to walk to the campus. I'd have a look at the library, find the photocopiers, ask if they had word processors, a fax. I would read job ads in the major newspapers, write up a c.v., make lists of potential employers. Having goals made me feel optimistic.

It was a good two miles to the campus, and when I had worked there I had biked, but this did not worry me. I was used to walking. In London I walked regularly to Harrods from our flat in Fulham, and sometimes on to Liberty's.

Mother had left for work, cheerful and pleasant, but noticeably not offering her car. I might have explained that I could not afford to rent a car as I had last time I visited, but the subject hung uncomfortably in the air between us, and I could not bring myself to say anything.

I set out in white walking shorts, sandals and a peach cotton shirt, fresh and confident; by the time I got to the end of the street I was ready to turn back. It was so humid, my shirt stuck to my back and my shorts were wrinkled and sweaty. I looked down at my sandals sliding oddly along the gritty pavement. My feet were already dirty.

I pressed on. I had forgotten that most of the way would be along a four-lane boulevard. I was soon beyond Clearview and houses; on either side of the boulevard were brown, idle fields of wispy scrub. I passed NEW MID-PRICED HOMES and turned under the freeway. Cars and trucks whipped past, spewing hot dust; above me, concrete and steel pulsated.

Soon it became clear that a walker was an oddity. Male voices from dirty vans shrieked inarticulate, unfriendly comments. A patrol car slowed with interest as it passed. I passed University Place and was beginning to wonder whether I had missed the entrance to the campus when I saw it. I was desperate for something to drink.

I turned off the boulevard and walked down the long drive that led to the college. The drive had been repaved since I had last been here, but there were still thickets of uncleared trees and brush on either side; the bayou meandered along one edge. There was, conspicuously, no sidewalk for pedestrians. Nobody was expected to walk to this campus.

Then, suddenly, the trees cleared and a lush, rolling lawn

appeared. At the end of the drive I could see a large parking lot, serviced by electronic gates and two new, squat buildings of black glass connected by an enclosed walkway, hiding the old red-brick school where I had worked.

I walked through the parking lot. To one side of the black glass complex was a large pond near a cluster of trees, like an oasis. Ducks sheltered in the shade, away from the water glaring in the full sunlight. At the entrance was a small sign with discreet lettering. It looked like a cross between a secret outpost of the CIA and a Swiss investment bank.

Inside, however, was innocuous and busy. Everything was sparkling new, carpeted, tiled, polished. I walked down the hall. Announcements were neatly pinned on bulletin boards. Every door was labelled with a metal plaque describing the room's function: *Classroom, Storage room, Registrar's Office, Admissions Office.* The toilets were marked with international symbols and had handicapped facilities.

Neatly dressed people who all looked alike strolled through the halls, chatting. It was impossible to tell who were students and who were staff or faculty; they were like a marketing segment: predominantly white, twenty to forty years old, well-dressed, employed. They had innocent, untarnished faces. They all seemed to know one another.

I found the cafeteria, which offered plastic-wrapped sandwiches and salads, like at an airport. I drank a glass of mineral water and decided I would say hello to Washington State and thank her for bringing me along the night before. I had said goodbye to her briefly, feigning tiredness and explaining that I had found a ride.

I found her office easily. The door was open and I pushed it gently; but instead of a small, plain woman in jeans, there was a platinum blonde in a pale green linen suit. She was sitting at the side of the desk, legs crossed, writing.

She didn't bother to look up. 'She isn't in.'

This caught me off-guard; but after a moment I replied coldly, 'I beg your pardon?'

She glanced up. She was in her forties, carefully made up, and attractive in an expensive, calculated way, as older women with time and money are. She was obviously single – probably divorced. She appraised me briefly and then returned to her papers.

I saw at once that she had taken care to avoid camouflaging her age too obviously. There was nothing cheap about her. Her hair, though clearly dyed, was probably close enough to her original colour and arranged in a simple, longish bob, parted in the middle, with a thin fringe. After a moment, I saw that she had managed to make it appear longer than it was, and that her hair, like everything else about her, was meticulously considered and played a particular part in the overall effect. The hair lightened her skin and disguised a certain amount of ageing. Her clothes were neither too young nor too old; her nails were short and lightly polished, and did not distract. Her shoes were low-heeled and her hem mid-knee.

'I said – ' She raised her eyebrows languidly and spoke with the soft vowels and long syllables of the mythical southern belle: *I say-ed* – 'she's not in today.' Straight out of *Gone with the Wind* and clearly put on. She virtually oozed sex, the pure heterosexual kind. I immediately pictured her in bed with some man, raunchy, confident, always conscious of her best angle.

'Then I'll leave her a message.' I walked over to the desk and took a pencil and pad. She continued to write.

I wrote a note, folded it, and placed it on the desk. As I turned, she said, 'Aren't you a student?'

'No.'

'Oh, sorry,' she said indifferently. 'These students don't believe in office hours.'

In another fifteen minutes I had seen every square foot of the two new buildings. The old school was now used for storage. The library was minuscule, but it had photocopiers. There were no out-of-state newspapers. There was no fax service. The only word processors were for staff.

I walked down the hall, looking at the bulletin boards. The film schedule for the semester was posted: three films, all of which I had seen years before. A *Cercle français* was advertised at somebody's home. A car pool was being arranged for those who wanted to go into the city to see the season's operas.

I thought of London and its fringe political groups, the subway by Tottenham Court Road where young men sold *Socialist Worker*, students on the tube carrying *Marxism Today*, neo-Nazis, Young Conservatives. The smooth texture of this place would never be torn by polarized opinions.

I couldn't believe I had to walk back.

I opened the dark glass door and felt a wall of heat hit and then envelope me. *I have no money, I have no money, I have no money,* rang in my mind as I began the slow walk back to Mother's.

What could I do? I remembered climbing the stairs up to my apartment on 35th thinking, *What I need is a drink.* Working for a large company had been like joining an all-male football team. I recalled my overflowing desk; knowing I did not have to go back still made my knees weak with relief. And I could not start another business; I knew no one who would lend me money. I turned on to the boulevard, feeling hot pavement around the edges of my sandals, licking my lips, tasting dust and exhaust.

I started taking off my clothes as soon as I closed the front door behind me, dropping them on the floor. In my damp bra and underwear I walked straight to the thermostat, and turned it down as far as it would do. Mother kept it at 80 degrees to save money.

I went to the fridge, took out a bottle of orange juice, and drank directly from it, standing with the fridge door open, the dirty tracks of sweat on my skin evaporating, the cotton of my bra and underwear fusing to me like a milky film. I stood for a moment with my back to the fridge, and then closed it. I found a clean white bed sheet from the hall closet and flung it across Mother's itchy orange sofa. Then I lay down, imagining myself to be somewhere, anywhere but here.

I thought about the future, a malevolent, humid jungle; not the clear, austere path I had always seen, rocky perhaps at times, but whose obstacles I would meet with conviction and the coolness of a razor intellect.

I had no money, no one who could help me. I had always found money through the wonderfully impersonal medium of institutions – scholarship boards, personnel departments, recruitment firms, bank managers – where all that mattered was my grades, my ideas, the quality of my cover letter, my interview technique.

I longed for that simplicity. Yet I had already complicated my life by an impetuous one-night stand, which I knew would not be a one-night stand. Of course I would see her again. Sex with women always restored my self-confidence.

I thought of my last affair, a disastrous fling before leaving New Mexico with Dewitt, a name I will always associate with a sad, disappointed man, and my own weakness. I would never be like Naomi, a strong, independent woman, because I slept with men like Dewitt. I had wanted him because I wanted to be flattered, because he was available, because he was persistent. He had wanted me because I had always refused him. It had been the kind of affair that you know is wrong the moment you uncouple. Cigarettes are lit;

distaste saturates the air; blame and regret hover mid-air, waiting to be flung across the sheets.

The only time I could remember sleeping with a man, and not feeling something too considered or obligatory or purposeful, was when I slept with Meredith's boyfriend, Didiet. Why did I do it? I was curious to see his body; I knew he would be easy, uncomplicated. I was greedy; I wanted to see what Meredith was getting when she wasn't with me.

He came to the house one day and, finding Meredith out, asked for me. I came down. We sat in the television room for a few minutes and we talked about wind-surfing, expecting Meredith to return at any moment. I watched him talk, watched him move under his clothes. He was thin and muscular and brown. His hair was parched and white from the sun. I suddenly wanted to have him. I wanted to feel that I had once had him.

I asked him to come up to my room: I would make him a coffee. I said the opposite of what I wanted, the way French talk when they want something: *Tu veux pas aller en haut et boire un café?* It was not difficult to distract the only lay nun on duty: she was the eldest, and nearly deaf. And I had an emergency plan: my window led conveniently out on to the terrace roof.

He sat on my bed and I handed him coffee. He took a sip, put the cup down, and looked up at me. My body was inches from his face. I touched his shoulder and he reached up, ran a finger from my collarbone, over the nipple of one breast, down my body, and along the inside of my thigh, an excruciatingly precise path. I was flooded, aching. He unbuttoned my blouse and unzipped my jeans. I pushed him down on to the bed and lowered myself, swollen, relentless, implacable, just above his open mouth, where I held myself suspended and intent.

69

After a very short time, I closed my eyes briefly and opened them again. Then I froze at a movement on the stairs and the sound of Meredith's voice. We scrambled off the bed, groping for clothes. Didiet was out of the window so quickly I could hardly believe he had been there. It had lasted no more than five minutes.

I pulled on my jeans and shirt and kicked my underwear and bra under the bed as I opened the door.

'*Salut, chérie*,' Meredith said as she kissed me. She was carrying her books and a plastic *Monoprix* bag. 'You're looking flushed.' She put her things down on the tousled bed. 'What have you been doing?'

At that moment the bell in the hall rang to let us know that a visitor had arrived. We opened the door and heard Meredith's name called. She went down to Didiet and I lay on the bed, feeling my clothes against my skin, delaying the moment when I would get up and take a shower.

Lying on Mother's sofa, I must have seen, however unwillingly, the gist of how things would go. How could I not?

Perhaps I tried to convince myself otherwise. I may have told myself she would tire of me as I knew I would of her. Women tired of one another – it could never be any other way. It did not matter whether they were lovers or friends; they tired of one another for the same reasons: a new lover, boredom, familiarity, a snide comment that brings envy painfully, irreversibly to the surface.

I knew I would sleep with her a few more times, obsessively, and then less and less, as the fever cooled. I would notice that the sheets had not been changed. I would tire of squatting over the toilet seat, unable to bring myself to sit down on it, as I had the morning after our first night. I had washed my hands and then dried them on toilet paper, revolted at the sight of the stiff, grimy towels.

I did not know then, of course, as I lay on the sofa, what habit or irritant would suddenly provoke me. I did not know whether it would be the constant flicking of her cigarette, or her bitten nails, her bad teeth (she was afraid of dentists), her terrible, unbearable self-abnegation. The towels and toilet seat could be cleaned, changed; she could study, go to the dentist, stop biting her nails. But she could never, would never transform into whatever it was that would keep me. I knew I would begin to make excuses to not spend the night. I would arrive later, leave earlier, feign fatigue.

Of course, I would get a job and leave; I would have that excuse, I thought, lying on the sofa, wanting to hold those shoulders again, to kiss the back of her neck, to feel her hands moving down my body, up my thighs: I probably counted on a clean break.

I hoped it would happen quickly and before too much desperation set in, before that terrible moment when she would be compelled to inflict her pain on me; before I would make that perfunctory and cruel effort at – what a horrible pat phrase – *being friends*; before having to watch her cling to any form of contact with me, the other, the indifferent and resigned beloved.

I saw which way it would go. Even if I did not foresee the details, I knew that what I was doing was consciously, predictably, inescapably wrong. But nothing would have stopped me from seeing her again. Not even knowing what I know now: that I would kill her.

6

I was sewing my gold linen shorts at the kitchen table when Mother came in from work. I had just stitched the side seams together, and the pieces lay on the table, flat and ironed and perfect, like stillborn wings.

Mother was in a good mood, the bustling, competent, career woman I had seen at her office during my last visit. She poured us each a glass of wine and proceeded to tell me in detail about her day and people I had never met.

I listened dutifully as I cleared the table. She began making a quiche. She had started making new foods the past few years – quiches, curries, gumbo, stir-fry. She liked to pretend that she had always cooked like this, but I knew better: I remembered the chilli setting like cement in my stomach, meatloaf stretched with oatmeal, mushy vegetables, tuna casseroles with canned mushroom soup.

We made coffee after dinner and washed the dishes. I looked in the television guide, but there was nothing on. Then the phone rang.

'It's for you.' Mother handed me the receiver with ill-disguised annoyance.

She went to sit on the sofa and began reading the evening paper the way she had ever since I could remember. She never held the paper; she sat at one end of the sofa, sideways, with her legs crossed, turning the pages upright against the back of the sofa, reading the print that lay spread in front of her.

'Hi, it's Lynette,' said a familiar, nervous voice.

Lynette. I tried to match the face, those shoulders, with

that name. It sounded like a country-western singer. How did anybody get a name like that?

I stood with my back to Mother, trying to sound natural. 'Hi.'

She was silent for a moment. I could hear her breathing. Then she said, in a mixture of anxious expectation and fear, 'I hope you don't mind I called.'

This annoyed me, but I controlled myself. I saw immediately that this tone of voice would soon become chronic, and tedious. I said brightly, 'Of course not. How are you?'

'Oh, all right, I guess. You don't want to come over do you?;'

'Sure, I'd love to.' I tried to sound as if she'd invited me to have a drink instead of go to bed. 'You mean, tonight?' I looked at my watch: it was nearly 9 o'clock. 'Can you hold on a minute?'

I held my palm over the phone. 'Mother, do you mind if I go out tonight?'

'Why should I mind?' Her tone was edged with sarcasm; she pressed her lips together and returned to her paper.

'Great,' I said into the phone.

'I'll pick you up. What's the address?'

'Oh, I can use the walk.'

'But I have the car.'

'Okay, I'll start walking and you can meet me. It's a nice evening and I really would like a short walk.' I told her the name of the street. The last thing I wanted was for her to meet Mother.

I hung up and said, 'That was one of the group I went out with the other night.'

'I see.' Mother continued to read, holding herself stiffly away from me, with a restrained, severe air. She had been to the hairdresser that day; her greying, athletic cut had been trimmed. I looked at her, thinking how different she was.

73

For years she had worn her hair in a puffy bouffant, like a helmet. And she was old now, or at least older. I realized that I did not know how old she was. Yet she was the same, like an immortal old witch. I had often seen her like this; she emitted her moods like radioactivity, permeating everything around her.

I felt suddenly claustrophobic and went to the bedroom to fetch my purse. I simply had to leave, right then. I hated her moods, her indirectness, her false politeness. She had slapped Alicia frequently as a child for such moodiness. *Don't you sulk, young lady.* We children did not have the right to our feelings. I, of course, was better at hiding mine.

It would never have occurred to me, then or now, simply to say, *Is something wrong?* I would never have invited such a direct confrontation. As a child I avoided her anger because I knew I would lose in any battle. Now I did so because I feared her condemnation. Not my *mother's* condemnation, you understand; I feared hearing the words that would condemn me to my own self-loathing. *Pervert. Lesbian. Dyke.*

For a week I lied, shamefacedly, made excuses, came home at 1 or 2 or 5 or 6 in the morning, smelling of cigarettes and sex, shedding my clothes and heading for the shower and bed.

I could have tried to explain, but I said nothing. I didn't want to 'come out'. I didn't want a heart-to-heart talk with my mother in which we spoke honestly to one another for the first time in our lives. I didn't want honesty.

Anyway, what could I say? *Look, Mother, I've met this girl and I'm sleeping with her. I'm sorry for being such an ill-behaved guest, but I simply cannot stop myself. Please bear with me. It will be over soon.*

What would happen if I said this? I knew the sky would not darken, the world would not end, we would not slip

74

through a time warp and disappear. And yet merely thinking these words produced in me such explosive anguish
and shame that I knew we would never recover if they were
ever said.

I wondered whether it would be even worse if she were
to say, *Oh, well, nothing that a cup of coffee won't cure.*

In the evenings she was irritable and frosty; in the mornings, pleasant and chatty, as though she could not bear
broaching the subject any more than I. Perhaps she also
felt this knot of words inside and feared their irreversible
damage: the knowledge that, however gently and vaguely
rendered the details, I made love to women; that I caressed
and kissed them, ran my hands and lips and tongue over
their bodies, just like her own.

In the evenings, I manufactured my lies, brushed my
teeth and hair in the bathroom, took my second shower of
the day, and left the house wishing I could simply stop, yet
unable to put down my purse, sit on the sofa and turn on
the television, drink another cup of coffee, make small talk
with Mother about movies, the news, her job. I wished that
it would end, and could do nothing about it.

Mother busied herself in the kitchen, saying goodbye
with a cursory turn of the head. I had a bizarre fantasy that I
would one night walk in and Mother would follow me
around, saying, *Whatever it is that I've done, please forgive me!*

Towards the end of the week I decided to call my sister. I
called her Chateau Estates apartment, but her phone was
disconnected. I found her work number in Mother's red
plastic phone book, under four or five other numbers under
the word *work*, all crossed out.

'I've moved,' she explained.

'Why doesn't Mother have your new number?'

75

'I don't want her to.'

'Oh.'

We chatted a bit, feeling each other out. I made the proper conciliatory signals, which meant I wouldn't mention drugs, criticize her job or ask her when she would get her life together. And she was less cold, less sarcastic than usual. Finally, she said, 'I don't know if you want to drive all the way over here.'

'Where is it?'

'Downtown. I can give you directions.'

'Oh. Well, I suppose I could ask Mother about borrowing the car.'

'Why don't you rent one?'

'I'm broke.'

'Well,' she said reluctantly, 'I guess I could come get you.'

I didn't reply.

'Well, it's only an hour's drive. I could come tomorrow. I don't work tomorrow.'

'Tomorrow's fine.'

'Yeah, okay. Mother'll be at work, won't she?'

'Yeah. Where are you working?'

'Oh, you know, another one of these shit jobs.' Usually she said, *Well, it isn't something* you'd *do*. 'I'll pick you up around noon. Oh, yeah, Krystal? You won't tell Mom about my moving?'

'Alicia, I'm not stupid. Of course not.' Whether we were getting along or not, a basic loyalty endured from earliest childhood which we never breached: *Don't tell Mother.*

The last time I had been home, I had gone to the Chateau Estates apartment in Clearview, which she shared with two boys, Larry and Sam. They were not more than nineteen or twenty.

In the main room, two futons, a bean bag and a maple

76

chair I recognized from Mother's pre-divorce dining-room suite encircled a low coffee table placed squarely in the middle. The table was littered with bags of marijuana, cigarettes, ashtrays, rolling papers, and comic books. In the midst of all this was a bong, brown and crusty with the dregs of marijuana, and two lit candles, a foot apart, as if on an altar.

The walls were covered with amateurish charcoal life drawings, the stilted attempts of a first-year art student. I looked at them without comment.

'I'm like really into the human figure, you know?' said Sam. He had shoulder-length hair and was trying to grow a moustache. He looked at me like a friendly hound. 'It's like the only really beautiful thing. It's so *perfect*, you know?'

Larry, Alicia told me, did not merely make art; he *lived* art.

Larry had a crew-cut and Andy Warhol glasses. He sat in one chair and stared at me, trying, it seemed to me, to look artistically intense. Around the apartment he had attached tacky souvenirs from the beach on to the walls and ceiling: glossy black and pink shells, sand dollar mobiles, mermaid statuettes. Rubber crabs and lobsters were arranged like alien invaders, coming up from between the folds in the futon, creeping out from behind the refrigerator, hiding under the fronds of a dying palm. One large red crab sat on a bookshelf holding joints in each claw.

There were art books on the shelves – *The History of Art, Renaissance Sculpture, The Impressionists*. I recognized a few from my undergraduate days, and tried to start a general conversation. This turned out to be impossible. Sam's opinions of various painters ranged from 'really weird' to 'like wow he must have been on drugs when he painted that'. Larry did not cease staring at me. Alicia said nothing.

The telephone rang and Larry picked it up, announcing in a surprisingly young voice, 'Starship Enterprise.' After his

77

call, he left the room and returned with two love-birds in a cage, named Art and Life, Sam explained. Larry filled a pipe with pot and, as he smoked, exhaled into their cage. Later, he said, we could watch them fly around the room, stoned.

Alicia sat on the sofa, smoking from the bong, ignoring us. Sam asked me if I had really lived in England; he thought it would be really far out to drop acid, sit in the middle of Stonehenge and trip out on the Druids.

Alicia chopped up some white pills on a mirror with a razor blade and added them to the tiny bowl. I watched the water gurgle in the vase underneath. She exhaled and I asked her what they were.

'Qualudes.' She did not look at me. She sat up, regally, and smoked the pipe as though this required all her concentration.

She had changed, gained weight in her hips and thighs, but her arms and shoulders were still thin.

She strode in, her black leather bag swinging, and stood impatiently in Mother's living room, tapping her foot restlessly. Her mouth was set and she folded one arm across her body. She was wearing jeans, despite the heat, and a sleeveless cotton shirt, pale blue, so short that a finger of skin bulged above her belt. She held her sunglasses in one hand, her keys in the other.

Her hair was the same: thin, a colourless brown. She could have had cut it into a neat bob, tried for a gamine look. She could have had it streaked with discreet blonde highlights. But she had grown it unbecomingly long, to its limits in fact, since it fell to nearly the end of her back in split, wispy fragments. She had cut bangs in a resolute line across her eyebrows, and tried to forge some body out of their stringy limpness with a curling iron and hairspray, creating a stiff, metallic curve.

She wore two or three silver chains around her neck and silver bangles on each wrist. Her fingernails were long, and painted burgundy. On each finger were one or two rings, some set with stones. In one ear were two studs; in the other, two studs and a silver loop. I noticed additional pierce marks without earrings. Between her sharply plucked eyebrows were indelible, parallel creases. Her mascara was emphatically, glaringly black.

'Let's get out of here.' Alicia looked around Mother's living room suspiciously. 'This place gives me the creeps.'

I picked up my bag. 'Where should we go?'

'I don't care. Out of here.' She jangled her keys, waiting for me.

She still had her 1967 metallic brown Pontiac. I got in, and felt split leather and disgorging foam against my thighs. She put on her sunglasses and parked an elbow out the window, holding the steering wheel with one finger. She backed out of the driveway with a jolt, scraping the muffler. She pressed on the accelerator and we screeched down Mother's street.

I suddenly found this very funny and laughed out loud. I had been obsessed by my crisis, my complicated life, my problems with degrees, careers, countries, lovers. Now I was in Alicia's banger, cruising on to the freeway at top speed, the exhaust pipe rattling, hot air blowing my hair, a DJ on the radio announcing, *The sounds of REAL country music.* I lit a cigarette, leaning forward towards the dash to shelter from the wind. I held my hair back with one hand and smoked. We were cruising, like we did during our parents' break-up. The hour or two that stretched out before us seemed endless. Nobody knew where we were.

She drove without looking at me. We were in the fast lane headed north.

'When did you move?' I shouted over the sounds of the engine, wind and radio.

'Two months ago.'   ·

'Why is it a big secret from Mother?'

'I just don't want to see her. I don't want her dropping by.'

'Mother makes it sound like you call her weekly.'

'Well, I don't. And I don't want her coming over and commenting about everything, you know, my apartment and stuff.'

I didn't reply. I knew what she meant: *Oh, that's nice, dear.*

'The reason I want to get away from Mother is that she's always doing that – stealing my life.'

I tried to imagine Mother stealing my life.

'She's always *using* my problems, you know what I mean? To make herself look good. I mean, she really *liked* my drug problem.'

She rummaged about in her enormous black handbag and drew out a long cigarette and silver lighter. The car ashtray spilled over with half-smoked menthol cigarettes.

We passed through a tangle of merging and splitting highways. Signs appeared, committing various lanes without warning to alarming, sudden places: DALLAS, SAN ANTONIO, VICTORIA, as though once on, there was no turning back. Alicia moved within this amazing flow without hesitation or anxiety.

We passed Gulfway, a half-empty, deteriorating mall, where we had shopped sometimes before the move to Clearview. It looked like a worthless family relic nobody had yet had the heart to throw away. Plywood had been nailed on store windows; an enormous *For Rent* sign was posted on the flat roof of the department store.

'*Aids*-way,' said Alicia.

'What?'

'Everybody calls Gulfway *Aids*-way now. Blacks and druggies hang out there.'

We passed alongside dozens of road-building machines sprawled on empty sections of pristine, slate highway. Then the freeway widened to ten lanes. I read billboards: *Dial F-r-e-e-d-o-m for instant bail bond; Living Hope Temple; La cerveza de Tejas, Zany's check cashing – No ID required!*

After a while, we exited the freeway and drove through some busy streets until we were in an area of older houses and tall, overhanging trees.

'Mother thinks you're still living like you were at Chateau Estates,' I said, recalling Larry and Sam and the drugs.

'Mother doesn't know everything,' she replied shortly, and parked the car.

I followed Alicia up the walk to her house. This girl was my sister, my blood; we had been children together. Now she was suddenly, obviously, grown-up. But she still had the same features. She was still a collector of items; I was cool and uncluttered in my olive linen skirt and pressed cream blouse. I remembered how I had slapped her once for using my make-up. We used to hang out our bedroom windows and smoke, exhaling into the dark night. Now she lived in a house converted into four apartments on a tree-lined street. She had friends, earned money, drove a car. She paid her electricity and rent and bought groceries. Why should all this surprise me?

Her apartment was shabby, but surprisingly nice, like an impoverished but creative student's studio. It had parquet floors, high ceilings and a large fireplace. In the curve of an enormous bay window she had placed a lumpy grey sofa covered with bright cushions. Between the sofa and two armchairs was the low coffee table I remembered from the Chateau Estates apartment. Against one wall was a pile of enormous pillows and a wicker magazine rack, overflowing with women's magazines. The walls were covered with watercolours, a woven tapestry, a board on which were pinned postcards. At the other end of the room was a work table and easel.

'Alicia!' I exclaimed. 'Have you begun to paint again?'

'Oh – that,' she said with some embarrassment. She threw her bag and keys on the coffee table, next to stacks of the same art books as at Chateau Estates, a set of porcelain ashtrays, a pale green ceramic platter filled with odds and ends – pens, a string of beads, a tiny address book, paper clips.

I walked over to her work table and saw jars of brushes, a set of coloured pencils, paper pads. I nearly picked up a sketch book, but resisted. I turned and followed her into the kitchen.

The kitchen was as tiny as a closet, with a gas stove and half-size fridge. She took out a Chinese teapot, white and blue, I recognized from years before, unchipped. I was sure Alicia still had every possession she had ever owned.

'How did you start drawing and painting again?'

'I took a course at the museum. Last year.'

'It's great that you've started painting again. I always thought you should have stuck with your painting.'

'Yes, I know you did, but it's not your business.'

This stung me. I looked away. 'I only meant to be encouraging.'

'Well, I didn't want to do it. I don't want to be a painter. I don't want to be scraping for money all the time. You have no idea how hard it is to paint.'

'Of course I do!' I couldn't believe she was saying this. It was I who always told her she would have to work at painting if she wanted to do something with her talent. *I* was the one, after all, who knew something about the struggle of the artist.

'I just don't like it when you get all *enthusiastic* about things, you know?'

'Sorry,' I said, somewhat sarcastically. 'I just couldn't understand how you could not do it, with all your talent.'

'Not everybody wants to *do* something with their lives you know, Krystal.'

'What do you mean? Of course they do. You must, even if it's just being happy.'

'Oh, you know what I mean. You always wanted to do something important, like be famous or write books or something. I'm just not that ambitious.'

She poured water into the kettle and put cups on a tray. I returned to the main room. How had things started this badly? I examined her bookshelves. Just like Alicia, on every shelf in front of the books were objects: little painted bowls of beads, photographs, a woven bookmark, an old pencil box.

I stepped over to look at the postcard collection and was surprised to find that they were all mine, from France, England, New Mexico, New York. Had I really sent all these? I now remembered each: a fifteenth-century black Madonna in Sante Fe, *Déjeuner sur l'herbe*, Salisbury Cathedral, a campy tourist photograph of Concord, Massachusetts. I had driven there one weekend from New York in a rented car.

They were carefully pinned to the board, arranged in an overlapping mosaic. I heard Alicia come in and put the tray on the coffee table. I turned around and said, carefully, 'You've really made this place comfortable.'

'I had to. It's where I live. It's all I've got.'

We talked about the costs of renting, comparing prices in New York, and about the neighbourhood, the crime, Alicia's drive to work, which was twenty minutes. She worked at a place that restored antique furniture, one of the reasons she decided to move downtown. She was an apprentice, learning about French polishing, rebuilding old furniture, re-upholstry. 'There's actually a lot to it. You have to know something about the history of old furniture.' She stopped abruptly and looked away. 'Well, you know all about that.'

I did not reply. I knew nothing about the history of furniture. I had studied painting and French. But I knew Alicia would not have believed me. 'Why haven't you told Mother about this? She thinks you're still dispatching taxis.'

'Because she'll be so *understanding*. She'll say, *Oh, isn't that nice, Alicia, it's so interesting. You've always been so good at doing things with your hands.* And she'll go around telling everybody how pleased she is that I've finally found something to do and that it doesn't matter at all that I didn't go to college.'

'Alicia, what Mother says can't steal you from yourself.'

'Oh that's easy for you to say, you don't live here. She makes me feel that everything I do is for her to analyse and scrutinize and judge and talk about with everybody. Anyway, my therapist says I shouldn't tell her if I don't want to.'

I should have guessed that Alicia would be in therapy. 'Have you been in therapy long?'

'Two years.'

I nodded. 'Is it good?'

'I love her.' She looked away and lit a cigarette. 'She's saved my life a few times.'

Of course, that was what sisters were supposed to do for one another. I remembered sometimes telling people that my sister was a painter. I had done exactly what Mother had done: I had stolen Alicia's life and reformed it into something I could use, talk about. I said, 'It's been two years since I last saw you.'

'Yes. Are you divorced now?'

'Oh, yes. It was simple – uncontested. And he didn't try to get any money out of me. He knew he couldn't.'

'Did he ever publish anything?'

'No.' I felt old anger swell up again. I had thought of myself as discriminating, as knowledgeable about art, and had not seen how self-indulgent and shallow Tomas's writing was. 'The bastard. I can't believe I fell for the oldest line in the world: *my wife doesn't understand me.*'

'I remember your telling me that his wife hadn't been very supportive of his writing,' Alicia said neutrally.

I had imagined Tomas's first wife as unattractive, comfortable and frumpy, although I never met her. Tomas never said anything explicitly nasty about her: I created her myself, although of course he encouraged me to dislike her, to think of her as bourgeois, materialistic, conventional.

He once pointed to a woman in a restaurant, seated a few tables from us. *'C'est un peu le genre de ma femme.'* The woman was short, slightly plump, wearing a conservative dress. I wondered now, had he lied? He wanted to implant an idea in my mind: *She is nothing like you; you are a different type, a woman who appreciates art.* He wanted me to support him; he made sure I knew he hated his teaching job. If he did not have to work, it was obvious, he could write.

Alicia and I went out to lunch, at a Mexican place, then shopping in a mall, and things got better. She decided to take some time off from her job. For the next few days, she drove down to Clearview in the mornings and took me into town. We went to art museums and the Galleria. We went to Walgreens and filled plastic baskets with pink nail polish, lipstick liners, brushes and eye shadows from buckets with labels like *Only 49 cents each!* We went to Mexican diners and ate hueavos rancheros and milk shakes and cheeseburgers.

We talked and talked, contented, saying nothing. I did not tell her about Lynette, or about getting fired. Released from the need to be serious and responsible or making intelligent conversation, we talked about make-up, our skin, our hair.

We read Alicia's old *Cosmos* and *Vogues*, side by side, flicking our cigarettes. We criticized the models and dissected the outfits we liked best. We drank tea and painted our nails with colours called Cotton Candy and Peaches n' Cream until the afternoon, and then opened bottles of wine. We tried on Alicia's collection of second-hand clothes. She had closets of them, black cocktail dresses, bolero jackets, three-quarter-length kid-skin gloves.

We rented old videos which we watched on Alicia's tiny television screen: Cary Grant, Barbara Stanwyck, Bette Davis. We watched *Kiss Me Deadly* and *Backstreets*; we watched *Double Indemnity* twice in a row. We cooked pasta and enchiladas and chocolate mousse and had pizza and Chinese food delivered. After dinner, she rolled joints from a blue enamelled box she kept under the futon sofa, which I watched her smoke.

I supposed that our relationship would always be like this, infrequent visits beginning hopefully, antagonism quickly rising to the surface, then reverting to the old, the familiar, girlish silliness. We would do anything to avoid the pain of intimacy.

7

Mother was sitting on the sofa, watching television, when I walked in. She did not look up, but said, 'Your friend called.'

'My friend?'

'I wrote it down next to the telephone.'

Her tone was abrupt. Was she irritated? Hurt? I walked over to the telephone as I combed through the possibilities. Perhaps she was annoyed that Alicia had left without coming in. Perhaps she guessed that Alicia had moved and resented our conspiratorial silence.

Then a thought came to me and blood rushed involuntarily to my face: could Mother have guessed about Lynette? Or, worse, had Lynette said something suggestive?

I dismissed this almost immediately. It was probably to do with Alicia. Mother had always been jealous of anything that smacked of closeness between us and therefore excluded her. She sometimes said, ambiguously and maliciously, 'Well, Alicia doesn't have your abilities.' She said *abilities* with distaste, as if they were a particularly unpleasant handicap; at the same time she seemed contemptuous of Alicia for not having them. I thought of Alicia's words: *She's always doing that – stealing my life.* Then I remembered Mother's display of me at her women's group during my last visit, and that I had felt, like Alicia, used; I didn't notice as much because I was rarely here.

Mother said, 'Did you eat at Alicia's?' Her tone became neutral; she was giving out no clues.

'Yes, thank you,' I said politely. I looked at the counter next to the telephone and found the message.

As lovers do, we told summaries of our lives which were, of course, as all such collections are, selective. I did not want to relive the humiliations of my marriage; I said, shrugging, 'Oh, I don't know; he was a bastard, but I suppose there must have been something good about him if I once loved him.'

This was not true. I did not love him. His body was long and lean and hard and it hurt my neck to sleep on his shoulder. He trimmed his beard too lovingly, shaved the errant parts along his throat and neck to achieve the most becoming shape. I had been attracted to his careless elegance. Only when we lived together did I see how painstakingly he worked to create that slightly unkempt style, the aloofness. He had long fingers, with fine black hairs growing on each. He did not like sex. How odd, and how fitting, that I should marry a man who did not like sex with me. He seemed to dislike women's bodies; certainly he disliked mine.

He had married while still a student. I had always felt disrespect for men who married young; it seemed to me an impulsive bid for security and predictability, an excuse to avoid the lonely task of forging a sovereign path.

I first saw Tomas coming out of the remedial French class he taught, which the Japanese girl at our boarding house attended. Meredith and I passed the building on our way to our Baudelaire class as Tomas's class let out. His longish dark hair looked sufficiently intellectual and insouciant to offset the consciously elegant shoulder bag and well-cut, slightly worn, clothes. He would never have carried his keys, chequebook, money in his pockets. He was very strong and lithe; he had been a competitive skier. He was originally Czech, and had been living in France since a child.

We saw him three or four times before we were convinced that he was also watching us. We discussed at length whether he was interested in Meredith or me; I always claimed that I could not tell, but she insisted that it was me and I knew she was right.

I agreed to marry him one night after making love in his car. This was the beginning, when we were still having sex. He lit a cigarette and rolled down the window slightly. It was November and getting cold.

'We have nowhere to go,' he sighed with calculated despair. He spoke beautiful French, perfectly accented. Because it was not his first language, he took particular care with it. 'There is no place for people like us.'

I knew I would marry him when he said that. His helplessness and pessimism worked on me like an aphrodisiac. I saw through the steam and darkness a gloomy European slumped in the car seat, and me, full of American energy and optimism. I wanted to tear apart what I thought were absurd constraints on us – his marriage, our different nationalities, his need for money. I believed I could release him, save him. He needed me. He would write; we would be in love. I was sure that my desire for him was love. He was what I always wanted.

In fact, Tomas was not as powerless and confined as I had thought. He had taken care to obtain a legal separation, which was one reason why his divorce went through so quickly. We got married a year later in a sunless registry office in Kensington by a woman who looked at us forbiddingly, as though doubting our seriousness. She may have thought ours was a *marriage blanc*, an arrangement of nationalities, an exchange of work permits.

The other reason for his easy divorce was that his parents gave his wife money so that she would release him.

I met his parents briefly, once. They had moved to Germany when Tomas went to university; a country where, they explained, they spoke the language better and felt more at home. They lived in a new, suburban house outside Stuttgart. It was the most Central European sitting room I had ever seen, and curiously incongruous with the pale-brick newness of the house itself. Inside were chairs of fine, dark wood, heavy green brocade curtains, lace runners, a large piano, dozens and dozens of books on glass-enclosed shelves.

They treated me with courtesy and reserve. Regret and surprise overlaid their every sentence, although they said nothing to indicate disapproval of me. They seemed terribly sad, and I knew I appeared to them a strange American girl who was taking their son away from his wife and child to a foreign country.

I asked Tomas about the money they had paid his wife. 'Eastern European parents,' he said, shrugging, 'will do anything to make their children happy.'

Several of the girls in our house had a crush on Tomas and were terribly jealous that I had landed such a boy-friend, when they had to make do with poor students, Moroccans, or nobody at all. They rarely left the house; I went to Florence, Nice, Paris. I went skiing on Mont Blanc and to Oktoberfest in Munich. I saw the Palais des Papes, a bullfight in Arles, walked among Rodin sculptures, drove along the Côte d'Azure and woke up in Tuscan countryside. That was when he had money, before he quit working.

Why did I do all I did for him? I moved out of the boarding house, and into his flat in town. The lay nuns wrote to my university, who threatened to withdraw my grant if I did not move back. I ignored them; I would not be going back anyway.

I went to London with him, although I did not want to live in an English-speaking country. I had to study for my degree from the beginning; my college did not accept my credits from France and the States. I worked full-time for an advertising agency in the West End and studied while he scribbled in notebooks, producing nothing. Finally, I went to New Mexico with him, because he wanted to see the American West. I did all this because I wanted him.

I *wanted* him; it was as strong as my desire to leave Clearview, go to university, and to France. But I also married him because I enjoyed having something nobody else had, but wanted. And I married him because he was a writer and because I did not want to go back home.

And because I wanted to hurt Meredith, who had become possessive, jealous, and even histrionic over the past few months. She stood at the end of the hall, screaming at me, shortly before I moved out. The entire house resonated with her words: *Fucking bitch, you fucking bitch. You have to have everything. You have to fuck everything. Everything you touch you blacken.*

Now I could look back calmly on Tomas. What he did was the worst kind of humiliation: he left me after two years in New Mexico for a nineteen-year-old girl, the daughter of a local artist, a man I and everyone else in town knew. It was, in fact, the delicious story of the season.

He had slept around almost since we arrived. Nobody dared talk to me about it. I perfected a discouraging look, much like the one I used during my time at South Bay High. I knew they felt sorry for me.

I looked back and I thought, humiliation hurts, but it can be healed, exorcized, purged. He humiliated me as a woman, but I had one act up my sleeve: I had not loved him. That was my salvation; it allowed me to go on.

After he left, I cleaned the house and threw everything of his away. I found one of his notebooks and read the elongated letters written in black fountain pen, his nearly illegible, European script:

Novel: a man who goes out for a pack of cigarettes and disappears for three years, crossing the seas, living only for the moment, at the edge of existence, and then returns, up the stairs to the wife and children sitting in their little apartment in front of the television, exactly as he left them, and the wife says, 'Didn't you get the milk?'

I felt humiliated that I could have wanted this man. I had wanted to make him into a successful writer; I had wanted to be responsible for having produced an artist. I had not done what I wanted with my life; I had put my energies into a worthless man. I thought, as I sat in my house alone, *I have never loved anybody.* This comforted me. My failure was a success because I had not loved.

And yet I would have hated to admit I married someone I did not love. I sat in Lynette's bed, smoking. 'I suppose I must have loved him,' I said.

'How did you break up?'

I lied without a second's hesitation. It was simply none of her business. 'I left New Mexico when I saw that it wasn't going to work.'

'How did you know – it wasn't going to work?'

'It just didn't,' I said impatiently, shrugging. 'Who knows why marriages go wrong?'

'You didn't know when you married him that you were gay?'

I did not answer for a moment. *Gay.* I would never think

of myself as gay. Gay meant happy. Gay people were not happy: I knew that. They were lonely, went to bars to meet other gay people, drank too much, lied to their colleagues, were disinherited from their parents, never had children, or money. People made jokes about them, or distrusted them. How could anybody want to live like that? They were like spies, always lying, always hiding. 'I had slept with women before,' I said carefully.

'Did you think of yourself as bisexual?'

I never think of myself in *labels*, I thought wearily. Annoying questions always made me reckless. 'I do not care about words like that. I sleep with whom I like.'

'Men always dumped me. I think that's why I started being attracted to women.'

'Well, you should have dumped them before they dumped you,' I said harshly.

'But if you love somebody – '

'Oh, love – there are more important things than love.'

'Like?'

'Self-respect,' I said, caustic and arrogant, my head high, an Amazon warrior, the solitary artist, the committed intellectual. Things I was not, had never been, and could pretend to be only because she believed everything I said.

She looked down, aggrieved, and did not reply. She wanted me to reassure her that I too had done humiliating things, loved stupidly, been weak and insecure. I knew this, and I held her disappointment in my hands as if it were a cheap garment hanging lifelessly on a rack, arousing momentary, idle interest.

Lynette told me her story. She had lived in California. There had been a man, a major affair. 'It took me a long time to get over him. I moved back in with my parents. I couldn't seem to do anything for a long time, maybe a year. Then my parents left for Melbourne and I just worked. And slept. That's all I did. I worked in the deli at Safeway.'

Then followed 'coming out': therapy and support groups, soul-searching, desperate crushes on older, inaccessible women. She had kept a journal throughout this period. I had always disliked the sort of woman who keeps a journal. I did not listen very carefully.

The next week, I agreed to go out with her friends after class. I looked forward to it; I felt like a sociologist invited to an obscure cult gathering. I knew they would dislike me, the interloper, but I decided I did not care.

The interesting short-haired woman, who turned out to be half-Cuban, called Mara, and apparently the teacher, was there again. She looked at me curiously. I had no doubt that she already disliked me for masquerading as a straight woman and now showing myself to be involved with Lynette.

We were in a place called Henry's Wine Bar, although it served all kinds of alcohol. It did not look English at all, but imported from California. Innumerable baskets of thick ferns hung from the ceiling rafters; the windows were fake stained-glass and the bar polished wood with brass rails. On the menu were hamburgers with avocados and tacos made with wholewheat tortillas.

I sat next to Lynette and smoked. The others were discussing a course at the university on third-world economic development. It was taught by a man and did not encompass the particular situation of third-world women. I listened half-heartedly; I knew nothing about third-world economics.

I had hated the two compulsory economics courses I took for my MBA, Accounting, marketing and finance I could manage; money supply and liquidity and theoretical explanations of market forces barely penetrated my literal mind. I spent graduate school longing for the material simplicity of the gallery: calculating the percentages I took from the artwork I displayed, my electricity and rent, the prices of the butter and eggs and bread that became the cakes and sandwiches I served in the café. I had to see goods arriving and bills paid to understand business; I could not conceive of learning to make money from a book.

I should have realized from the beginning that the MBA was a waste of money, that I had made a mistake – but I could not admit failure. I was proud that I could competently manage work I disliked.

I now saw what a mess I had made of everything. I had taken all my money from the sale of the gallery and spent it on my divorce, the trip home to Houston, on doing my entire MBA without having to work, the move to New York, working clothes for my new job. It was all gone.

How could all that money have slipped through my hands? I had assumed that the business degree would buy me a very lucrative job. But living in New York was expensive. And the job had not paid as well as I expected. I was in the midst of the MBA glut; I had rushed into it like so many of my generation, thinking it was the answer to finding myself unemployed.

Mara leaned over towards me and said, 'You live in New York?'

'Yes.' I thought of my empty sub-let; the tenants would be back by now. *I live nowhere.* I recognized Mara's accent, and said, 'You are obviously from New York.'

'The Bronx.'

'Do you miss it?'

'Can't stand the place.'

I nodded. I avoided these discussions with those who

loved and hated New York. I had heard it all too many times: it was glamorous; it was filthy; it was exciting, innovative, friendly; it was insane, dangerous, a prison.

It was no more dangerous than Houston, I reflected, thinking of the evening news, which my mother called 'the body count', the ubiquitous gun stores. Hardly a day went by without a murder.

I knew Mara was about to embark with a convert's passion on the marvellous advantages of living here, so I said quickly, 'You're teaching this class?'

'Yes, and English as a second language and Spanish.' She spoke pleasantly. 'I do everything but sweep the floors! That's the way it is here, you have to do a little bit of everything. The pay is shit but the students are nice. What do you do?'

'Oh, I was a marketing consultant. Actually, I've just quit. I'm out of a job at the moment. I'm staying with my mother.'

'What does a marketing consultant do?'

'Research and interviews. Then you tell your clients how they can make more money.'

'Marketing what?'

'Oh, anything: laundry, detergent, cars, electronics, credit cards. Consumer products, mostly. You try to find out if the market's growing, or if you can expand it by differentiating the product, if there are any obstacles to buying it, like distribution.'

'Like inventing a new kind of cornflakes and getting the supermarket to put them on an eye-level shelf.'

'Exactly.'

'What if people don't want to buy the new kind of cornflakes?'

'Well, then, you made a faulty analysis and your client loses money.'

'Or maybe the new kind of cornflakes wasn't different enough from the old kind.'

'Yes, of course, that's possible. You can't force people to buy something. You can only offer then a choice.'

'Is that true?' That you can't force people to buy things?'

'Of course. You can only try to persuade them.'

'I was just wondering if you think, say, the amount of money women spend on clothes is a form of manipulation, which, because of the subservient economic nature of women's relations with men, could be called a kind of *force*.'

I felt my eyes glaze over. She went on, 'I mean, if women didn't care about attracting men, would they continue to spend as much money on their clothes?'

'I don't know.' I knew this was a jab at my appearance and my obvious bisexuality – why would I dress so well if I didn't like men? – which was a crime in her eyes. I wasn't going to go along with it. I didn't care that other, usually gay, women wanted to shave their heads and wear ragged jeans, and I didn't want to argue about it.

'I mean, can you really talk about free choice outside its historical and political context?'

'I've never really thought about it.' I lit a cigarette. I did not want to discuss free choice with a woman who thought I was a victim of a sexist society.

I glanced at Lynette. She was still talking with the others about the third-world course, although it seemed now that the man who taught it rather than the course material was at issue.

I had been right about Mara from the first: intelligent, political, stringent. I had wished for years to be this kind of woman, but I never would. I felt guilty: I ought to be more serious. I knew I was shallow; I liked clothes and money and make-up. I was cowardly: I needed men. I was dishonest: I slept with girls like Lynette, shabby, inferior girls;

97

or girls like Meredith, girls who wanted a man, girls like me.

Mara was demanding, uncompromising: an adult. I felt meagre next to her. She was very attractive but her exactness, her sureness, intimidated me. She would never like a woman like me, and I would never tolerate a lover with whom I felt inferior. I knew when I talked to her that I was far from the strong woman and intellectual I had once hoped to be. I turned away and reached for another cigarette.

Mara took the hint, and changed the subject, saying, 'Are you going back to New York?'

The abruptness of this surprised me; I said, 'I don't know.'

She must have taken this to mean that it depended on my new relationship with Lynette, because she nodded knowingly.

This annoyed me and I added, 'I would rather go back to Europe.'

'Oh, where?'

'I studied in France and England – I did my degree in London. I'd rather live in Paris though.'

I did not mention why going back was almost impossible. Apart from my lack of money, I now had what every American abroad knew about, discussed at parties, tried to resolve: the work permit problem. I had been able to work before by being married to Tomas, who was a citizen of an EEC country. But I was now divorced.

'I see,' she said severely. 'So you're fluent in French?'

'Oh, not any more,' I said airily, in the tone the English use when they want to imply the opposite. Not that it mattered. I didn't have to care what this woman thought of me.

Three hours later, Lynette and I were sitting in bed, sweaty and tired from sex, smoking. Out of the comfortable silence she suddenly said, 'I don't think we should see each other again.'

I blinked and looked sideways at her. I tilted my ash into a jar lid balancing on her thigh. She held the sheet across her ribs with one arm and her cigarette near her mouth with the other. She stared straight ahead.

'What?' I could not tell whether she was joking.

'You don't know me very well and I think we'd better leave it that way.'

'What are you talking about?'

'We've had a good time and I'd rather leave it that way. I've got a lot of problems right now and I think I need the space to work them out myself.'

'What problems?'

'Oh, you know . . .' She shrugged. 'I've slept around a lot, since I came – here.' She turned away, blew out smoke and looked back at me with eyes bright with tears.

'I see.'

'After – California. I was starting to get my life together out there when – well, when he dumped me, this guy I was living with.'

I did not reply.

'He dumped me for this other woman. Don't you think it's just a crock of shit to think you can be heterosexual and a feminist?'

I shrugged. Ideological struggles bored me. Besides, she sounded on edge, and I didn't want to start an argument.

'I mean, how can women care about each other if they're stealing each other's men and hurting each other? I mean, really *invading* each other's lives, you know?'

'I don't know.'

She looked at me. 'I think women should help each other.'

'Yes, of course,' I said mildly.

She drew a breath and went on. 'Well, I got back and my parents were about to leave for Australia. They had the house up for sale. I didn't have anywhere to go, and they offered to let me rent it. But I had to pay, you know, the house note and all.'

'Yes, you've told me that.'

'Well, that was why I got roommates, you know. But anyway, I was broke and pretty fucked-up for a while, and I slept around and stuff.' She paused and launched into her speech, which was clearly planned. 'I'm in love with you, you know. You're the most wonderful person who's ever looked at me. I know you'll leave me and I just wish you'd go now.'

I knew this was a carefully orchestrated attempt to get me to declare me intentions. I said, 'I don't know what all this – our relationship – means.'

She was silent. Then, 'I was just beginning to get it together again before you came along.'

'In what way?'

'Oh, you know, going to college. I've been saving to move out of here. I wrote to my parents to tell them I wanted to get an apartment on my own.' She worked as a cocktail waitress, a fact she had kept secret from her gay friends. 'I know you think this place is a dump. Well, it is. And since George – oh, you don't know him; he's my roommate's boyfriend. He's practically moved in and it's just too many people.'

'Well, I think that's great,' I said matter-of-factly. 'I think you should get an apartment if you want to.'

'Oh, but don't you see, you've changed all that. I'm like so in love with you and I can't stop thinking about you. And you've torn all these stupid ideas up. My stupid little dreams of living in an apartment and going to this rinky-dink college, and here you've done all this stuff and studied and lived in Europe. It's as if you've showed me another whole world and I can't be part of it.'

I was silent, thinking, *Here we go.*

'Are you going to leave?' She turned to me desperately.

I laughed a little. 'I don't have anywhere to go. I don't have any money, for one thing.'

'Oh, but eventually you'll get a job and some money. People like you always do.'

'I don't know when or how. I don't know what I'm going to do for a job.'

'Yes, but you will.'

'Yes, I suppose.'

'And then you'll go away.'

'Well – yes.'

'Without me.'

I hesitated, disliking my cowardice. 'I don't know.'

'Probably without me. You've always left your lovers when you're sick of them, haven't you?' *People like you always do.*

'I don't know where all this will lead.' I suddenly realized the script I had prepared for was going off track; I had no idea where this conversation might lead. It was too early to have this talk, too early to break up. I didn't want to stop seeing her yet. I needed her.

'But you do know there's no chance we'll stay together.'

'If that's the way you feel – '

'You *know* that's not the way I feel! But I have to know how you feel!'

'I don't know.'

'If you loved me, you would know; you would try to find a way. So I want you to leave and not see me again.'

'But I want to see you again.' I was calm, rational. Her

attempt to control me rankled; I would not let her have the upper hand.

'Until you dump me.'

'No, no, I didn't say that.'

'Well, what *are* you saying?'

'We have to see how things go.'

'You mean there is a chance?'

'Well, I suppose we can't know what will happen.'

She crushed the end of her cigarette against the lid and left it to burn. She looked at me. 'I know I'm a mess and you could have somebody much better. But if I had a chance, I could really get it together. Really, I could. I always wanted to be – the kind of person that doesn't get dumped.' She spoke in a rush. 'We could move into Houston and get jobs. It's completely different there. There's museums and women's groups and feminist bookstores and – '

'Yes, I know what it's like,' I said, picking up the lid and putting out the cigarette.

'I really love you, you know. I could take care of you while you look for a job.'

'I don't know if I want to live here.'

'Well, we could save and go somewhere else. We could travel.'

I smoked. 'Perhaps.' I knew I wanted to continue to see her, for the moment, anyway; I told myself, maybe I did want to see where this relationship would go. It wasn't a lie. Anyway, what was the truth? Telling her my gut feeling that it would never work out might mean a major scene, name-calling, a screaming match. How did I know it wouldn't work out?

'Perhaps you don't want to live with a woman.'

'Don't be ridiculous.'

'You appear – it's really important to you to act and look straight.'

'What of it?' I demanded aggressively.

'Well, maybe you don't want to commit yourself to a woman – '

It was a dare; I knew she did not want it to end yet either. She simply wanted me to give her hope that we had a future together. She wanted time. She wanted enough time to make me fall in love with her.

I examined myself for some sign of love. Perhaps, I thought briefly, this is something I ought to do. Perhaps this is where my life has now led. I could not be, was not, devoid of feelings for somebody I so wanted to sleep with. And I was willing to do certain things for her, some things.

But I did not want to live with her: it came to me with unmistakable simplicity. I could not deny it. Did I feel the slightest tremor of guilt? I cannot remember. Did I see that I would never do something good for someone out of pity? I did pity her, but in an impatient way; I thought, *Well, if you don't like your life, then change it.* I knew things were not that simple; it *was* unfair that Lynette was unhappy, had so little, had been dumped by this man, had never finished high school, was not beautiful or particularly intelligent. And I had so much. Yet I knew I did not love her. My pity was not kind; it was harsh and callous.

Then I lied: I told myself, maybe it could work out, you never could tell, perhaps I should give it time . . . But the truth was that I felt the pull of loneliness and boredom, and the need for her inferiority, her admiration.

I drew a deep breath. When I opened my mouth, I heard myself take refuge in that traditional line men seem to have imprinted on their genes, so naturally, so universally do they use it: 'I just don't want to be pressured about the future.' And I felt this lie set to work into my life like a fungus, spreading with long, searching arms.

8

The moment I awoke, I knew it was late. The bed was empty and light poured through the sheet covering the window. I sat up painfully; I couldn't decide which was worse for my back, this mattress or my bed at Mother's. This one felt like a centre of lumpy porridge contained within a perimeter as hard as a tyre.

I pulled on my shirt. I felt as if I'd been beaten up: puffy, dazed, indistinct. I had spent the night ineffectually clinging to the hard edge of the bed, and rolling towards the middle, against Lynette, in an awkward heap.

She must be in the bathroom, I thought. I pulled on my underwear, sat back down on the mattress and brushed my hair, trying to remember the last time I had had a decent night's sleep. Then I thought of the ridiculous verbal game of the night before. Suddenly I was angry. Like a man who has been tricked into a premature proposal, I wanted to escape. I would not let this silly girl blackmail me into declaring eternal love.

This was it: the breaking point. With every stroke of the brush through my hair, I banished our affair further into the land of the past, the realm of minor escapades.

I got up and finished dressing. I found some hand lotion and tissues among the disorder on her walnut dresser and wiped sweat and the dregs of my make-up away. I needed to use the toilet, but decided to wait until I got to Mother's. I wanted to leave immediately.

I walked out to the hall, past doors I normally saw closed. The bedroom next to Lynette's was nearly bare but for an unmade bed, trampled male and female clothing on the floor, a clock radio, a lamp.

The one across the hall emitted a masculine smell; heavy woven orange and brown curtains, a hastily made bed, a chest of dark wood signalled unkempt bachelorhood. As I passed, a large glass aquarium on the chest caught my eye and I paused and stepped back.

It did not have any water; a layer of sand lined the bottom. I stared at it for a few minutes before I could take in what I knew I had seen: the black and gold mosaic of snake skin. It was a python, as thick as my arm, coiled upon itself. I could not see the head, but its vigorous, gleaming skin left no doubt that it was alive.

I could not believe that I had been creeping in and out of this house in the dark, sleeping on a mattress on the floor, for two weeks, with a loose python on the other side of the wall. Yes, loose: the aquarium had no cover.

I walked through the living room, which I had never seen in daylight. It was almost identical to Mother's, but dirtier. The walls were wood-panelled; the carpet, matted brown shag. The sofa and matching chair, also brown, slumped as if abandoned on a kerb. Under the television was a VCR, with a few tapes in plain white boxes, their titles scribbled on the ends with felt-tip pen: *Freddie III, Mad Max II, Predator.*

I went into the kitchen and stopped. A man and woman were sitting at the folding table. I had never seen him before, but I recognized Charlene from Mother's group at Janet's house.

The man was in jeans, no shirt; Charlene was wearing a dark blue bathrobe. They were smoking a joint. On the table were coffee cups, an ashtray, a plastic bag filled with marijuana, plates with crusts of toast, the bone handle of a knife protruding from an open jar of strawberry jam. The telephone rang.

'Oh, fuck,' said the man, drawing on the joint. Then he saw me.

'Well, *go* get it,' the man ordered Charlene without taking his eyes off me. She handed him the joint and scurried, gaping at me, into the living room.

Lynette appeared from behind. 'Oh, hi. Do you want some coffee?' She walked to the stove and picked up the kettle. 'This is George. This is Kris. That was Charlene. Terry's our other roommate – he's gone to work.'

George said, 'Hi Kris,' in an insinuating way I did not like at all. He was bearded and his hair was long enough to be tied back. I could tell he was not tall, but he had a tough, powerful body. His bare chest and arms looked completely at rest, and yet latent, primed. He continued smoking the joint, watching me.

'I can make coffee,' said Lynette.

George looked me over top to bottom as he drew on the joint. 'Yeah, Kris, have some coffee.'

I turned around to Lynette and said, very carefully, 'No thank you, I have to go now.' I had to pass him to reach the back door. I half-expected his hand to reach out and touch me, block me. I heard his breath as I passed his chair. As I walked down the drive, I felt eyes watching me from the kitchen window.

I was half-way home before I began to calm down. I was surprised at how rattled I was, both by George and by the coincidence of coming across Charlene. My anxiety focused on George, but disparate thoughts about Charlene raced through my mind without clear connections: she was Lynette's roommate; she knew Janet or knew someone who knew Janet who knew Mother. She knew I was sleeping with Lynette. She was somebody who knew me when I was

Krystal, went to South Bay High. She lived in a house exactly like Mother's, but worse. A house I had been sleeping in the past two weeks. A house with a python and a man who looked and acted like a rapist. George.

I had seen the full force of pure, masculine hatred and it unnerved me. He seemed to take my presence as a deliberate insult; he was the kind of man capable of attacking me for the sheer pleasure of hurting a woman who – he no doubt assumed – rejected men. Although I had dealt with plenty of aggressive men, I had never confronted what I knew to be danger so closely. This man would not hesitate to use force to subdue any woman; and he would clearly use it on me. I looked at my hands; I was shaking.

I turned with relief on to Mother's familiar street. I passed her neighbours: neatly shelved tools lined an open garage; a tricycle lay on a gravelled drive. Even the rusty sail-boat seemed a sign of safety. I felt this man diminish in importance. I did not have to cross his path again; this was the time to break it off with Lynette: what had started last night would only get worse. And the python! That decided it: nothing would bring me into that house again.

Mother had already left for work. I went immediately to the toilet and then stripped and showered. I washed every inch of my skin. I shaved my legs and underarms. I plucked my eyebrows and trimmed my toenails. Then I went into the kitchen wrapped in two towels and made toast and coffee; it was nearly 11 o'clock.

I sat down to my breakfast and tried to think about the future. I had been here for over two weeks and had done nothing to find a job. I had annoyed my mother by my behaviour. I was spending money, going around town doing silly things with Alicia. I had to get serious now.

I drank more coffee and my mind felt clear and sharp: Lynette took her place in the scheme of my life, a casual, somewhat dingy and mildly embarrassing episode; it was now over. I knew that she would eventually call, and I would have to talk to her, but for the moment, she simply disappeared. I thought how presumptuous she was to try to force my hand. How absurd to think that she could have any power over *me*.

Women did not have power over me. Tomas had, for a while. Until I finally said, for the first time, *No*. I suppose I always knew that our marriage would end the moment I decided I would not move and make yet another life from scratch simply because he was restless. And so I was not surprised when he left with someone who would.

After Tomas left, I spent nearly a month alone. I sewed: a white silk blouse, a cashmere jacket the colour of young fawn, an elegant silk and wool suit which I would wear to my job interviews two years later. I drank coffee, made in a tiny espresso pot I had bought in a French shop six years before.

I sat in a straight-backed pale blue armchair in my silent, white living room, by a window. The house was an adobe copy of a seventeenth-century house built by Spanish Jesuits. I watched the winter sky, and the snow fall erratically and then melt on the wet trees and the glimmering, dense undergrowth that covered the slope falling below me.

I asked my nearest neighbours, Gary and Annette, also gallery owners, to bring me groceries so that I would not have to leave the house. I decided to wait until I was strong again. How important my pride was to me then; it was my weapon, protection and strength.

Then one day, I was ready. I decided to walk into town.

I left my house early. It was snowing very softly; minute flecks of white rested briefly on my black coat before suddenly metamorphosing into clear droplets and vanishing. I stopped from time to time and looked around as if I had never before noticed the beauty of where I lived.

My road was unpaved, and descended down the hill. I continued walking carefully through the slush, looking for dry patches. The road was less than a mile long. I passed Gary and Annette's house and, at the end of the hill, came to the interstate. To my right was Arizona; to my left, Texas.

I crossed the interstate and walked up the side street towards town. It was the most European town I had seen in the United States. The streets were narrow and winding; the houses closely placed and strictly kept in the original six-teenth- and seventeenth-century Spanish and French designs. In the middle of town was a square, lined with shops selling Native American jewellery, blown glass, cer-amics, textiles, leather.

It was February and the streets were empty. Most of the shops were closed. There were no tourists; the Christmas craft fairs were over. We received little traffic from skiers, who made for higher, more northerly mountains.

I walked up to the grocery store. I would pick up my *Times* as I had so often before and take it to Rosita's for a breakfast of huevos rancheros, buttermilk biscuits, and numerous cups of weak coffee.

It was about 9 o'clock. A few cars were parked in front of the grocery and the hardware store next door. Then I saw a dented pick-up, dull black. The tailgate was open and Dewitt was loading lumber into it, his strong arms carefully sliding the planks across the tailgate and into the bed of the truck. I had known Dewitt almost as long as I had lived in town, nearly two years. He was a potter, and lived in his studio in a converted barn outside of town. I sometimes took his pots on consignment in my gallery.

'Hello, Kris,' he said, continuing to load the lumber on to his truck.

I watched him. 'Building shelves,' he explained. After the rush of Christmas, people in town spent two or three months resting. They cleaned their studios, made improvements, experimented with new designs, slept, and threw parties. By Easter, it was time to begin again producing the enormous stocks of glass, pottery, jewellery, stained-glass and leatherwork they would sell during the remainder of the year.

Dewitt was the last sort of man I ever wanted. He had dropped out of a Ph.D in English at an eastern university ten years before, for obscure reasons having to do with student protests against Vietnam. He was a draft-dodger, a convicted felon. He had appeared for his induction and torn up his draft card in the face of the reception officer. He was immediately arrested.

He had become a potter on an impulse. He had heard of our town, which was known as an 'artist' colony', and arrived suddenly, with all his possessions in his black pick-up. There was talk of a child he had left behind. He was thirty-five or thirty-six, but looked older, from the hard, physical work of the past few years, from disappointment perhaps, or having made too many mistakes. His hair was roughly cut and his beard nearly covered his face, as though he no longer wanted to know what he looked like. He was not unattractive, and he was known for being extremely gentle and kind. He never had any money; he never left to visit his family. He seemed completely alone.

Except that he wasn't. He lived with a young girl at his studio. She was, he told everyone, his apprentice. She had been there two or three years, but few people saw her or noticed her. She did not go to the parties, or if she did, stayed in the background. She helped him set up his booth at the fairs and then disappeared. She was often in his truck, waiting for him when he came into my gallery with his pots. I never met her. She was nameless; she was 'Dewitt's apprentice'.

I watched Dewitt and understood that he knew Tomas had left and would not bring it up unless I did. He smiled briefly, the wrinkles around his eyes deepening. I felt unequivocal sympathy wash over me and tried to resist it, although I knew there was no cruelty or pleasure in his pity; he looked as if he was incapable of amusing himself at another's expense.

We talked for a few minutes. He had turned off his kilns, he told me; he had stopped firing for the moment. He wanted to pour a new plaster wedging board. He thought about building a new kiln to try some salt-firings. He had not sold much at the Christmas fairs. I was not surprised: Dewitt's pots were solid, well-made, but unimaginative.

I turned to leave. He said, 'Are you going to Gary and Annette's tonight?'

'Yes,' I said. I had already thought about this. I had attended their previous winter parties and I wanted to show that I was not afraid of being seen.

'Do,' he replied with concern, as though what I did mattered, and he had thought about this and felt it was the best thing for me to do. I watched him pick up another pine plank. He held the soft wood in his hands. Suddenly, the loneliness of the past week rose to the surface and I felt exposed and open beneath his concern. I thought of my curt, polite answers in response to Annette's restrained questions as she handed me groceries through the door; and the brittle surface that seemed to cover me cracked and fell away.

I wanted to put my head on his shoulder and weep, to feel the strength of his shoulders. He was a tall, large man. He paused for a moment, still holding the board, and leaned against the truck. I imagined myself surrounded by his solid arms; I wanted to be told what to do. I wanted to cry out that I was no longer certain of anything: I had spent the last six years looking after a man who did not love me.

Dewitt reached over and touched my shoulder, saying, 'You have nothing to be afraid of.'

I smiled and moved away, pretending not to notice the touch, and went into the grocery to fetch my paper. I came out and walked along the square past the darkened windows of my café, decorated in art deco black and white. I had written each menu myself, in black ink: sandwiches, quiches, cakes, pastries. Italian espresso was dispensed from an enormous, gleaming gold machine. On the walls were watercolours and photographs by local artists; the other half, the gallery, was empty now; I usually had sculpture, ceramics, blown glass and jewellery on consignment.

I had nothing to be afraid of. I walked to Rosita's, thinking of the party that evening; I had prepared myself for ironic smiles and malicious comments. But Dewitt would be there as well. He would protect me by his presence; he would stand near me and make normal conversation and nobody would dare say an unkind thing to me. People respected Dewitt.

This made me afraid. I had spent my time alone, my recovery, preparing for what I had thought would be the most difficult part of being betrayed: having to be proud. I now saw that I had not built defences against the stronger effects of tenderness and false masculine comfort.

Later that night, Dewitt touched my face and said, 'You have a harshness I've always liked – an arrogance that I admire.'

We were standing alone in front of a painting I looked at, but could not see, as though my brain had been disconnected from my vision. Gary and Annette usually exhibited a young and unknown artist for their winter party; nobody but locals came, and few paid attention to the paintings. I glanced down, hoping nobody was watching us. Most of the party had gathered around a large table where Annette poured out cups of hot wine and passed platters of carrot cake and tiny pastries filled with cream cheese. I forced myself to laugh lightly, disparagingly.

He ignored this. 'But I've also always seen a kind of passion under all that control.'

I already knew this was Dewitt's assessment of me. He always spoke to me as though saying, *I can see through you. You can't fool me.* I had never had a conversation with Dewitt that was not in some way flirtatious. He spoke with an edge of humour and suggestion, as though we both knew that we were attracted to one another and had to pretend that we weren't, like children trying to behave and wanting to giggle. I always found this a strain.

'One day, you should let go of that control. It's the other side of your passion. You're always trying to keep it in check. Tomas did not understand that, but I saw it at once. He wanted you to punish him, for being a bad boy. He thought your hardness was a need to dominate.'

This was true. 'Yes,' I said. I found myself seduced by the sharpness of his perceptions, although I also knew that he was flattering me. And I knew that every experienced man knows a woman loves to be analysed, loves to watch him create a layer of complications that then fall away like silk under his shrewd touch, revealing a simple, beautiful core. It annoyed me that this man, whom I thought so unsuited to me, should be so clever.

I smiled at him scornfully, trying to keep us from that point at which a man knows you will go to bed with him. I kept telling myself, *I can still choose.* But I knew I would not go home alone.

Dewitt and I left Gary and Annette's gallery, awkwardly, with his arm around me, through the slush. We decided to walk to my house. We stopped at his pick-up – he needed something, he said. He turned his back to me, but I saw him leave the keys under the driver's seat. For his apprentice, of course, who must still have been at the party. The studio was a good fifteen miles from town. I wondered briefly whether this had happened before, how many people Dewitt had slept with. I wondered whether I would regret this. But, I thought, I have lived here two years and never slipped once. I deserve one ill-considered fling, one reckless night.

The next morning we woke up in my bed, polite and wary. I did not want to see him again, and knew I would. A one-night stand would have been to admit a mistake. I hated mistakes.

He left, refusing a ride. He would walk into town, he said.

I thought, *I don't have to see him again. I don't even have to stay here.* The gallery had been closed since Tomas left. The two girls I employed to serve food had gone to Aspen to work until Easter. I thought about an offer I had had around Christmas, which I had rejected out of hand. There were always people looking for small businesses, wanting to get away from city life, wanting to live in the mountains, particularly in our town.

I drank another cup of coffee and, after a while, showered and dressed. It was about noon; I expected Dewitt to call that evening, out of courtesy. The day stretched before me, empty. Then I saw Dewitt's pick-up pull up and he got out.

I opened the door and let him in. He ran his hand through his hair and said, 'Got a cup of coffee?'

'Sure.' I let him in and went into the kitchen to put the kettle on. When I got back, he still stood in the hall. 'Is something wrong?'

'She's gone. Linda's left.' He looked around the room and then back at me, expectantly.

For a moment, I did not know whom he meant; then of course I did. 'Oh.' I remembered the keys. This must have been one time too many. 'What happened?'

He told me. He had walked into town to try to get a ride out to his place. Someone at the hardware store told Dewitt he'd seen the pick-up at the bus station. Dewitt walked there, found the keys under the seat, where he had left them the night before, and drove the pick-up home. The studio was empty, all her things gone. There was no note; she was simply gone. She had apparently caught a Greyhound early that morning. He didn't even know where: there had been three buses the night before, and the station refused to tell him which she had boarded.

'I see.' What could I say? That I was sorry I had run off his girlfriend?

But he looked so distraught that I realized I had to comfort him. He needed a friend, and in a way I was glad of the opportunity to change the tone of our relations. We could forget about the night before. I could sympathize with him, listen to his sad story.

I said, 'Do you want to stay for dinner?'

'No, no. I'll – go home.' He had not taken off his coat. I noticed it for the first time. It was a thin leather jacket. The lining was ripped. It occurred to me that Dewitt was probably always cold. I had been to his studio once. He had no heating apart from the kilns. It was an uninsulated barn, with an open loft, in which he had a bed, a refrigerator, a table and stools, and dozens and dozens of books, all in boxes stacked against one wall.

I suddenly felt great tenderness towards him. 'If you need company, or a hot meal, just call.'

He did. He drove over the next night, and then every night for a week. I slept with him out of pity and loneliness. How horrible two lonely people are.

Finally, one night, I said, 'We have to stop doing this, it isn't doing either of us any good.'

He looked relieved, and I nearly blushed with the humiliation of it: he had been sleeping with me because he had not wanted to insult me, he had not had the heart to tell me he didn't want to. And then, because he did not have to sleep with me any more, he talked to me, an unbearable flood of words, sudden and gushing, as if released by drink, or therapy or confession.

He had picked her up hitchhiking on the interstate three years before and taken her home, initially for the night. She was carrying a cardboard box tied with string. It contained a hand-stitched quilt her grandmother had made and a few clothes. He had taken her home and fed her. She had not eaten in two days. She was seventeen. I found this story oddly, reluctantly touching.

She had stayed. He taught her how to mix glazes, wedge clay. She kept the studio clean, and cooked for him. She read his books, systematically, one box at a time. She had never read books before; they talked about them. Even as he told me how he had discussed with her *Emma* and *Middlemarch*, I heard in his voice the freshness of discovery, and I saw a layer of graduate-school cynicism drop from his face.

He had not known how much he loved her until she was gone. And, no, he had never done this before. He had not slept with anyone else since her arrival.

'Why did you do it?' I asked, as though he had slept with someone else, as though I were a disinterested friend.

'I think,' he said carefully, 'I did it because I knew she was going to leave me.'

It was, in its own convoluted way, clear and logical: he

had slept with me to induce this girl to leave, a girl whom he loved and could not bear to lose. He drove her away because he feared she would soon, or one day, leave him, and he wanted the pain to be sharp, quick and self-inflicted.

When I flew to Houston, a few weeks later, I put aside the affair as if my actions belonged to another person. Dewitt was one of those impulsive mistakes, the result of loneliness and depression, a pain-induced reaction. I would not dwell on it.

But I knew that I had to find some place safe to be, a place where I would be told what to do. I knew I was dangerous; I could not trust myself to make decisions. I went home as a wounded animal seeks a cave; I decided to apply to graduate schools as if I knew a debilitating illness were about to overcome me, and I would be, for some time, incapable of looking after myself.

I finished my breakfast and rose to wash my dishes. Then I noticed a note in Mother's handwriting by the telephone. She had scribbled my name and a local number, nothing else. I dried my hands and dialled the number before wondering who could be calling me.

A woman's professional, busy voice answered, 'Department of Romance Languages.' I told her my name and explained that I had received a message without a name.

'Oh, yes, Mara mentioned you to me and said you might be able to teach French. I understand you are quite fluent.'

Mara? Then I remembered that she had said, *You're fluent?* I faltered, and then managed to answer, 'Yes, but I haven't taught it. In fact, I've never taught anything.'

'Well, we're in a bit of a bind over the summer – we've lost two of our faculty and classes start in two weeks.' She sounded cautious, but desperate, as though she were crossing her fingers that I was the godsend she needed. 'It's not like teaching kids. Most of our students are older and highly motivated. We're a commuter campus, catering to working and returning students – '

'Yes, I know.'

'As long as you know your material – '

'That shouldn't be a problem.' In fact, I had no idea how my French was. I hadn't spoken French since Tomas had left; not a word in two years. But this was a job handed to me on a platter. 'My grammar is good and I know the . literature.' I tried to sound confident.

'That sounds fantastic,' she said distractedly. She explained she was a languages programme director, whatever that was, and would like to interview me as soon as possible, if I was interested, of course.

I was, and a time was arranged. I put down the phone and stood at the kitchen counter, in my towels, freshly-showered; a fine layer of perspiration had formed on my skin. The woman's bright, professional voice echoed around me like another life. I had a job interview.

9

The following day I made a list from memory of my under-graduate reading – Camus, Gide, Mauriac, Flaubert. I felt diligent and purposeful for the first time in months. My love of French came back to me: I felt a surge of childish excitement. I remembered how I read absolutely anything and everything in French: detective novels, women's maga-zines, road signs, advertisements in the supermarket: *Seule-ment cette semaine: Vache Qui Rit, dix-huit francs le kilo.*

I learned French with a sense of amazement and delight: I could actually *do it*, put these funny sounds together and make sense, be understood, hear myself whip out idiomatic expressions, attach subordinate clauses, use subjunctive, pluperfect. It was thrilling, like learning to ice-skate or ride a bicycle. I would read along, carried on a wave, thinking, *I am reading this*, remembering how as a child learning to read my own language had aroused in me the same zeal for more, the same assurance: it was so easy once you knew how.

I was not too worried about the intermediate courses. ·Even as a freshman I recognized how poorly the teaching assistants, and even the professors, spoke compared with Mme Smith. And my French had been very good; Tomas and I rarely spoke English together. I walked around the house for the rest of the day, talking to myself with surpris-ing ease, hearing myself speak French for the first time in two years.

All this made me very happy.

I arranged for Mother to drop me at the college and spent

119

a day preparing for the interview. I skimmed novels in the library. I went to the lab and read tattered women's magazines stacked on a shelf: *Marie-Claire, Elle, Marie-France.* I browsed through the bookstore. I found the introductory and intermediate textbooks, paged through the lists of verb conjugations and the sweetly simple dialogues that reminded me of the Dior-suited *Mme Dupont* of my high-school days:

JEAN: *D'où venez-vous?*
ANNE: *Je vien des Etats-Unis.*
JEAN: *Est-ce que vous aimez la France?*
ANNE: *Oui, je l'aime bien.*

The languages programme director turned out to be a small, middle-aged woman in a business suit named Eleanor. She was nervous and busy, with hair that flipped up at her ears like wings.

'Oh, yes, do sit down.' She waved at a chair. 'I do hope you can help us out. You know, this is such a nice campus, and the students aren't like regular students – they're much more motivated because, you see, they're older – '

'Yes,' I said. 'I worked here once, a long time ago.'

'Oh, I see. Well, you know then. And the faculty are really very nice – ' She stopped. 'You do have a degree?'

'Yes, from the University of London.'

'Oh, I see. Well, I suppose that will do.'

'In art history – painting mostly. But I've studied in France.'

'Oh, fine, fine. Well, you see, if things worked out, well, if you wanted to stay, there's a possibility, but of course, you don't have a Ph.D – '

'No.'

'Well, it doesn't matter in the summer, you see. And we

had this terrible mix-up – well, that doesn't matter either. The thing is, can you teach introductory conversation and composition as well as one intermediate course – they're not really intermediate, of course, don't worry about that – I'm sure your French is far better – and one course in French civilization? In English, of course?'

'Well, the language courses shouldn't be a problem. Is there a syllabus, or a programme or outline or something?'

'Well, not really. There's a textbook and workbook. And the lab book, of course.'

'The French civ I'd have to read up a bit. Is there a text-book for that as well?'

Her face fell slightly. 'Well, no.'

'I see.' I wondered how much they would pay me. 'Can I expect any help from anyone in the department?'

'Oh, of course! The faculty are *so* nice.'

I bet, I thought. I wondered what the 'mix-up' was about. I knew about office politics. However, I needed a job. I needed money. I said, 'Well, I'd be delighted to give it a try, if you'd offer it to me.'

'Yes, you seem perfect. I'm sure it will work out fine. We start in two weeks. Oh, and one other thing – Mara said you were looking for a house?'

'She did?'

'Yes, she said that you might be interested.'

'In a house?'

'She reminded me of a house, it's in University Place – you could practically walk to campus – of this really very nice man – he was in the economics department, and he's on sabbatical, in Washington, DC, as a matter of fact, at a research institute. It isn't much rent. He wants to sub-let it to an academic, and you are more or less, or at least, you are now – '

I walked out ten minutes later with a job and a place to

live. I walked down the hall, and suddenly these newly carpeted halls, with their placid students and labelled rooms and neatly arranged bulletin boards, did not seem so bad after all.

Mother said, 'Well, it's something to do while you look for a job.'

I ignored this. I was too pleased with the prospect of reading French again. 'I think it'll be fun. It's just for the summer.'

She nodded. 'I see,.'

Then I told her about the house in University Place. I had not seen it, but I knew it would look like Janet's, and the thought of a skylight, the little terrace in back, my own kitchen, excited me. I thought about the summer ahead, having a job. I would make friends, perhaps with Washington State. I would be speaking and reading French. I could take my time finding the right job. Everything would turn out all right.

'Oh. Then you won't be staying here any more,' she said guardedly.

'I think I might as well go ahead and take it.' I spoke in an off-hand manner, as though I had no strong feeling about it one way or the other. 'I don't want to impose on you the entire summer.'

She pressed her mouth together, mildly insulted that I wanted to leave, but also relieved. 'You do what you want, dear.'

'Well, I think I'll do that then.' A weighty silence followed; I could think of nothing to say to break it, and I felt her deliberate, grim resolve not to speak.

I have met other people like my mother, people who believe that they are well-behaved and polite and do not say rude or cruel things and yet have the ability to emit an aura of disapproval and anger more powerful than words, and more hurtful. Her sulking was manipulative, spiteful. Yet if I said, *Stop it! Stop doing this to me!* she would have been shocked and uncomprehending.

I tried to stifle my anger. We set the table and sat down. I said, conversationally, 'I haven't looked at it yet, so I don't know. It's probably a bit of a dump – it belongs to a man, a bachelor who's on sabbatical.'

She said nothing.

'I hope you'll come over and have dinner with me,' I said, with an attempt at lightness, but my voice sounded cheerless.

'Of course,' she replied, like a jilted woman whose lover has said he hopes they'll be friends.

I said, without thinking, 'Mother, is something the matter?' I felt suddenly hot and my breathing stopped; I could not believe I had said it.

'No.' Her voice was sharp, indignant.

I had committed myself; I plunged on. 'Well, you sound like something is the matter.'

'Well, there isn't.'

'Do you want me to stay here?'

'You can do what you want.' Petulant, angry, martyred, self-pitying.

I braced myself. I knew my mother well: a moment of . honesty was an excuse for her to air resentments and anger. She would do nothing to deflect this, nothing kind to alleviate this horrible feeling between us, and I felt the tension over the table stretch unbearably.

I could have stood up and walked out, but this would have meant a rupture between us. Why didn't I do it? I was afraid of tearing apart the tenuous fabric between us, this frail bond of obligation and accident, devoid of love or understanding. It was not much, my relationship with my mother, but it was the only thing of substance I had. And though this was still a time when I thought I could march through life, taking and leaving whatever I pleased, I simply could not do it; I knew I could not live cut off and rootless. I would have to find a way out of this.

I tried to speak calmly. 'Mother, has my being here inconvenienced you?'

'You could say that.'

I was relieved at this admission, which gave me the courage to go on. 'But why?'

'Krystal, you are not the only one who has problems, you know.'

I waited; she said nothing more. I saw that this was going to be like pulling teeth, a game of twenty questions: guess-what-Mother-is-talking-about. I started at the most obvious. 'Is it money?'

'Well, of course that's always a problem. Food is not cheap. Electricity isn't free.'

'I'm sorry, I should have been buying food, and contributing. How stupid of me. It's just that I have so little right now and I didn't think about it.'

'No, I suppose you didn't.'

'I suppose,' I added carefully, feeling my heart rise to my throat, 'that I've been a rude guest.'

'Oh, I don't care what you do. You're an adult. But you're not the only one who wants privacy.'

'I've overstayed. I'm sorry; I'll be gone soon.'

'It's not your staying. It's that I never know when you're going to be in or out.'

I bit my lip with embarrassment; I couldn't say anything.

'And I do have a private life, you know.' She continued to eat, more calmly now.

I looked at her. *What?* What was that supposed to mean?

'I *am* involved with someone.'

I stared at her. I nearly asked, a man or a woman?

'And it isn't very pleasant to have him over when I don't know whether you will be coming in during the night. Or not at all. Or if I want to have dinner and I don't know what your plans are.'

I caught my breath. My mother had a lover. My *mother* had a *lover*. I felt an immediate, involuntary twinge of shock: who would want to sleep with my mother? I stared at her. Then I pushed this ugly thought from my mind and said, 'I am sorry.'

There was a silence, and the air cleared, lifted. Something had changed now between us. Was this what it meant to become an adult? To acknowledge that your mother had a private life apart from you? I felt the irony of my arrogance: our relationship had altered, and it was not because of my sex life. I almost laughed.

Mother looked up and smiled briefly when she saw my face. 'When do you think you'll be going over to University Place?'

I began breathing normally again. 'I don't know. I guess I can go any time since the guy has left already. He asked the department to sub-let it for him.'

'Well, you can tell me if you need anything, if there's pots and pans and things.'

'Thank you, Mother,. I would like it if you came over to
· see me. I don't know any' – I caught myself – 'many people.'

'You can go visit Janet.'

'Yes. I'll do that.' We got up to make coffee. 'Mother, I really do appreciate your being here and all. I mean, leaving my job and not having any money – it's all been a bit frightening. I wouldn't have had any place else to go.'

'Well, of course you can always come home.'

'I suppose it was a bit of a surprise.'

'Yes, well, I never expect you to come back.' *Nor do I, I*

125

thought. She went on, 'Last time was a bit short-notice as well.'

I blushed slightly. I had flown home the day after calling her, exactly as I had done this time. Was I really this glaringly rude?

'But of course, you were between things then, too.' It was true; I only came home when I needed to rest, sew, plan, send letters. I had spent the time organizing my divorce and applying to MBA programmes.

She went on, 'You were always anxious to get away.'

I did not answer. What could I say?

'Even when you were very small.'

'Really?'

'Yes. I remember when you were four or five and you told me you wanted to be a pilot so you could fly all over the world. I don't know where you got that idea.'

I laughed a little. 'I don't remember that.'

'You were born wanting to get away.'

I looked at her. 'Did that bother you?'

'Oh, I don't know. You always knew what you wanted. You didn't really need me. I felt like a caretaker.

'And with Alicia?'

'Alicia didn't need me either.'

'Mother, that's not true. Alicia often tried to please you.'

'Alicia cannot accept ever being wrong. She always tried to provoke me so that I would be the wrong one. She has always blamed me for everything wrong in her life.'

'Mother, that's absurd. She was a child. She couldn't manipulate you, not then.'

'Children have a lot more power than you think.'

I remembered Alicia saying, *Mother really liked my drug problem.* Of course, that could not really be true; Mother was not a monster. But I did see how it would have justified Mother: it was something Alicia did to herself; something

126

Mother did not have to fault herself for. And it was concrete; Mother could use it to explain Alicia.

How had things between us turned out like this, simply gone wrong? My mother must have had children thinking she would love them. She did not know she would not have the strength or discipline to manage either of us.

Mother looked ahead, glancing at me sideways, as if she were driving. 'Perhaps she couldn't have manipulated a different kind of mother. I just felt defeated by it all. By you, because you were so independent. And then when Alicia came along, I didn't know what to do with her. I didn't understand her. She never talked about herself, or what she wanted to do, or what she liked. She was withdrawn, always in her own world. She resented me trying to help her in any way.'

I was silent.

'I just felt so – unnecessary. Used, I suppose. I cooked and cleaned and changed your clothes and you both went off and did whatever you wanted. I was never a part of either of you.'

'And I guess your marriage didn't help matters much.'

'I'm, sure you know he was sleeping around. I was – so tired. It's hard to explain how very tiring it all is. You wash clothes every day, and they get dirty and you wash them again. My back hurt from just picking up things all the time and I felt so old. I remember when I was thirty, I felt like an old lady. I looked old. I wasn't surprised that he left me. I didn't want sex; I didn't want anything; I didn't feel anything; I just wanted to sleep.

'Look at you,' she went on, matter-of-factly. 'You're almost thirty and you look so young. You've lived, you've had fun and gone to college. You don't have any children.'

This was what my mother thought: my life was good because I had no children. 'I'm sorry.'

'Oh, it doesn't matter. It's just that now, all those years of feeling like that are beginning to wear off. I have a normal life now.'

'Yes. I'm sorry, I didn't realize – ' I could not stop saying, *I'm sorry.*

'Oh, it doesn't matter,' she said again, waving her hand. 'You just can't expect me to always be giving you things, Krystal. I don't have anything more to give you. You can stay here, of course, if you like. You can always come here. But I'm getting older. I'm going to retire in less than ten years.'

'You mean, you wish Alicia and I would settle down and get married and stop worrying you.'

'I'm not worried. You and Alicia know what you're doing. You think I don't know Alicia has moved. Well, I know she doesn't want me interfering. That's fine. I never meant to interfere. I was just trying to show some interest in her life. I don't have a lot of energy left to worry about anybody but myself.'

'You don't care about us?'

'Oh, yes, of course. I mean, I care about your safety and your health. And I hope you both have enough money to live well. You won't get any from me; all I've got is my pension. But you must see that I just can't give a lot of myself to two people who have given me so little the past twenty years. The well has run dry.'

And so it was out: all my convoluted interpretations of my mother's behaviour were empty and self-serving. My mother was irritable because she had a lover and I was in the way. My mother wanted to have a normal life, without the clutter of children. She wanted to feel again, after the numbness of her life. She wanted to feel loved.

And although I felt I had never needed her, her indifference now lodged in my heart like an old pain I thought I had long since healed.

10

My offer letter arrived in the mail two days later. The same afternoon I bought a very old and used dark green VW bug. It was tattered and dirty and did not have air conditioning, but I could trust it to drive to campus and back, and down the freeway for the occasional visit with Alicia.

I transferred my suitcases from Mother's to my new home. When I opened the front door and walked in, I stood perfectly still for several minutes. My first impression was of standing in a blood-spattered colosseum.

I saw a sofa of dark red and burnt-orange plaid, flanked by end tables decorated with metallic bull fighters. Between two red and orange armchairs sat an enormous coffee table of glass under which an ornate fresco of carved bull faces, complete with ring-pierced noses, stared out. On the walls were pictures of bulls, bull fighters and guns. Above the fireplace an antique rifle was mounted.

I looked up and saw the expected beams and skylight, but any lightness they offered had been massively over-powered. I realized at once that any attempt to transform this house was doomed. I would simply have to accept it.

I brought my suitcases in and looked around. The other rooms were ugly and beige, but inoffensive. I decided I would simply close my eyes when I crossed the living room.

I put my jewellery on the bedside table and my make-up in the bathroom. I hung up my clothes in the closet, and put my suitcases in the spare bedroom. I walked out to the living room again. I would make one change. The rifle would have to go. I took it down; I could not tell if it was loaded. I found the ladder to the attic and carried it up, the barrel pointing away from me. In the attic I found other assorted firearms. I laid the rifle down and descended. I hoped I would be gone before meeting the man who owned this house.

As soon as I put the ladder up, I heard the telephone ring. I picked it up and immediately recognized the echo of anxious breathing. She waited a moment and said, 'Why haven't you called me?'

I had not seen or talked to her since the morning I saw George and Charlene the week before. I sighed. 'Because I am busy. Look, I'm sorry, Lynette. I've moved and started a job –' I stopped. 'How did you get my number?'

'I called your mother.'

'Right. Lynette, I'll call you in a few days. Just try to ease up a little, okay? Try to understand. I'm *busy.*'

'Where are you working?'

'I'll call you in a few days and fill you in. I have to go now.' I hung up.

About fifteen students showed up for my first class; they filed in holding the introductory textbook and matching exercise workbook, blue, called *Cahiers.* I sat at the desk, glancing through my notes. I could see a few of them flipping through the textbook towards the back chapters, to the future of their French.

When they were all seated, I looked up, rose slowly to my feet, scrutinized each face and said, politely and clearly, *'Bonjour tout le monde.'*

They stared at me. I said it again, more emphatically, and gestured towards them, as if to sweep the entire class to me. I then leaned towards them and gestured to the front of the class, indicating that this was the expected response: *'Bonjour, Madame.'*

They mumbled something back and I saw immediately who would be dropping the class.

'*BONJOUR TOUT LE MONDE*,' I repeated, hearing my voice bounce against the walls. They made a slightly louder reply.

That would have to satisfy me for the moment. I carried on. '*Prenez vos livres*.' I picked up my book and showed it to them. A few looked quite angry by this time, but they all picked up their books.

'*A la deuxième page*.' I held the book up and pointed at the page number.

'*Répétez après moi*,' I commanded, pointing with my finger to illustrate each conjugation. '*Je suis*' They stared at me in dismay: was I really going to speak nothing but *French*?

I repeated '*JE SUIS*.' Their response was nearly inaudible. I went on '*Tu es. Il est. Elle est. Vous êtes. Nous sommes. SOMMES! Pas some. SOMMMME Ils sont. Elles sont*.'

They repeated dutifully, without the slightest feeling or vigour.

'*Très bien*.' I drew a happy face surrounded by little stars and exclamation marks on the blackboard. Then a few faces smiled. I thought, *Maybe this will work after all*. I smiled back and taught them their first sentence: *Je suis américain(e)*.

By the end of the hour, the entire class *looked* dazed and in shock, but most seemed pleased: they were already speaking French.

Now it was Thursday, my second week of classes. As soon as the bell rang, I folded my French civilization notes and walked out of the classroom towards my office. I now had to stay in my office an hour for student visits: then I would teach my last class of the day.

I hated having to observe office hours. As much as I liked teaching the classes, I found that I actually disliked my students. What I enjoyed was the language, of course, and the theatrics of standing in front of a captive audience and trying to persuade them to love French as much as I did. I gesticulated, mimed, used props, drew pictures. I fought to bring my students out, make them laugh; I berated, cheered, rewarded them.

But my enthusiasm was wasted. Many were high-school drop-outs. They worked in the petro-chemical plants in Beauvue, or in menial local jobs. They had returned to school, as they called it, to 'get their degree', as though there were a sea of unclaimed degrees waiting for them with their names attached, like lost luggage.

The students who came by during office hours were invariably the worst, the ones who wanted to chat, to complain, who did not study and wanted to know why French was so hard and why I didn't give open-book exams and how could I expect them to go to the lab when they had to go to work. French was just another requirement fulfilled, another exam to pass. My language students would never use French; for the French civilization students the words Racine, de Musset, Colette, Manet, Rimbaud would soon ring only the vaguest of bells.

My dislike did not keep them away. I could be cold and abrupt; they would merely return at the next opportunity. I tried putting a note on the door saying that all students had ·to make appointments with me; I would not keep office hours otherwise. The next day I found a memo from the Dean in my pigeon-hole. He thought the note 'unfriendly', 'discouraging' and 'demotivating'. The decision to build the offices with glass doors had, after all, been made, he informed me, to 'promote student-teacher interaction.'

When I got to my office, I closed the glass door behind me and found a tissue to blow my nose. It was oppressively hot now, in June, with worse to come, but the building was glacial; I had acquired an unshakable cold from the extremes of temperature. I put on my cardigan and sat down at my desk. Behind me, I heard students pass by, hesitating outside my door. If I kept perfectly still, I told myself, they would give up and go away.

My desk overlooked the now abandoned pond: the ducks had gone in search of better shade. I had always thought of ponds as serene, filled with glittering fish and gentle, floating greenery. This one was still and brown, with a few cat tails around the edges. An alligator lived in it, a migrant from the nearby bayou; it devoured an occasional duck.

Just beyond the pond was the parking lot. Heat rose from the cars; the trees just beyond, along the bayou, broke apart into strange, fuzzy green wavelets. Outside looked uninhabitable, encased in a primordial, radioactive heat; yet my fingers were stiff with cold: it was like looking out on to a treacherous planet of hot gases from the safety of an icy capsule.

I had started out energetic, idealistic, open-minded, excited. I was determined to do a good job. Eleanor had mentioned again that my contract would be renewed if I stayed to do a Ph.D. I had thought, *Three or four years wouldn't be that bad.*

Then I showed Eleanor my French civilization course plan, a four-page outline covering literature, art, and political and economic history. She read it with distress on her face.

It was very interesting, she said with embarrassment. But the French civ course, she informed me regretfully, was intended to familiarize students with French food and the like. She had thought I could show them one of the classic films, or have a wine tasting. Perhaps they could each do a project, on Impressionism or the Resistance.

She sighed and went on. I certainly knew a great deal

about France. It was a – here she swallowed – challenging programme, with many good ideas. But, she had to explain, I really couldn't expect them to do all this.

She handed the papers back with a regretful smile.

I simplified my material, but went ahead with my outline. I refused to indulge my students with glasses of Chablis and cheese platters while watching *La Grande Illusion*. Instead, I faced three times a week twenty-two obedient, unquestioning heads following their pens to and fro for fifty-five minutes. They never looked up, but wrote down everything I said. They never expressed an opinion or contested a point.

After an hour of sitting in my room, I walked down the hall to my last class of the day.

I was introducing the verb *faire*, their first irregular verb. Ten minutes into class, the door opened. I glanced over in annoyance and saw Lynette poke her head into the classroom.

I stared at her in silence. She had found me, and now, I was sure, had come to cause a scene. I braced myself. But she said nothing. She walked in, stumbling, and closed the door behind her. She was holding the blue textbook and matching workbook. She smiled childishly and said, 'Is this introductory French?'

I took a breath. 'You have missed two weeks of class.' I felt the students' faces turn from Lynette to me as we spoke, sensing a drama. I could not believe she would have the nerve to do this.

She shrugged and waved a pink slip at me. 'I'm enrolled.'

'Then sit down.' My students stared at me. They had seen me exasperated with a student, but not hostile. I immediately switched back to French, and ignored her for the rest of the class.

She sat at the back, gazing at me, an elbow planted on the

desk, her chin resting in her palm. She wore a loose shirt that she allowed to fall seductively off one shoulder. Her hair was pinned up untidily, strands carefully extracted to give a sensual effect.

As soon as the bell rang, I closed my book. Lynette was on her feet and at my desk before I could leave. She said, 'Can I make up the work I've missed?'

'I suggest you do, since you will receive a zero for all quizzes and homework you do not turn in. Since attendance is part of your trade, you are already at a disadvantage. I expect all students to do ten hours of lab work a week.' I picked up my books, walked out of the class and returned to my office.

It was now four o'clock. I was supposed to stay in my office until five, but I could not bear to talk to her again. I packed up my books and papers. Then I locked my door and walked down the hall to the department office.

I imagined teaching in a different place, perhaps in New England, I imagined an old, well endowed, prestigious college, lecture halls with well-trodden, irregular, wooden floors; interesting faculty, trips to Europe, research grants, film societies, theatrical productions, intelligent, serious students.

Did such a place exist? I did not know. But I had applied to several graduate schools to do a Ph.D. It seemed inevitable that, having failed in the real world – the world of men, competition, money, where people produce and create – I should retire now to academics, which was demanding but not difficult, and, as I had always suspected, a repository for the mediocre. There seemed no other place for me to go.

I would not make much money, but I couldn't be fired easily once I found a place in this sheltered world of few incentives and small rewards. And I did like the work. In my spare time, I scouted about in the library for research ideas. I discovered I liked rooting through academic journals and reading my favourite novels and poems with a view to dissect and interpret. For the first time, I began to understand why I liked a poem, a story, a particular writer.

A feeling of disappointment still haunted me, but I was not niggardly. I was grateful that I could do this, earn money, live, even if it seemed a poor substitute for what I thought I should be doing with my life. But what was that? What had I thought I would be doing? At the ad agency in London I had been a glorified secretary without the typing. The gallery had been a lark; the MBA a stroke of sheer poor judgement.

I walked on, absentminded, and would have gone straight past Mara had she not stopped me.

'Kris.' She touched my arm gently. 'How are you getting on?' She was wearing brown cotton trousers, a white shirt, and silver and jet earrings. Her hair was more striking in daylight, ebony black, sharply contrasting with the streaks of grey. I thanked her for both the house and the job referral.

'Oh, don't thank me; it was just a fortunate coincidence. They needed somebody and it sounded like you needed a job.'

I detected an allusion in her voice that I could not place. Had she suggested me for the job in an attempt to engineer a long-term relationship for Lynette? Did she feel sorry for
. her, want a stylish lover to motivate her, raise her self-confidence? *Well*, I thought, as we parted, *Mara will have to find lovers for her students elsewhere.*

I went into the department office, and pulled papers and envelopes from my pigeon-hole. As I looked through my mail, I heard something and glanced up. A small, plump man stood at the doorway with some files. 'Hello, Kristina,' he said, looking pointedly at my books and bag. His name was Tom; he was assistant to the Dean.

137

'Oh, hello – ' I spoke with a calculated mixture of disinterested politeness and boredom. Then I turned away and continued to look through my mail. Nothing that looked like a request for an interview. There was something about my envelopes that had rejection written all over them.

I consciously ignored Tom. I had thought at first that he was gay. But gays were usually the darlings of universities and everyone here was terrified of this little man. He seemed to vibrate with latent possibilities, as though he kept a record of everyone's activities. He stood upright, his trousers belted across a plump stomach. he had a small moustache.

I turned towards the door, and he followed me. I nodded politely to him and turned away.

'No office hours this afternoon?'

'No, no students came by, and I'm going to grade some papers at home.'

'That student,' he pointed out smugly, 'seems to be waiting for you.'

I turned around. I caught sight of Lynette, peeping idiotically from around a corner. She smiled and trotted towards me.

'Well,' said Tom, smirking, 'have a nice day.'

I could not think just then what it was that this girl had once inspired in me.

She wanted to go and have coffee. Dozens of excuses came into my mind although I knew I should accept; she looked fragile, almost brittle, as though she were capable of causing a scene.

'Are you angry that I'm taking French?' she asked plaintively.

I knew I should talk to her, but at that moment, her need and pain disgusted me. I did not try to fob her off with lies. I said, 'Lynette, you can enrol in whichever classes the college allows you to. But I don't want to have coffee with you. I want to see you, but later. You must see that I cannot sit around drinking coffee with you here.'

'Because you don't want people to know we are lovers.'

I wanted to say, *We are not lovers*. 'I don't advertise my personal life.'

'You wouldn't mind if you weren't embarrassed to be seen with me.'

Of course, she was right. I was not particularly proud of having been involved with her. If it had been Naomi, Mara, or even Washington State, who had gone home for the summer, I would not have been so furtive. I felt angry that this stupid girl was making me feel guilty and shallow. I said, 'That is not true. It's just a lie you tell to make yourself feel worse. Do you think the other faculty go around publicly announcing their latest lovers?'

This was also true; if I were sleeping with a Naomi, people would know, but it wouldn't be discussed indiscreetly. Such a lover wouldn't feel the need for exhibition.

'What do you care what people think? You've told me a million times how much you hate this place.'

'Lynette, I'll call you tonight. There are things I have to do.' I sat down on one of the chairs near the door, waiting for her to go away. After a few minutes I stuffed my mail into my bag and rose to leave. Then the blonde from Washington State's office, whose name had turned out to be Georgine, walked in. *Walk* was an inadequate word for Georgine's entrance; she *sailed* in, a whirl of white and blue linen, a few hairs dislodged, slightly winded, as though escaping from a throng of admirers, but magnificent, a boat gliding into port, the Queen Mother making gracious progress through a crowd. I automatically looked behind her to see what followed.

I had met Georgine once or twice, but had made no effort

to get to know her better, assuming I had nothing in common with her. Besides, I couldn't figure her out. I did not like people I could not figure out. Georgine was sick of teaching and made no secret of her wish to find a rich husband. Yet all her friends were women, and many were gay. She wore glamorous clothes, but was tenured and considered highly intelligent. She had published – unusual for this college – but now was utterly indifferent to her work. She was late for classes, late grading papers, never attended meetings. Nothing about her made sense.

'Hitler been after you?' she asked casually.

I smiled. 'Oh, yes, but it doesn't matter.'

'What d'you do? Call the Dean a prick?' She was looking through her pigeon-hole.

'Office hours,' I replied in explanation, but she had ceased listening. She glanced through her mail and tossed it in the rubbish bin. Then, as though we had known each other for ages, she said, 'Oh, to hell with that little creep. Let's go drink.'

She insisted on going to her house instead of out. 'I have the entire makings of a pitcher of Margueritas on my bar.'

I followed her baby-blue Honda out of the parking lot. Georgine's house turned out to be at University Place, three doors down from mine. The inside had been completely redecorated. The living room was sunk a foot into the floor, like a giant rectangular bath tub, carpeted completely in white and lined with three white sofas, each sprinkled with multi-coloured silk cushions. Steps led from this to a dining room, at the end of which was a bar of white leatherette and very pale wood.

I had never seen anything before that I could, without hesitation, call a bachelorette pad.

Georgine ordered me to sit down and disappeared. She

reappeared in an orange velour jumpsuit, floor-length, with a scoop neck and a white belt. She pushed her hair back in an unconscious, yet perfectly arranged, movement. I wondered briefly why she was wasting all this artifice on me, but I soon realized that she so lived this persona that she never turned it off.

We walked over to the bar. As she had said, a bowl of limes, bottles of Triple Sec and tequila, and a crystal bowl of rock salt sat in a still-life on the bar. I wondered if she had planned this for someone else, or if she always kept drinks ready-made on her bar.

She took ice out of a tiny refrigerator and poured liquor into a cocktail shaker, expertly, without measuring. 'You see, Kris,' she said familiarly, as though we knew each other intimately and were continuing a long-standing conversation, 'I've met somebody.'

'Oh.' What could I say? I knew, as anybody who had met Georgine knew, that she was after a man: she did not bother to hide it.

'Jack.' She took champagne glasses out of the freezer, rubbed them with lime, dipped then into the bowl of salt. 'I met him at church.'

'*Church?*'

'Oh, not here,' she explained, as though I was surprised that she would meet someone appropriate at a local church. 'On the west side of town. I drive there to go to church.' She seemed not to consider the possibility that anyone would not attend church. She poured out our drinks and added, unnecessarily, 'There's a better class of men there.'

'Oh.'

'I saw him in the parking lot. He took me to lunch.' She sat down on a stool at the bar, crossed her legs, twirled the greenish drink around and gazed around dreamily. I sat in my hot and dirty clothes, now cold and stiff with congealed sweat, and listened for at least ten minutes to the possible outcomes to which an affair with Jack could lead. I nodded occasionally and drank. I listened patiently. I would be going shortly anyway.

Suddenly, she stopped. 'But it probably won't go anywhere. I sleep with men too quickly and then they drop me.' She said this quite matter-of-factly, almost cheerfully, without any self-pity, as if this self-knowledge were sufficient to protect her from unhappiness. She seemed to believe that doing what she wanted was more important than denying herself for the overall goal.

'Perhaps you will meet someone some day who does not play such games with women.'

'Oh, it's not a game. They want to go to bed, and so do I. It's just that their assumptions are different. They say they are in love like children say they hate you.' She was pulling all sorts of cocktail food from the fridge – salami, cheeses, pâtés. She poured things out on to plates and opened boxes of crackers.

'Now, what about you, Kris?'

'Oh, me.' I was taken aback. I could say, *I've crashed here, like on a different planet, yet it's my planet. I need to build a new rocket and take off, go back to my own voyage.* 'I'm just looking for a job, really.'

'You were in New York before, weren't you?' She looked at me sideways, guardedly, as if she were asking me if I was divorced, or had taken drugs or was underdoing psychotherapy. I remembered my mother once excusing a neighbour's bad behaviour with the comment, *Oh, but they're from New York.* New Yorkers were more particularly badly bred than other Northerners.

'Yes, but I didn't like it or my job.'

'But you won't stay here.'

'No.'

'I didn't think so. I've met your mother, by the way. She goes to those things at Janet's.'

'Oh, I see.' Another unlikely, unwanted connection; my skin prickled slightly. I tried to change the subject. 'You don't go to that group, I take it?'

'Oh, no. They don't like me. I'm not dogmatic enough. We West Texans are live-and-let-live.' She stood up and drained her glass. 'I know what we should do. Let's go dancing?'

'*Dancing*?'

'Yes. I'll change and we'll stop by your house and you can change. It's a cowboy bar. Do you have any cowboy boots?'

'No,' I said, somewhat indignantly.

'Oh, well, that doesn't matter,' Georgine replied, ignoring my tone. 'You can wear jeans.'

'I don't like dancing.'

'Well, you can watch. I'll dance.' She left the room once again and returned in a cowgirl skirt and blouse and boots. She twirled once and the skirt flared out. 'Let's go.'

After I had changed, we drove south down the freeway. When I saw the exit, I nearly told her I was ill and had to go home: we passed directly by the Christmas light-strung parking lot of Harmony Bait and Tackle. Georgine pulled into a gravelled lot and parked in front of Maybelle's.

It had not changed since my childhood: a glaring pink beach house on rickety stilts, covered with net and plastic sea shells. The parking lot was packed with pick-up trucks and cars. It was country-western night. Georgine explained.

We went in and, as if being transported back fifteen years, paid a cover charge, and a doorman pressed our hands with a stamp visible only under fluorescent light. A highway patrolman stood chatting to a waitress in black fishnet stockings, his holster snapped shut on his right hip. The band was playing 'Honky Tonk Angel'.

We found a table. Before I could speak, Georgine ordered

143

two Lone Stars from the waitress. 'You have to drink Lone Star on country-western night,' she said. 'It's unpatriotic not to.'

The dance floor was packed. I simply could not believe that all these people were real: women in white and gold cowgirl outfits, with white boots; men with enormous bellies hanging over turquoise and silver belts. But of course they were real. I had seen them in our town in New Mexico, spending money, driving Cadillacs with longhorns strapped across the grill, or in campers, plastered with stickers.

Within five minutes, a man in cowboy boots approached and Georgine disappeared on to the dance floor. For the next hour I saw her only briefly between dances, when she stopped to drink some of her warm beer and wipe her face with a tissue. Every man who asked her to dance seemed already to know her.

I drank steadily. I supposed I could have found all this amusing and camp, except what I really wanted to do was crawl into bed with a book. I couldn't move. I sat rooted to my chair and poured more beer into my glass.

Georgine came back when the band stopped for a break, panting, waving her hand at the waitress. She ordered fresh beers.

'So you got caught sneaking out during office hours.' She smiled as the beers arrived.

I returned her smile. 'Yes, is that a capital crime here?'

'Oh, it'll go down against your name in Tom's little black book.'

'Who is he anyway?'

'The Dean's spy. I wouldn't worry too much about him. I doubt if you're useful to him. At the moment, anyway.' She took a swig from her bottle in the most proficient and lady-like fashion I had ever seen, as though she were on a hay ride, or a horse. I had assumed Georgine was a southern belle, but now she looked as if she had been swigging beer her entire life.

I said, 'I cannot see how a summer teacher could possibly be of any use at any time.'

'That depends on if you stay. You're good at teaching. People have noticed. He needs you. He needs somebody he can do a favour for. He needs allies.'

'I see.' Did I?

'Do you like the kids?'

'No,' I admitted. 'Well, a few of them. Is that terrible? The sign of a bad teacher?'

'No, I can't stand most of them either. What did you expect? Milk-fed East Coast brats? Honey, third-rate is a *kind* description.'

I told her about my French civ class. No questions, arguments, passion or interest. I told her how I hated taking attendance; I found it insulting that I had to count attendance as part of their grade. And how it enraged me that they attended religiously.

I told her about my fantasy of reading out of *Mein Kampf* or *Das Kapital* or telling the story of my life to see if they would react or merely continue to write everything down.

'Oh, yes, they're just in it to spit back whatever you say. But there's the odd one or two that make up for the others.'

'Yes,' I thought, *I was that for Mme Smith: 'Don't give up your French.'*

'It's perfectly acceptable to dislike students. Most people do.'

I laughed; it was simple for Georgine. I wondered whether I was useful to her. Why was she being kind to me? It occurred to me that she might simply like me. I found, to my surprise, that I liked her.

'Do you enjoy it?' I asked her. 'The students, the teaching?'

'Oh, I've done it for too long,' she said vaguely. 'I suppose I have burnt-out.'

It was not reckless for her to admit this; everybody on campus knew how carelessly she treated her classes. But I liked her honesty anyway. I thought, *Perhaps, for the first time, I will have a friend.*

How odd that I should find one in Georgine. She interested me, but as an alien, or an exotic animal would. I found I was beginning to enjoy hearing about her affairs; it was like knowing a lifetime of men in one evening. And she never bored me. I was surprised to find she was an ardent feminist and had once spent the night in a sleeping bag in front of City Hall with hundreds of other women in some kind of protest.

'I suppose,' said Georgine, 'that I always liked the research better than teaching.'

'I prefer it, too.'

'Then you should do it. It's the only way to get out of the drudgery of teaching. You'll get sick of it eventually.'

I knew I would; this did not surprise me. I knew what I really wanted to do was putter about in the library, do research, read, write papers.

'Just don't let anybody here persuade you otherwise. Our dean thinks that wanting to do anything besides teach is insurgency. You get tenure here by turning in your grades on time and getting good student evaluations.'

'So keep my nose clean, hide my research notes and mark my exams *tout de suite*.'

Georgine smiled. 'You're going to do fine, honey.'

146

11

The next morning, I walked across my Spanish Mediterranean living room into the kitchen. I plugged the coffee machine in and sat down at the table to read the mail I had picked up the day before.

There were two we-read-your-c.v.-with-interest-but-are-sorry-to-inform-you letters, and one from a university in Pennsylvania acknowledging my application. I threw the rejections in the bin and stacked the acknowledgement on top of the fridge with two others.

The coffee was still dripping. I wrapped my robe around me and decided to fetch the morning paper my absentee owner had never cancelled. I usually glanced at it and threw it away.

I crossed my horrible living room and opened the door. Early morning humidity rushed past me into the cool house. Behind me I heard the coffee machine gurgle to a halt. I picked up the paper, closed the door and returned to the kitchen, sliding the damp plastic wrapper off and tossing the paper on to the table.

I poured a cup of coffee and spread the paper out on the table. The telephone rang.

She hesitated, breathed into the phone. 'You didn't call me.'

I saw dark mouldy corners, dirty sheets, a sink edged with brown soap scum. 'Hello, Lynette,' I said briskly.

'You said you would call me last night.'

'Well, I'm sorry. I went out.'

'I waited until midnight.'

'I'm sorry you waited.' I tried to keep the impatience out of my voice.

'I went out, too.'

'Really.' I took an audible sip of coffee, not bothering to move the mouthpiece of the telephone away.

'To a bar.'

I was silent.

'I picked up this guy.'

I lost patience then. I put my cup down. 'Lynette, what do you want me to say?'

'I didn't sleep with him.'

I didn't reply, thinking, *I am not interested in what you do.*

'When I asked him to leave, he hit me.'

'Fine,' I said brusquely. 'You go ahead and do stupid things like that. Just don't bother me with a report.' I nearly slammed down the phone, but caught myself in time.

I scoured my body in the shower and pulled on my clothes in a frenzy of outrage. How dare this little idiot attempt to manipulate me?

I taught my classes. When I went to my afternoon intro class, she was already at the back of the room, studiously writing in her workbook. She wore her tight black Levis and the same shirt as the night we had met. She did not look up.

I remembered the first night, slowly unbraiding her hair. Why on earth did I ever give in to that inexplicable urge to go after this girl? Sex was inseparable from exposure. Desire was an appetite, an itch, inviting weakness and humiliation. *Please do this to me right here.* I watched this girl at the back of the class, and rage gripped me. I could do nothing to keep her away from me, and she knew it. But she would not win.

She thought she could hurt me, blackmail me, make me feel guilty, but I knew more dirty tricks than this little idiot would ever know. I wanted to hurt her, punish her. I wanted her to know that her insolence was powerless against me. I stood at the front of my class and knew, finally, there was no such thing as pure, isolated desire, sex without domination. Just looking at Lynette's smug face at the back of the class, her T-shirt sliding down a bare shoulder, and then her hand pulling it up slowly, filled me with a ferocity I had not known myself capable of. I now knew what the term *blind rage* meant.

I taught with atypical reserve, and my students were duller than usual in return. I was careful to call on everybody, including Lynette, once.

A week passed. It was now the end of June. Lynette attended class faithfully and turned in work daily. She sat at the back in her usual seat, her chin in her palm, gazing at me, trying to imitate my words with her flat, nasal voice. I saw no marks on her face; I doubted whether the story about the man had been true. She did not bring up the phone call, or come to my office after class. She had decided to back off; she knew she had pushed me too far.

My rage subsided; my new life carried on. I went out with Georgine a couple of times; I drove into town to see Alicia. I told no one about Lynette. I wanted to believe that she would simply disappear.

Finally, on Friday, she appeared at my office. I was sitting with my back to the glass door, staring out the window. I saw her in the reflection. 'I don't have much time today, Lynette.'

This did not bother her; she was impervious. She sat down and examined the surface of the desk between us.

I sighed ostentatiously and put on my professional voice. 'What can I help you with?'

She took out a *dictée*, a composition, and two exercises, all covered with red marks. 'I guess I didn't really understand this.'

I didn't take the papers, so she laid them on the desk. I didn't move for a few minutes. Finally I picked them up, glanced at each and then returned them. 'Lynette, what do you want me to do? You simply have to study. If you come to class regularly and do your homework and go to the lab, you will learn to speak French. All it takes is studying.'

'I don't understand why I make all these mistakes.'

'Because you have not studied enough. You must do the exercises in the *Cahiers* and read the examples in the textbook.'

'I don't really understand the exercises.' She looked at me imploringly. I glanced at the papers in her hand, hurriedly scored with red, and was close to admitting that there might be some people in this world incapable of learning a foreign language.

She said, 'I can't believe that if I memorize all those words which are just nonsense sounds then I will end up speaking something that other people will understand. I can't believe that all those rules matter. I mean, I speak English, and I don't know any rules.'

I leaned towards her, across my desk, and stared intently into her face. 'Look, Lynette. I know this is hard. Believe me, I didn't grow up speaking French. You have simply got to work harder. *Anybody* can learn French.'

'Yeah.'

'You *are* going to the lab?'

'Yeah.' She paused. 'I mean, I put on the headphones and listen, but, you know, when the tape says to repeat, I just can't say anything. It's too embarrassing. There are other people around.'

I imagined her there, with the headphones on, looking at the battered copies of *Marie-Claire*, *Elle*, *Marie-France*, at the thin models marching through the streets of Paris, Milan, New York, as if the city belonged to them. I thought, *Poor*

Lynette has never had anything belong to her, and yet this thought did not move my heart one millimetre. I wanted her out of my life, and if it hurt, well, that was too bad. I looked at her and said in a deadly quiet voice, 'Do not call me any more and do not tell me anything again like you did last week.'

She smiled an embarrassed, satisfied, childish smile. She said, 'Okay,' as though I had asked her not to call me after a certain hour, or not to embrace me in front of other students. As though we were still lovers, and she had made a small breach of etiquette. I held my breath, waiting for my irritation to subside.

She played with her pen, tapping it against my desk, examining it, taking the top on and off. 'The car broke down.'

I exhaled and glanced out my door. For once, I wished for a student to come by. 'I'm sorry to hear that.'

'Could you take me home?'

I sighed. It was time for the big talk. 'Yes. All right.'

I told her I had to remain for my office hour. I made her wait for me in the corridor. I read for a while, and then packed my books and papers slowly. I left thirty minutes later.

I drove the familiar route to her house. I stopped in front, but did not turn off the engine. I said, 'Look, Lynette – '

She sat, head bent, staring at her knees. She said, 'Can't you come in for just a minute?'

I turned off the engine. If this was how she wanted it, I was ready. I could no longer expect her to figure it out for herself and gracefully disappear from my life. It was obvious to me that if someone did not want you any more, you simply did not cling. Well, if she wanted it explained in excruciating, humiliating detail, all right. It was time for her to understand that she could not cling to me.

I gave silent thanks that the house was empty. I followed her through the kitchen and down the hall, past the closed bedroom door behind which lived the loose python. We went into her room. I looked at Virginia Woolf and thought, *She lived without sex; why can't I?* But, of course, she killed herself. I sat down on the chair.

Lynette sat on the unmade mattress, on top of a confusion of sheets, pillows, the patchwork quilt. She drew her knees to her chest, and wrapped her arms around her legs. She looked at the floor, not speaking.

I sighed ostentatiously. 'Lynette, you must see that this is not going to go on.'

She did not answer.

After a moment, she released her arms and reached towards me. I remained perfectly still, although I wanted to shrink back from this nail-bitten, nicotine-stained hand.

She took a lock of my hair and twisted it gently. It took all my self-control to restrain myself from slapping her hand away. I waited a few seconds and then gently pulled my hair from her grasp. She buried her head in her arms and rolled over on to the mattress, her back to me. I could see her shoulders shake with weeping.

I rose and left without looking back.

12

The telephone rang early the next morning. I picked it up, and Georgine, without preamble, said, 'I was just thinking maybe we should go out to dinner tonight.' Her voice was a picture of bored New Orleans heiresses in white dresses, hot rooms, fans slowly rotating, iced drinks on a tray, the sort of woman who need not bother identifying herself on the phone.

'Hello, Georgine,' I said, pleased and relieved that it was not Lynette. I wanted light conversation, girlish gossip, the simplicity of Georgine's life, an evening with someone with whom sex was an impossibility. 'Yes, I'd like that.'

I arrived early, holding flowers, feeling awkward. I realized I had never brought a woman flowers before.

Georgine threw the door open. She was wearing what used to be called pedal-pushers. Her backless, high-heeled sandals clattered as she turned and waved me in with a perfectly manicured hand.

I followed her past the sunken white sofas into a gleaming green and white kitchen, newly tiled, with crisp, expertly hung curtains the colour of spring leaves, matching dish towels, polished appliances. She was not alone.

Mara sat in a white wicker chair, at the glass-topped table; the last person I expected to see at Georgine's. She sat comfortably; she had obviously been here before, and apparently had also been invited. She wore her usual cotton trousers and T-shirt. I wondered whether her presence meant the evening would be serious, rather than girlish. We said hello.

Georgine had made Bloody Marys and placed on the table a platter of squares of toast spread with shiny black caviare and slivers of lemon. 'I was telling Mara about Jack.'

I nodded. I thought, *This I want to see: Marilyn Monroe meets Gertrude Stein.* I took a square of caviare and sat back.

'So you see, he has his own company.'

'Doing what?' Mara said neutrally as she bit into a square of toast.

'That's part of it – I don't know. He's explained it to me a . dozen times, but I still don't understand.'

'Um,' said Mara, non-committal.

'But he seems to be doing well.'

'How can you tell?'

'Well, his townhouse is very nice.'

'Anything else?'

'Well, he seems to live very well.'

'Georgine,' said Mara patiently, 'does he *own* the townhouse?'

Georgine hesitated. 'I don't know,' she admitted.

'How long has the company been going?'

'I don't know that either.'

'Have you been to his office?'

'No.'

Mara looked at her hands. 'How many employees does he have?'

'Oh, it's just him.'

Mara coughed, and then said gently, 'Georgine, I want you to do one thing for me. Get a piece of paper and make this guy write down his assets on one side and what he owes on the other. And see if the number on the assets side is bigger.'

'Mara, I can't do that.'

'Why not? What does he expect? To marry a bimbo?'

'*Marry?*' I exclaimed, nearly choking, sitting up in my chair.

'He's asked me to marry him,' Georgine explained.

'How long have you known him, Georgine?' I was flabbergasted. I imagined there would be half a dozen Jacks to console Georgine during the course of the summer.

'Three weeks.'

I looked at Mara, who raised her eyebrows. She turned back to Georgine and went on, 'He can't object. You have to find out what your financial position's going to be.' She picked up another square of caviare and looked at it. 'You can offer to do the same.'

I took a gulp of my Bloody Mary: Mara, the resident radical lesbian, was giving her friend, the campus easy lay, advice like a mother would.

'Well, we'd keep everything separately,' Georgine said.

'Georgine, you know it's just not that simple. Are you going to keep your house and live separately? Who is going to pay for the upkeep of wherever you live? What if he goes bust? Are you going to refuse to support him?'

'Yes, I know we need to discuss all that.'

'Why do you have to do all this now?' I asked. 'What's the hurry?'

'He doesn't want to live together. He wants to get married. He's a Christian.'

.   'Don't you think you ought to – ' I had trouble keeping the irony out of my voice – 'get to know each other a little better?'

'Oh, I don't know.'

Mara was silent. I felt an edge of disapproval from her and saw that my words had inadvertently wounded Georgine, a tiny, effective barb. I felt cruel and inept; I had overstepped my place and had not been very helpful. I saw now that I hadn't had much experience as a friend. Logic and reason did not help somebody who needed talk and discussion, who had laid herself open, exposed her loneliness and need.

'Well,' said Georgine, gliding over the tension, 'we can't decide anything over an empty stomach. I need a platter of nachos and a Dos Equis.'

We went to a Mexican place and drank Margueritas and beer and ate platters of food that had different names, but were all made of beans, cheese, meat, tortillas, avocados, peppers. I ate everything greedily; it was all greasy, cheap and delicious. I could not remember ever having liked enchiladas and tamales and nachos so well.

'Is your place all right?' Georgine asked me.

'Well, it's ugly,' I said. 'But it's okay. It's just for the summer. It's not like yours, of course.'

'Oh, don't envy me, I've thrown tons of money down the drain on that stupid place. The only reason I don't move is I can't afford it.'

'Where would you live?'

'In town. I'm sick of driving in just to meet unmarried men. If you stay, you could live in town.'

'I don't know,' I said, looking at the table, feeling idiotic. I was an adult, and I did not have any idea what I would be doing in two months' time. 'I suppose it depends on where I get a job.'

'Will you do the same thing?' asked Mara.

'No. I don't know why I've even been sending out c.vs. My heart's not in it, and they know it; all I get are standard rejection letters, you know, printed straight off the computer.'

Georgine reached for another nacho. 'You could sell real estate. You could go to law school. Law school's a good place to meet men.'

I smiled.

'I know.' Georgine waved for the waitress and held up three fingers to indicate three more Margueritas. 'Let's open a restaurant. The three of us. Mara can do Cuban, Kris can do French, and I'll do West Texas Barbecue.'

More drinks came, and we went on like this, making up silly plans. We laughed and complained, and talked about our lives, and what we could do and couldn't do and had done. It was like being in the hostel in Paris, in the boarding house with Meredith, except now I was not in a rush to get away. I thought, *How strange it is: I am happy.*

On Monday, Mara stopped by my office. She collapsed in a chair. 'Good God, poor Georgine, that man's going to steal what little money she's got left and there's nothing anybody can do about it.'

'What? How do you know?' I glanced at her. Although Mara never dressed particularly well, she still managed to look trim, cool, unwrinkled. I noticed her woven brown sandals, a plain silver bracelet encircling one wrist. Her arms were dark. She crossed her legs, and beneath one trouser cuff I noticed with some surprise that she shaved her legs.

'Oh' – she waved her hand – 'I don't. It just sounds so suspicious. He's aching to get married and she's got a house and a job. It sounds to me like he's going bankrupt.'

'I thought she was looking for somebody with money.'

'She was. But she's just dying to get married again and has convinced herself this one's true love. She's afraid of holding out for Mr Rich.'

'I thought Georgine was so, well, cunning.'

'No, she's a complete idiot. About her life, I mean. She's very intelligent, of course. I mean, she's very respected academically, or she used to be, before she stopped publishing. But she's lonely. She only looks like she's tough as nails.'

'Surely you must find all this – well, wrong, Mara.'

'What?'

'Chasing after men, marrying for money. Well, wanting to marry for money. I mean, how can you encourage her to do it?'

'Well, it's what she wants, isn't it? I mean, of course, it's all a crock of shit, but if that's what she wants, she might as well not get screwed any more than necessary.'

I was at a loss. 'I thought you would be more – doctrinaire.'

She ignored this. 'The problem with Georgine is that she's a soft touch. Her kids exploit her, she gives money to every goddamn charity that comes around. I mean, she's only got the state pension coming, and when she inherited her parents' money she gave half of it away.

'Her son lives on a commune and calls her up for money, and that worthless daughter of hers studied for five goddamn semesters and dropped all her classes every one. So Georgine ended up paying all that tuition and the kid hasn't got a single credit.'

'Oh.'

'Well, anyway, I didn't come here to talk about Georgine. I wanted to know if you're going to the faculty party Friday night.'

'Oh, I don't know. I don't know if I'm invited.'

'Of course you are. Everybody is. It's so horrible that anybody can go. You probably threw the memo away. It didn't look like an invitation.'

'Well, I don't know. Are you supposed to?'

'Oh, yes. You have to go and kiss the Dean's hand. Would you like to go together? We can make an appearance and go somewhere afterwards to recover.'

'Sure, that sounds fine.' I felt pleasure and anxiety rise up my spine. I had to find out what sort of an invitation this was. Did she want to see me alone? 'Shall we go with Georgine?'

'I doubt if she'll want to. She's tenured. She's not supposed to talk to plebs like us. I don't want to, you know, put her in an awkward position.'

'Okay.' I kept my voice carefully even.

'Right, I'll pick you up about seven.'

'Oh, Mara – '

She turned at the door.

'Thanks again, about the job, I mean.'

She shrugged. 'It's okay; you sounded like you needed a job.'

She left, and I sat for a few minutes. The pleasure of her invitation had been slightly dampened. Had she suggested me because she knew I needed a job? Had I really appeared hard up? Or had she wanted me to stay?

Georgine had told me a bit about Mara. She was one of those women who helped people. She had done volunteer work settling in Laotian and Vietnamese refugees. She was on the board of a shelter for battered women. She had been a delegate to a National Women's Conference.

And now she had asked me out. Why was she interested in me? Perhaps she had simply done me a good turn, as she no doubt had done to other women she hardly knew. It was no doubt part of her politics to help other, anonymous, women. She probably thought of me as another one of her small political acts, a woman in need. I thought, *I am a woman in need*.

13

Friday morning, a week later, I put on the coffee and went to get the paper. It was now my fourth week of teaching. I was beginning to enjoy my morning routine, sitting in my bathrobe, smoking and drinking coffee while I graded papers at the kitchen table.

I crossed the living room, opened the front door and froze. Lynette was standing facing me. My first reaction was fear; I nearly slammed the door shut. Then I saw the rope wound around her neck, the ends dangling in parallel lines down her chest.

I drew back. I thought, *She has gone mad.* She stared at me with a catatonic gaze. Then I realized her expression was one of surprise. She blinked.

'How long have you been here?'

She smiled a queer, twisted smile. 'Since seven.'

My voice hardened, as it had when she first walked into my class. 'Please move. I want my paper.'

She stepped aside and I reached down, expecting a blow, a touch. But she did not move. I picked up my paper and closed the door in her face.

I sat down at my kitchen table and opened the newspaper. I read slowly, drinking my coffee, filling my ashtray. There was one column of international news, of which I read every line. The rest was made up of local murders, burglaries, *Dear Abby*, a gossip column, supermarket advertisements, human interest articles. I read it all, taking my time, drinking coffee.

When I finished, I rose, chose a tape, *Vesperae solennes de*

Confessore, and put it on. I dressed for the day. I chose my clothes with care. I brushed my hair and tried on three pairs of earrings before deciding on the silver and lapis. Before I put on my make-up I thought I might as well check the front door. I opened it casually, but I knew she would be gone.

I returned to the bedroom and looked for the necklace that matched my earrings. I found my blouse was slightly crumpled and I changed it. When I was ready to leave the house and get into my VW, I looked perfect.

I knew about intimidation. I had been through it before. But this time I was in control. This girl was not going to get to me.

I went to my classes prepared to be charming, vivacious, at ease; she did not show. I rehearsed a calm, poisonous speech if she appeared at my office; she did not.

I left campus at 5 and went home to change for the faculty party.

Mara was slightly late; I was at my front window, watching for her, when she pulled up. I locked the door and ran out to her car.

She reached over and opened the door. 'Hi.'

I smiled. I knew I looked good, and I wondered again why she had asked me out. As I settled into the car, I realized that I was acting as if we were out on a date, and forced myself to calm down; I knew nothing about this woman and I simply couldn't expect her to show interest in me. She was probably just being friendly.

Mara did not seem to find anything different between us. She chatted as if we often drove to campus together. She was completely composed, and I thought, *If she is interested in me, she will always be the one in control. If I were to fall in love with this woman, there would be no lies.* She would want a serious relationship. My life would change profoundly.

But, of course, she could not be interested in me. She

knew about Lynette; she disapproved of me: I was not 'out'. She often did women good turns. Women were her politics. I meant nothing to her.

The party was in three conference rooms, joined together by their removable grey-panelled partitions. At one end was a long table, with food and wine. The room was packed with all kinds of people, some in business suits, some in jeans or shorts. They all balanced plastic glasses filled with white wine on paper plates crowded with *hors d'oeuvres*.

It was not until several minutes later that I saw George. I had not seen him since that morning in Lynette's kitchen. He was wearing an open-necked shirt; the muscles of his neck and chest were disagreeably exposed. I avoided his eye, but I knew he would approach me.

'We haven't seen you around much lately,' he sneered.

I did not answer. I tried to look at him calmly. Mara was at the table, pouring wine into clear plastic cups. I noticed Georgine at the other end of the room talking to Janet.

'We're colleagues now, Kris, you and me.'

I looked at him in surprise.

'Yeah, I'm teaching here. I'm doing a Ph.D in development. I'm teaching economics.' His smile dared me to doubt him.

I tried to keep my face neutral but I felt distaste and suspicion distort my features. I had to remind myself that this man knew nothing about me, except that I knew Lynette. He had nothing on me. What did he think he could do?

But he saw that he had a slight edge, and went on, 'You've ditched Lynette, I hear.'

I glanced over his shoulder, hoping to catch someone's eye.

'That's really one fucked-up chick.' He watched me

closely and I stepped back. He moved nearer. 'Lynette's pretty pissed off with you from what Charlene's told me.'

I froze involuntarily to listen. Did she have some kind of plan to harass me? Would she try to hurt me, physically?

He knew he had my attention. 'I know your kind,' he whispered close to my face. 'You're the kind of dyke that fucks around. Well, you might have fucked Lynette, but let me tell you, baby, Lynette will fuck you.'

Now I was angry. '*Piss off.*'

I turned around just as Mara walked up and handed me a glass of wine.

She looked at me and then at George. He said conversationally, 'So what department are you in?'

'Spanish,' she said flatly, still looking at him, completely expressionless, as solid as a mountain, unwavering.

'I'm in economics.'

She did not reply, but did not shift her gaze. To my delight, he shuffled his feet slightly, and then tilted his glass as if just noticing it was empty. 'Well, time for a refill. See you around, *Kris*.'

Mara watched him walk off. She said, 'Do you know him?'

'No. Except that his name is George. I guess he teaches here.'

'Yes.'

. 'Do you know him?'

'Yes, I've heard of him. He's a teaching assistant for a guy in development economics. Who isn't a bad guy, by the way, but stupid.'

'For taking George on?'

'Yes, that, and, oh, you know, knee-jerk. Free market and all that. The invisible hand is the answer to everything. If the market doesn't solve it, it's not a problem.'

'Oh.' I felt boredom fall around me like a veil. I certainly did not want to get into another discussion with Mara about free choice. 'Well, I don't know much about that,' I said politely.

'You know,' she said, warming to the subject. 'If you go around doing what you want, it all works out; everybody's better off.'

'Mara, you must know it's not that simple.' Even I knew, as much as I hated economics, that this was as lame interpretation of market theory. I tried to change the subject; we would never get on a personal level at this rate. 'Anyway, why are you so interested in this?'

'I'm interested in development, especially in Latin America. Literature bores me, actually. It's economic policy I'm interested in really.'

I blinked. 'Oh.' It was becoming more and more obvious that everything I had assumed about Mara was wrong.

'But you know, people have to do their best with whatever resources they have. Which are not, of course, the same for everybody.'

'Yes, well,' I said mildly, 'people aren't and never will be equal.'

'No, but they should have equal chances.'

'Um.' I changed the subject again. 'You were telling me about George.'

'Oh, I'm on the doctoral applications committee and I saw his file. Everybody fawned over him because he was in Bangladesh in the Peace Corps. But from the sound of it, it sounds as if he didn't do much there. He probably sat around and smoked hash for two years.'

I did not know what to say. I certainly was not going to volunteer that I had seen George smoking pot in Lynette's kitchen.

'Well. Enough of George. Tell me, how did you end up in

New York? I'm sure we talked about it the other night but my memory tends to fade after the third round.'

'I got a job there. I was only there for nine months. Most of which I spent working. I don't really know New York very well.'

'Why didn't you like the job?'

'Oh – ' Dozens of responses came into my head, but I said, 'Oh, I don't know.'

Mara did not answer, and I went on, 'It wasn't what I expected.'

'In what way?'

'Well, I suppose business school does prepare you for a certain amount of competitiveness. I mean, you do get a thick skin studying for two years with people who will do anything to get better grades than you. But I guess I expected to be treated – professionally.' I knew I sounded naïve. Had I been naïve?

'How were you treated?'

'Oh, I suppose it was just pettiness. I liked the work at first . . . I suppose I'm not the corporate type. You know, I guess I couldn't take the kind of back-stabbing most people get used to dealing with.'

'Don't underestimate that kind of intimidation. The women I know who went into business have all told me that it's a very stressful, very sexist, difficult environment. It takes years to do anything in your career anyway, and the men usually try to get the women out before they have a chance.'

I had always avoided this kind of thinking; it had made me think too much of whining. For Mara it was simple, a political reality; for me it was a question of pride. I could not blame my failure on men, the office. It was easy for her. She could dismiss people she found stupid. But I had desperately wanted to succeed; she did not know how I had worked for it, put all my money, hope and time into preparing for that career.

'The company was very proud of their training and career opportunities. I suppose that was why I took the job. They sort of threw me in the deep end and then turned away when I started to drown. Then I began to hate it. I suppose it was a shock to find people want you to fail.'

'That doesn't sound very professional. I'm sure you've figured out academics are the same. Petty and competitive, back-stabbing. But you seem to be doing all right here. Even though you irked the Dean with your office hours sign – '

'You heard about that.'

'Of course, that's a sin against student-teacher interaction.' We smiled at each other. Mara went on, 'But everybody else talks about what a great job you're doing. Anyway, the Dean isn't exactly well-loved. He has his enemies. Why else would he have Hitler running around spying for him? You haven't written your obituary yet.'

'I'm glad to hear it. Not that it matters. All I've got is summer contract.'

'Have you thought any more about what you'll do after the summer?' she asked. 'Do you really want to go back to what you were doing?'

'Well, I've got to do something.' I didn't want to mention the Ph.D idea; Mara would arrange the entire thing in a flash and then I'd be stuck here. I wanted time to look around.

'But not here.'

'I don't think so.'

'Why don't you like it here?'

I did not want to tell her the truth – that it was ugly, sprawling, a humid backwater. She lived here; she liked it. 'It's too hot for me. I know you do like it, though.'

'Yeah. It's relaxed. People like things because they like

them, not because you're supposed to like them. New Yorkers eat Tex-Mex because it's the flavour of the month; next month it's Thai or Vietnamese. They think they're terribly cultured, but they're really just people who read magazines and then do what the magazines tell them to do.'

'Yes.' I had heard this before, but was surprised that she should use the same old excuse to justify living here simply because she had a job. I thought she would be more honest than that. 'But it's so suburban,' I said a little aggressively. 'And there's no public transportation.'

'Well, I find that liberating,' she said pleasantly, not noticing my irritation. 'I grew up using the subway, and I'd rather sit alone in my air-conditioned car any day.'

'I suppose you think that New Yorkers and Europeans – are pretentious.'

'No, just narrow-minded. I don't think it's pretentious to like old houses and little shops instead of malls and all that, but I do think it's arrogant to refuse to admit there are other ways of living.'

'I mean,' she went on, 'I suppose I find it arrogant to attach moral implications to one's own definition of beauty. You know, people do think that if your environment is ugly, you must be stupid because you live there, or even wicked.'

'So you do feel it is ugly here.'

'It is not beautiful in the sense that British Columbia or · Norway or Italy is beautiful, no. But I like it.'

I thought of something. 'How did you know I was visiting, that first night?'

Mara hesitated and smiled. 'You looked lost.'

'Oh,' I said, stung. 'I see.' I felt frightened now that I liked this woman so well. It wasn't a game of words with her. I had met somebody with whom I would never win an argument because she was not interested in winning. I was not in control when I was with her. Then I thought, *Am I really somebody who has to win every argument?* Who was I? I was not sure of anything. Perhaps I had become permanently vulnerable, a frail, transparent egg.

Georgine came up from behind, pushed between us and whispered, 'Let's sneak out.'

'Don't you have to stay?' I asked.

She ignored me and, looking at Mara, said, 'Excuse me, I have to go to the ladies.' She walked away.

I looked at Mara in confusion. Glancing at her watch, she . said, 'How about something to eat?'

When we got to the parking lot, Georgine was waiting for us.

I hoped we would sit in a quiet restaurant and talk, but Georgine wanted to go to Maybelle's and Mara seemed happy to go along, and I did not object. We all climbed into Georgine's car.

It was mariachi night at Maybelle's and very crowded. We ordered drinks. Georgine and Mara talked about people at the college. I could barely hear their conversation and looked around idly. I watched the dancers, both Hispanic and Anglo, stepping to the Latin music, incongruously bathed in disco lights. My gaze floated towards the bar, where men and women sat and eyed one another.

Then I saw Lynette. She was leaning against the bar, drinking. I did not recognize her at first. She had pulled her hair neatly back and instead of her usual jeans and loose T-shirt was wearing a tight skirt, blouse, and high heels. She turned around and planted her elbows on the bar, thrusting her breasts out. She was heavily made up.

She turned away from a young man, laughing. He walked angrily away and she ordered another drink. As she waited for her drink, she surveyed the room. Then she saw me. Her eyes widened; then she smiled and tossed her

head. Her drink arrived and she turned to chat to the bartender.

Mara and Georgine noticed nothing. Georgine got up to
dance; Mara and I did not try to talk over the noise and
music. I glanced occasionally over to the bar. Lynette was
now talking to a man in a black cowboy shirt and jeans,
Stetson and lizard-skin cowboy boots. She leaned against
the bar, holding her glass, bending towards him in a
pathetically brazen, coquettish posture. He sat on his bar
stool, reserved and polite.

'Do you know them?' Mara asked me loudly, 'or are you
just observing?'

I hesitated. She obviously had not recognized Lynette. 'I
was just watching them.' I tried to think of something to say,
to distract her.

'She's a bit sad, I think, trying to flirt with that man.'

The music stopped and I knew I had to tell her before she
herself recognized Lynette. 'Don't you know who it is?'

'Who?'

'It's Lynette.'

'Oh, yes, it is. What is she doing? Why is she dressed like
that? What has she done to her hair?'

'I don't know.'

'Is she trying to pick up that man? Has she seen you?
Look, she's seen us.' Mara waved. Lynette waved back.

At that moment, Georgine returned to the table. 'Who are
you waving at?'

'A student,' I said.

'Oh.' Georgine was trying to flag down a waitress.

The drinks arrived, and I drank mine, feeling miserable,
anticipating a scene, wishing we would leave. I hardly said
a word the rest of the evening, but Mara and Georgine
didn't seem to notice. I kept my back to the bar. The next
time I glanced over, she was gone.

14

I felt almost pleased with my mild hang-over the next morning. For the first time in my life I did not feel guilty about drinking. I was not being reckless and irresponsible; I had a social life. I worked hard and then I went out and had a good time. I was like other people. I did not drink alone, trying to forget about a terrible job; I had friends.

I rolled out of bed, looked at my clock, feigned a groan. I imagined myself in a movie, acting out the part of a hung-over, single, professional woman. I said, aloud, 'God, my head. Coffee, coffee, coffee.' I got up and headed for the kitchen.

I wondered when I would see Mara again. Georgine had dropped her off at her car in the campus parking lot before driving us back to University Place. She had not mentioned Lynette again, but she must now know that we had broken up. I imagined her eyes, judging, reproachful. She would think I had acted badly. Why else would Lynette be out picking up men? I thought of Lynette's cinder-block book-shelves, the sheet tacked over the window, the speckled mirror, the mattress on the floor. If I simply told Mara, *It didn't work out*, I would be lying. I had aroused hopes and expectations in a girl I wanted nothing to do with.

The sun shone through the kitchen windows and I decided that I would not upset myself with speculations. I took a shower and dressed. Everything would somehow work out. I would take one day at a time. I would see how things went with Mara. I would see how my applications went. My life had always followed a line, a path determined by some objective I had settled on. I had rushed towards one goalpost after another, frantic and dissatisfied. Now I did not know what would happen tomorrow; my life now, I realized, was here and today.

I drank another cup of coffee and walked around the house restlessly, brushing my hair. It was about 10 o'clock. I wanted to take a walk, but of course there was nowhere to go. Finally, I decided to walk the two blocks to Georgine's.

Georgine answered the door in a pink satin bathrobe with matching slippers. She looked tired, but surprisingly good. Her hair was in slight disarray, but much the same as the evening before. She wore no make-up. She held a mug of steaming coffee. I apologized for dropping in too early and tried to leave, but she insisted that I come in.

I followed her into the kitchen and saw at the table a blonde girl, a young, unkempt Georgine in shorts and sandals.

'This is Sam.' She poured me a cup of coffee. 'My daughter,' she added, unnecessarily. She told Sam my name.

'Am I interrupting?' I felt the weighty silence of a private, possibly distressing, conversation.

Sam said, 'It's just that somebody I know died.'

'Oh. I'm sorry.' I stood up to leave, but Georgine handed me a cup of coffee and waved at me to sit down.

'I've never known anybody who's died before.' Sam was about twenty-five. 'And you know, the weird thing is, I didn't even like her. I feel kind of guilty about it.'

'You can't help your feelings,' I said uneasily, trying to finish my coffee quickly.

'She was kind of fucked up.' This took me aback. I never used language like that with my mother. I glanced at Georgine, who did not seem to notice. 'I mean, nobody liked her . . . You didn't go to South Bay High did you?' she suddenly asked.

'Yes, I did.'

'Did you have a sister?'

'Yes, Alicia.'

'Yeah, I remember her. What happened to her?'

'She lives in the city. She works for – ' I stopped; for the first time, I consciously tried not to lie about my sister. 'She's an apprentice for a place that restores furniture,' I said carefully.

'Oh.'

'You should be having a high-school reunion soon, shouldn't you? It's about that time, isn't it?'

'Yeah, it's year after next. The big ten years when you get to see who's got fat and divorced. What a joke. Well, poor old Lynette, she'll never get to see it.'

'I beg your pardon?'

'Sorry, that was a bit in bad taste, I guess.'

'No, I mean, what was your friend's name?'

'Lynette. Lynette. It was really Linda Annette, but she changed it after high school, to Lynette. Why?'

I felt dipped in numbness. I put my coffee cup on the table. 'Lynette?'

'Yeah, weird name, huh? She dropped out of school and ran away from home. When she got back, she had changed it to Lynette.'

'Where did she go?'

'I don't know; I didn't know her that well. Somewhere out west, Arizona or California or something. She only went to South Bay for a year. They moved here from Asia or the Middle East or some place. Her father was always getting transferred around. I don't think she even finished high school.'

I realized I did not even know that Lynette had gone to South Bay High.

Both Georgine and Sam were looking at me now. 'It's just that, well, I think she was in one of my classes.'

'Oh, Kris,' said Georgine. 'Are you sure?'

'Was she – did she have dark hair, long?'

'Yes,' said Sam. 'And she lived in her parents' place in Clearview. They were real shits. They split to Australia and left her to pay the mortgage. They told her if she missed a payment, she'd be out on her ass.

'I only know this,' she added, 'because I know her room-mate. I really didn't know her that well. Her roommate called me this morning.'

'Did you know her, Kris?' said Georgine, now very concerned. I must have looked upset.

'I don't know,' I said vaguely. 'I think she's also in one of Mara's classes. Women's studies or something.'

'Women in literature,' Georgine said. 'It's her only women's studies course.'

'Yes, that must have been it.'

'It's the gay one. All the gay women take it because she does Radclyffe Hall. Among others, of course'

'That makes sense,' said Sam. 'Lynette was always talking about coming out. But I don't think she ever slept with anybody. Any women. I mean, she was always going on about hating men and all, but it was weird. It was like she was just trying to be different. You know, trying to be gay, but she really wasn't. Like she wanted to be gay so that she wouldn't have to get fucked around by guys any more. She was always getting fucked over by guys.'

'Was she in your class, Kris?' asked Georgine.

'She was the one that was there last night, at Maybelle's.'

'What one?'

'The student at the bar.' Georgine looked puzzled. 'That Mara waved at,' I explained.

'Good Lord, Kris.'

I turned back to Sam. 'How – what happened?'

'Well, Charlene – that's her roommate – told me about it. Lynette was going around picking up guys in bars, you know, in cowboy bars. She did stuff like that. Charlene told her it was dangerous. She's really like I-told-you-so. I mean, the girl is *dead*. But Charlene thinks she's tough shit just because she's got this boyfriend who's lived in India or some place and was in the Peace Corps and has got all these degrees and all.

'Well, I guess some guy did her in. That's what Charlene said. He did it to her in their house. Charlene was out with her boyfriend. They got back and found her.

'I mean, that's the worst of it. Can you imagine, coming back and finding her there? On the floor and all? The police took fingerprints and pictures and everything. Charlene wouldn't stay there. God, neither would I. Lynette's parents are flying out, she said. She's moved in with George, her boyfriend, now.'

15

I walked home. Georgine had told me she would call me if she heard anything more. It was about 11; already the heat closed around me, bright and merciless. I went inside, found my purse and keys and then drove to Clearview, slowing as I passed Lynette's house. A police car was parked in the drive and the overgrown yard was cordoned off with police tape and cones.

I returned home, past the crescent of clipped hedges enclosing the sign UNIVERSITY PLACE CONDOMINIUMS, the neat complex of laundry and maintenance rooms. I parked in my drive. I went inside and closed the front door behind me.

The house felt large and quiet. I went into every room, even checking the closets and shower stall. Then I locked and bolted the front and back doors. In my months of living alone in New York, I had never been so edgy.

I sat on the sofa and tried to piece together what Sam had told me. *She was trying to be gay but really wasn't.* I could not believe that; she had been nervous that first night, but clearly not inexperienced. I thought of the name change and wondered why it disturbed me. Then I thought, *Of course. It must be because I too changed my name.* It was one of those strange coincidences. I put this out of my mind and tried to concentrate.

Sam had said, *She wanted to be gay so that she wouldn't get fucked around by guys any more.* That had not surprised me; Lynette had admitted it herself. She had wanted to be gay in order to protect herself. I had disliked her for *deciding* to be gay, for that cowardice, that need for cover. She had said, *Guys always dumped me.*

And I had said, *Well, you should have dumped them before they dumped you.*

I sat and waited for something to happen. The telephone did not ring; nobody knocked on my door. I thought, *I have no one to talk to, no one who knows I was this girl's lover.* I was certain that Mara knew, but I did not want to be the one to tell her about Lynette's death. She would find out soon enough from Georgine.

If I had known Lynette only slightly, the story I gave Georgine, I would have wanted to talk about it. As it was, I wanted to do nothing, because I did not understand yet what I felt. I sat, the knowledge of Lynette's random death germinating inside me. I waited to see what it would become. Her death was now part of my life; it would change everything. But I could not foresee the effects, not yet.

I watched the news, but there was no mention of it. This made it seem even more removed, as if she had never existed. I wanted to drive past her house again to check that I had not dreamed up the police car and cones. But, of course, there were murders every day and this one was probably insufficiently bizarre to warrant a story. I thought, *Poor Lynette will even die in obscurity.*

The sun went down; I still sat on the sofa. I tried to remember each time we had seen each other, the content of our affair. But it was a blur of cigarettes, sex, arriving in the night and leaving some hours later. It had lasted less than three weeks. We had gone out together a few times; the rest of the time we had spent in bed.

What remained in my mind was Lynette leaning against the bar, ordering another drink, smiling provocatively at some man, looking at me, smug, justified; or Lynette at my door, rope ends dangling down her chest. I imagined her drowning: I had not reached out; I had not tried to help her. I had rejected her appeals for comfort, for reassurance. I tried to remember if I had ever said anything kind to her. We had not talked much. Or, perhaps, I had rejected her attempts to talk. I had not called her when I told her I would; I had not talked to her about breaking up. I had turned my back on her pain.

Georgine called me an hour later. Sam had spoken again to Charlene, who had found out more details. Lynette had picked up a man at Maybelle's. People had seen them leave. Witnesses gave conflicting descriptions of the man; nobody was sure of his height or colouring. Some said he was dark; others, that he was slight and fair. I remembered the tall man in the Stetson, but said nothing. Like a murderer, I knew that the time had come for me to start covering my tracks.

'You didn't see her leave with anybody, did you, Kris?'

'No.' I thought, *I must remember now everything I say.*

He had taken her home and gone in. There were no signs of a struggle, but her clothes were torn. There were no identifiable fingerprints. She had been raped, struck on the head with some object and strangled while unconscious.

Charlene and George came in a few hours later and found her. Their other roommate was out of town. A neighbour had seen a white pick-up truck parked outside her house some time during the evening, but did not notice the make or the licence plate.

I got up Monday morning and went to my intro class. I wondered what people would ask me. Would Eleanor say, her little wings of hair bobbing nervously, *We feel it's best if you don't renew your contract this fall?* Was gossip spreading about me? Would I have to talk to the police?

Of course, the entire campus knew about it, and talked about it, in the way people do. Those who had seen her around claimed to know her better than they had. Those who did not know her at all talked of it with a kind of gruesome curiosity. People stopped me in the corridors, as if I had not known her any better than the next person. *Did you hear? Isn't it awful?*

I walked through the college, free now, but feeling links of chain gather together, slowly locking me in. The entire story would spread. Soon everybody would look at me with suspicion and distaste and interest. I thought, with revulsion, I will be *interesting*. People would talk about me; they would say, *Did you know they were lovers? Can you imagine?*

It was inevitable. Charlene knew, George knew. It would emerge that I was at Maybelle's with Georgine and Mara. People would know Lynette had enrolled in my class. Tom had seen her follow me in the corridor. All the bits of information would combine together, the pieces of a puzzle. and the picture would emerge of me, a murderer.

When I walked into class, my students were whispering; the moment they saw me, they fell away from one another with an embarrassed air. I thought, *I cannot avoid discussing this*.

I took a deep breath and said, 'I'm sure you have all heard about the tragic death of one of our students. For all of us this is a great shock, but especially for those of you who knew her. I'm sure that we will all need time to get over such a violent and senseless death. In the mean time, the only thing we can do is go on and hope that the police find whoever did this terrible thing.'

I looked at my notes. I was sure they all hated me by now and thought me completely heartless. 'So. *On continue*.' As I said this, I vaguely recalled that this was a line from Sartre's play *Huis Clos*. I thought, *Am I now in hell?*

As I opened my office door, I heard the telephone ringing. I picked it up and Alicia said, 'Oh, Kris, did you hear about that girl that got killed?'

'Yes.'

'She went to your college.'

'Yes, I know. She was in one of my classes.'

'Oh, my God.'

'Yeah, it's very strange.'

'Krystal – I *knew* her.'

A silence formed over the telephone. I thought, *Where will this end?*

'Krystal?'

I forced myself to think. 'How did you know her, Alicia?'

'She went to South Bay High.' Then I thought, *Of course: Sam, Alicia, Charlene, South Bay High.* I felt relieved that I did not have to construct a new link, expand and try to understand a larger picture.

At that moment, Georgine knocked on my door and put her head in. I waved her in, saying, 'Alicia, shall I come over tonight?'

'Yeah, do. This is so weird.' She added, with an edge of humour, 'You sure you want to risk the freeway again with that car?' Every time I drove up, Alicia teased me about my car. She couldn't resist: after all these years my little sister had something on me.

I smiled. 'I'll call you if it conks out.'

Georgine sat down. Her face put me immediately on my guard. 'Kris, do you want to come and stay with me?'

'No, thank you.' I spoke politely and firmly. Georgine had probably talked to Mara, and knew now that Lynette and I had been lovers. Why else the look of concern?

'Are you sure?'

'Of course,' I said bluntly. I didn't want to talk to Georgine. I didn't want to explain my feelings. I didn't want her to say, *Kris this is not your fault.*

I needed sanctuary. I needed a haven from anybody who knew that I had been involved with Lynette. I wanted to think, to sit quietly with the knowledge of what had happened. I did not yet know what to do with it. 'I'm going into town, to my sister's.' How strange that sounded to my ears. *My sister's.* It sounded like something other people, other women did. When you are in trouble, you go to your sister's.

'If you need anything – anything, you call, honey.'

'Right. Thanks, Georgine.'

I packed my books and was about to lock up when I saw Charlene walking down the hall. She had a bruised eye, nearly purple and swollen shut; her cheek was puffy and red.

We looked at each other a moment.

She said, 'Did you hear about Lynette?'

I wanted to say, *How could I not have heard?* I said, 'Yes. You'll have to excuse me, I was just leaving.' I would not ask her about the black eye. I never had sympathy for women who allowed men to hit them. I turned away.

'Isn't it terrible?'

I looked at her, and saw that my coldness had provoked her. I did not answer.

'I found her, I found her. It was awful.' She held her face with her hands and shook her head back and forth. I wondered pitilessly how much of this was an act, how much she actually enjoyed the drama of having been the one to find her.

'She was all – twisted, and naked. Her clothes were torn off her. And her eyes – '

I did not want to hear this. I said, quickly, 'Please don't

tell me any more.' I knew she wanted to goad me into a discussion, a confession of responsibility.

'Who can I tell? It was awful, you can't imagine.'

'I don't know. You have friends . . .' Then something she had said seemed to jar. Sam had told me that Charlene was with George. But she had said, *I found her.* 'You found her?'

'Yes, it was *awful*, I'm telling you.'

I assumed a more sympathetic tone. 'Did you scream?'

'Yes, yes, wouldn't you?'

I moved closer to her and said quietly, 'Yes, I would. Weren't you frightened that he was still there?'

She looked up at me in surprise. 'No, I mean, all I thought of was that she was dead. She looked so dead. I mean, she was all twisted, lying on the floor. I mean, he had done it and – left. Why would he be there?'

'Of course he wouldn't.' I glanced around, checking that we were alone. 'Did you touch her?'

'Oh, God, no! I just screamed and screamed.'

'Was she in the living room?'

'Yeah, on the floor by the coffee table.'

'In front of the TV?'

'Yeah, in front of the TV. What does it matter? Can't you understand? I've never seen anything like it. You can't imagine. In that house. Isn't it awful?'

'Yes,' I said. 'You must have been terrified. What was the first thing you did?'

She held her face again and shook it. 'I just ran out screaming.'

'Through the kitchen?'

'Yes, what does it matter? Through the kitchen and down the driveway.'

'Did you run to a neighbour?'

She sat up. 'No, because – well, I didn't really run out. I

ran over to George. He was there, too, you know. We both found her, George and me.'

'Was he behind you? Who went into the house first?'

'I did – I – saw her first.' She looked frightened now.

I looked at her calmly. I knew she was lying. If George had been behind her, she wouldn't have screamed and run out. She would have turned around and rushed into George's arms. She had not *walked in* with George. 'Why did you say *you* found her?'

'Well, I just meant – that we did find her.'

'Was George already there? When you got there? Did you see him and run out? Did he run down the driveway and bring you back?'

She did not answer.

'What did you tell the police?'

'We both found her. It's the truth.' Now she was angry, defensive.

'Why did he hit you?'

'He didn't. We – I – we drove to his place, he slammed on the brakes, and I hit the dash.'

I turned and began to walk away.

'Why are you trying to accuse George?' she said nastily.

'I have not accused anybody,' I hissed at her as quietly as I could.

She shook her head slowly, back and forth, as if disgusted. 'You bitch. You cold bitch. You don't even care. Don't you even care about *her*?'

I thought of several caustic replies. I finally said, 'Yes.'

'You ought to.'

'Please excuse me.' I picked up my bag.

'George didn't do it, you bitch.'

'Perhaps he didn't, but you must have thought he did. He was there when you got there, wasn't he? Otherwise why did you run out of the house screaming? Is that why he hit you? Because you didn't believe him?'

Her face seemed to twist in on itself with her anger. 'You cold fucking bitch. George didn't do it. You did.' She moved in front of me.

I stared at her. 'Please move out of my way.'

'You're the one who did it to her. And I don't mean that you're a dyke. I don't give a shit about that. But I know more than you think.'

'What are you talking about?' I suddenly felt a shift, a movement between us. Power is about the ability to ignore; and Charlene knew I was listening.

'I remember you from South Bay. You were always such a stuck-up bitch. You thought you were better than everybody. Changing your name. Going to France and all. Well, you're not.'

I looked at her, enraged that she thought she could talk to me like this. But I stood, fixed to the floor below me. Why did I not simply walk away? At any other time in my life I would not have given this woman two seconds' thought. But I could not move. I was afraid if I moved past her, I would slap her. I wanted to hurt her, and I sensed that if I did this, if I touched her, I would be lost for ever. I stood and listened, humiliated, watching these words, which I knew I had to hear, coming out of this ridiculous girl's mouth, a girl with a black eye and swollen cheek.

'Look at you. What are you doing here? Why aren't you in Paris or London or wherever? Lynette told me about you. You're divorced and you're broke and you had to come home and live with your mother. You must be pretty hard up to have to go home.'

'You know nothing about me.' I tried to speak with force, but I was on the defensive.

'I know enough to know you're a bitch and you don't care

about anybody. You're a dyke and you're ashamed of it. Don't you think we knew you were sneaking in and out of the house at all hours? We could hear you, every night you were there. The walls in that place aren't that thick and we were in the next room.'

I felt blood rising to my face.

'You didn't deserve her. She loved you. She told me you promised her you were going to live together and then you dumped her. You were embarrassed to be with her.'

'Get out of my way.' I made to go past her, willing my hands to stay away from her.

'You're garbage, you're nothing. You have no morals; you're completely selfish.'

'Get out of my way.' I spoke carefully; I was in control again now.

'Don't you see? She wanted to be like you. She wanted to be a winner. Like you. Somebody who doesn't give a shit about anybody else. Somebody who dumps people. Don't you see? That's why she was doing it. That's why she was picking up men. To dump them. To be like you. To sleep with whoever she wanted and not get fucked around. To be in control.'

I hated this girl now. My hands shook. I could have killed her at that moment. I pushed her aside and walked out.

I drove out of the parking lot and to my house. I pulled open drawers and chose clothing at random. I opened my closet. A pile of laundry was heaped on the closet floor. I found one clean, ironed blouse hanging on the rail. I threw everything into a bag and went back out to the car.

I drove through Clearview and on to the freeway as if on automatic pilot. Why did I have to be there, at Maybelle's, for her to exhibit herself? Why should I have the enormous ill-luck to be there? Why should I be responsible for this stupid girl? What was I being punished for?

Charlene said that Lynette had wanted to be like me, a woman men do not dump. But I had been used and dumped by men, by Dewitt and Tomas. I never told her that; she never knew I was a complete fraud. I had lived a role I had created for myself, an elegant, sophisticated woman. I had thought that if I lived this role, I would become it, and it would become me. But I was not that. I was a woman who got dumped.

My own father had dumped me. And my mother had loved him, not me. *My mother did not love me.* It came to me with searing, brutal clarity. I could not love because my mother had never loved me. She was what I thought women should not be: weak, intolerant, ungenerous. I had, from earliest memory, determined I would be different. My mother had loved my father and been thrown out as if she were garbage. *It would never happen to me.*

I had married a man who did not love me. I could not bear any real closeness with Alicia. I had never until now had any true friends. (And they would not be my friends for much longer.) Yet Lynette had loved me. Lynette wanted to be the sort of woman I was, the sort of woman who does not love. She too had been hurt and wanted to learn not to love, to have dignity, to be in control.

I was not in control. I drove on even as I thought I would have to pull over and call Alicia to come and get me. But I drove, I continued to drive, with pain and anger rushing through my body, as though I were on my way to a hospital emergency room, as though I were in shock, and would shortly be able to let go and have somebody else take care of me.

If I could reach Alicia's, I would be all right. If I could just reach Alicia, I could hide. I would be protected in her small, shabby apartment. I would not have to see anybody else. I would not have to talk if I did not want to. I would sit and drink tea and wine and smoke cigarettes and I could go to bed and sleep. And I would be safe.

16

By the time I got to Alicia's, I had partially recovered. I parked the car in front of her house and sat for a few minutes before getting out. I tried to pull myself together. What I really wanted was to throw myself in Alicia's arms and cry. I wanted her to hold me; I would tell her the whole story.

I had murdered this girl. I had slept with this girl and lied to her. I had hurt her and she had killed herself. I had never cared enough about her to tell her the truth: that I was terrified of vulnerability, of the loss of control. I had never loved anybody. And my mother did not love me. My life was empty; I had nowhere to go, nobody to turn to. Except to Alicia. I would weep on Alicia's shoulder and she would understand.

But, of course, that was impossible. I squared my shoulders and assumed my usual reserved expression. I could never bare my soul to my sister. She would look at me with those coal-black eyelashes, arched brows, metallic bangs, an expression of surprise and disgust, pull away and say, *Are you telling me you're gay?* Or, perhaps, *Krystal, I really don't want to hear about your sex life.* My relationship with Alicia was built on years of caution, misunderstanding and resentment. It was too late to try to change that now. Alicia had once been my audience, and she wasn't going to play that any more. Now that I needed her. How many times had she needed me?

She opened the front door and led me up the stairs to her apartment. I said, 'How did you find out, Alicia?'

187

'It was on the news this morning. I shouldn't have said I knew her. I meant, I remembered her. Isn't it creepy?'

'Yes.' I sat down, laid my bag on the sofa. 'Do you have a cigarette?' She handed me her pack and lighter. 'Did you know her well, Alicia?'

'No.' I returned the pack to her and she lit a cigarette as well. 'I just remember her. It's just that, well, I've never known anybody who's died. Much less been murdered.'

'No, I haven't either,' I said. 'Alicia, she was in one of my classes.'

'Yeah, you said. This is so weird.'

'She was in one of my intro classes. Alicia, do you mind if I stay here a couple of days?'

'No. Of course not. I wouldn't want to stay down there either. Who do they think did it?'

'I don't know . . . Do you have anything to drink?'

'Some gin. And vodka. And a little wine.'

'White?'

'Yeah, you want it?'

'Yeah. Thanks.'

She went into the kitchen. I said, 'Do you know somebody called Charlene? From South Bay High?'

'No.'

'How about Sam? Sam Brightman. Samantha, I guess.'

'I don't know, maybe.'

'They knew her. I'm friends with Sam's mother.'

Alicia returned with the wine. 'I remember Linda. She dropped out and ran away, I think. And came back. But I don't think she came back to school. I must have been a senior then.'

'Do you know where she went?'

'No, California maybe. She was weird. I mean, you have to be weird to hang around bars and pick men up. What a place to do it. Do you remember Maybelle's?'

'Yes. Do you remember Harmony Bait and Tackle?'

'What?'

'Remember? The place that said, *Eat and Get Gas.*'

'Oh yeah.' She laughed.

'Alicia, I was there that night, at Maybelle's. I saw her there.'

'What? Krystal, really?'

'Yes. All I keep thinking is, well, it could have been one of us. I mean, we've all done stupid things.'

'Yeah, I guess so. I've never picked up guys like that though.'

'Neither have I. I know it sounds weird, but I feel like it almost happened to me.'

'What do you mean?'

'I don't know . . . As if she was somebody I could have turned out like.'

Alicia looked at me with one of her cold, suspicious looks. The look she had whenever I talked about my feelings or asked her about hers, whenever we weren't talking about *Vogue* and nail polish.

I plunged on. 'What I mean is, she was lonely, and had problems.' I leaned forward, hoping she would understand. 'Don't you see, the only difference between us is that she had bad luck? She wasn't very intelligent or good looking. And she was all alone.'

'You mean her parents were gone,' said Alicia, not understanding, or refusing to understand that it was only chance that separated me from Lynette. 'Yeah, I knew that.'

'Yes, and she didn't really have any friends. After I heard about it, I was sitting there, in that house I'm renting, feeling really alone.' I added, 'I'm glad you're here.'

'Yeah, I know what you mean. I feel alone most of the time.'

'Alicia, are you going out with anybody?' I had been afraid of asking her about this; shock gave me courage.

'No.' She blushed slightly. 'Don't laugh, okay? I put an ad in the paper, you know?' She laughed nervously. 'A lonely hearts ad.'

'Really?' I was intrigued. 'Tell me what it said. Did anybody call?'

She explained how it worked: box numbers and letters exchanged, a neutral, safe, meeting place. She had met two men for drinks, neither of whom she liked. She shrugged. 'So what? Thirty bucks down the drain.'

I saw that what had happened to Lynette would never happen to Alicia, not in that way, not by picking up a complete stranger; she was too used to looking after herself. But I still clung to the idea; it *could* happen. A man she had gone out with a few times, a rejected boyfriend, a neighbour. Lynette was stupid and we were clever, but that was only luck. Luck was what separated us from Lynette. I decided not to press the point. I drank my wine. 'Did you know Mother has a lover?'

'No, but don't tell me about it. I'm not interested in hearing about Mother's private life.'

'Well, I won't, but she made it pretty clear that she didn't want me around. I don't know why I should feel surprised.'

Alicia shrugged. 'Do you think she's any different with me?'

'Well, yes. She always talks like she's so involved with you.'

'She talks that way about you too. She makes it sound as if you call her weekly.'

'Yes, of course, she would.' I should have guessed that. We had seen each other several times since my arrival and this was only the second time we had talked about Mother. 'I suppose,' I said, 'it's been even more lonely for you, in a way. I've been gone, and married and all. I've had college and Thomas – '

'Of course it has, Krystal.' She shook her head, and let out a light, amazed, slightly annoyed laugh. 'You can't imagine how hard it's been to put together what I've got. I don't mean to put down your degrees and all, but I've never had any help or been married. I feel really independent, but I tell you, I'd give away a lot of my independence for a relationship.'

So Alicia was lonely, and alone. Of course, I had known this, but I had always pushed the thought out of my mind. Alicia had struggled to put together a life, which on the face of it had little to show. All the struggles of a woman without money or education or skills or family are invisible. They are the parts of life that the educated, the articulate, never consider difficult: learning to interview for a job, balance a bank account, file a tax return. Learning to cope when your parents have told you your entire life you are stupid. Finding the money to put a deposit on an apartment, get the electricity turned on. Of all that Alicia had done, all that could be seen was a rented apartment, a job, a used car.

Alicia had had independence thrust on her, and had survived. She had created a toe-hold, a sanctuary, which she did not own, but had managed to make her own. I looked around at all of her collections on every bookshelf, every table top. She had created a life for herself. And now had found something to do, a job she liked. This had taken time, and had imprinted lines on her face, and hardened her mouth, but Alicia had survived. Alicia would be all right.

I thought of my suitcases, my pile of laundry, my tapes, my dilapidated VW. This was all I had at the moment. Would I be all right? I had, of course, in some ways much more than Alicia did: education, skills. But now that my luck had slipped, I was frightened.

Why had I been so proud? All I had was a streak of enormous luck, a wealth of resources. I was born with many gifts; I had been given help, scholarships. I attracted lovers easily. I had rarely been alone; I had never been without money or a job. Would I have done so well if I had had to struggle as Alicia had?

Alicia gave me her bed and took the sofa for herself. When I woke up, she had already left for work. She left me a note with a spare key on top. I made myself a cup of tea – she had no coffee – and dressed. I had to drive down for a class. I passed a flower stand and stopped to buy a box of roses.

I took the Clearview freeway exit and, instead of driving to University Place, drove past Lynette's house. The police tape and cones were gone. On the front door was a large black wreath. I parked in front and got out. The lawn had been mowed and the front door was now accessible. In the drive was a spotlessly clean American car.

I knocked on the front door. A large, red-faced man opened it.

'I'm sorry to disturb you.' I handed him the box. 'I knew your daughter. I'm sorry.'

I turned to go, but the man said, 'I'm not her father. I'm her uncle.' His accent was distinctly Australian. 'Don't run off like that. You can at least come in. Linda's mother is in the kitchen. I'll tell her you're here.' Hearing the name Linda in that home confused me for a moment; then I remembered the name change and wondered why it still bothered me.

I went in through the hall and into the living room. I noticed that the carpet had been shampooed, for it was fluffy and did not smell. The entire room was brighter; I saw then that the curtains had been taken down.

Lynette's mother walked into the living room, a small, dark woman, about fifty years old. I said, 'I'm sorry to disturb you. It's just that I knew your daughter. I'm very sorry.'

Behind her, I could see the kitchen through the door; the cabinets and floor had been scrubbed. The red vinyl table was gone. The windows sparkled. I realized that this woman had been here for two days, after a twenty-hour flight, and the house had already been transformed.

She took the flowers from the red-faced uncle and sat down. 'Oh, that's all right. Please sit down.'

I sat on the edge of the horrible brown sofa.

'You're the first person who's come by.'

'Oh.'

'Linda didn't have many friends?'

'I'm not sure. She was one of my students. I teach French.'

'Oh, how nice. You must be very talented.'

'Well – ' I stopped, for once in my life speechless.

'Linda had people living here, didn't she?' .

'I believe so.'

'She wasn't supposed to.' The woman shook her head at me as if scolding me for having failed to enforce this rule. 'We had asked her not to. But everything I said went in one ear and out the other.' She had a strange accent, a mixture of Texan and Australian; the tone sing-songy, like a patient, exasperated school teacher's. 'The police told us there were three of them. They haven't come around. That girl and her . boyfriend – ' She stopped.

I nodded. 'Yes.'

'This house never used to look like this. I can't imagine how she let it get into this shape.'

I smiled politely and moved as if to get up.

'Oh, you don't have to go. Do you want a cup of coffee?'

Thank you, no.'

'Oh, it's no trouble.' She rose and went into the kitchen.

The man, the uncle, spoke up then. 'She was always

193

doing stupid things like this. Ran away. Should have been put in a home if you ask me.'

I stared at him.

'Ungrateful. And stupid.' He shook his head. 'Girls like her, going out to bars. It's no wonder something like this happened.'

The mother returned. 'I put the coffee on. You see, we have another life now, in Melbourne. My husband has a good job there. We have a younger son. We have to think of him too, you know.'

She smiled kindly at me. 'The police will investigate. It's best if we leave it to them. I wanted to sell this house long before. We let her live in it, but we'll put it up for sale now.'

I drove to campus. This girl, whom I and others had fucked and dumped, was now gone. There was nothing left of her. A few clothes, a house, now cleaned, soon to be put up for sale. Her mother would go back to her husband and son in Australia. Was this what Lynette's life meant?

Her father had not bothered to come. Her uncle thought she had asked for it. Women who trusted men were fools. A woman should know a man cannot be trusted. If a woman is stupid, she should die.

And her mother was ready, after two days, to put the entire thing behind her. Did this girl have no one who loved her?

I taught my class, left campus immediately and drove home. The house already smelled uninhabited. I dropped my clothes from the day before on to the closet floor with the rest of the laundry. I would sort everything later, do the washing, and then go back to Alicia's.

I turned on the air conditioning and checked the fridge. There was only some butter, a pot of old yoghurt and milk. I washed the yoghurt down the sink and made a cup of tea.

I found some hardening bread and threw it out. Then I sat down at the kitchen table and took out my diary. I counted the days until the end of the summer term. Then I counted the days that I would actually have to go to campus. Then I subtracted the second number from the first to see how many days I would not have to go to campus, but could stay at home, or at Alicia's.

The doorbell rang.

I opened the door and saw Mara. She said, 'Are you okay?'

'I'm fine.' I looked at her coldly. She would not be interested in me now, even as a friend. She knew about me. I was a murderer. 'I was at my sister's.'

'I tried to catch you at campus, but you weren't in your office.'

'No.' What did it matter whether I kept office hours? Mara followed me into the living room. We sat down.

She looked around. 'So this is Dan's place.'

I realized I didn't know his name. I said, conversationally, 'Sick, isn't it?' She meant nothing to me now, nor I to her. She would be kind to me, even though I was a murderer; it was part of her politics.

'Look, Kris, the police are going to contact you for a statement. You know, because we saw her that night.'

'I see.' Her eyes said, *I came over to warn you.* I did not need her to warn me. I already knew I had to be very careful of everything I said.

'I've already spoken to them. I just told them what you'll probably tell them. You know, about Lynette hanging around the bar at Maybelle's. I told them we hadn't talked to her.' *Make your story simple and stick to it. Don't tell them you were lovers. Nobody knows but me, and I won't tell.*

'Right.'

'I can imagine you're pretty upset about all this.' *Having killed this poor girl.*

'I'm all right.'

'Do you want to talk about it?' *I will play therapist for you, but you know that means we can't be lovers.*

'No, I guess not.'

'Apparently a neighbour saw a white pick-up in front of the house about midnight, but nobody saw it arrive or leave. I told them I saw her talking to that guy at the bar, but . another witness said she left with somebody who looked completely different. You know the police talked to George, but he's in the clear.'

I looked up. 'Are you sure?'

'Yeah, too bad, huh?' She smiled ironically. 'He was with some guys at another bar in Seagate. He and his girlfriend arrived at the house about the same time and found her. You know he beat up his girlfriend?'

'Yes.'

She rose. 'If you need anything, or you just want to have dinner or something, just call.' *What are friends for?*

'Right, thanks.'

I sat on the sofa for a long time. Darkness fell around me like ash. I thought I could see particles of darkness suspended in front of my eyes. My hands grew faint. The edges of the furniture blurred. In the dark, I could not see the oranges and reds, the bull fighters and bulls. It was very quiet.

I knew that if I sat there long enough, light would again fill the room. I would eventually hear the thud of a newspaper falling against the front step; mail would slide into the box outside the door. The air would stir. I would get up and make coffee, shower and dress, go to my classes.

Life would go on. This would all happen some hours from now.

I did not know what time it was. I sat in the dark and did not move. I wished I was dead.

17

I decided to stay home instead of returning to Alicia's. The commute was too far, and I did not want to take Alicia's bed while she slept on the sofa.

A few days passed. I taught my classes and went home afterwards. Nobody talked to me about not keeping office hours. I stayed away from the department office and did not check my pigeon-hole.

Georgine called me once or twice, but I made up excuses not to see her. In the evenings, I sat on the sofa and watched television. I drank dry gin martinis and fell asleep where I sat. I woke a few hours later and turned off the television, which by then would be producing a monotonous tone and a rainbow of horizontal lines. I did not always bother to take off my clothes before going to bed.

A policeman called me and made an appointment. We met in my office. He wore a suit rather than a uniform and looked very young. He did not seem very interested in Lynette, or me. I told him she was in one of my classes and that I had seen her at Maybelle's on the night of the murder, as he put it. No, I did not see her leave Maybelle's. I did not know if she had a boyfriend. I did not know how often she went to bars.

He smiled and apologized for taking up my time. 'We'll do our best,' he said, 'but these random murders are rarely resolved.' He closed the file on his lap and stood up. We shook hands.

I stopped worrying about what I was going to do after the summer. I realized it did not much matter. If the college did not offer to renew my contract, or if none of my applications to other universities was accepted, I would do something else. I could be a waitress. I could clean people's houses. I could learn computer programming. I could learn to type.

It did not matter what I did because I had never done anything of value. Anything I did would be more important than what I had done before. I had thought it was important that I studied in Europe, learned to speak French, owned an art gallery. But in fact I had never done anything of substance. I had taken all the opportunities, the gifts, that life had handed me, and used them to imitate a successful, interesting woman. I imitated; I masqueraded. I was a party girl, dressed in flimsy, pretty clothes.

I thought with some amusement of my snobbery towards Alicia for not having become a painter. I had considered her afraid of risk. In fact, I was the coward. I had studied what other people created, afraid to create something of my own. I had tried to create a writer out of Tomas since I did not believe I could do anything myself. I had created one thing, loved one thing: my gallery. And that was making money from other people's art.

Charlene was right. I had thought I was better than everybody. And I had not deserved Lynette. I did not deserve anybody's love. I had never loved. Even now, since coming home, I had used people. My friendship with Georgine was a diversion. I had liked her because she amused me. I had seen Alicia to avoid Mother during the weeks I was sleeping with Lynette. And I had wanted Mara because it flattered me that a serious woman was interested in me.

I had done things not out of love and sincerity, but out of pride and egotism. I had liked the idea of being married to a writer, of having a sister who was a painter. I was no better than my students, who did not absorb and love French, but merely liked the idea of learning it. And I was no better than

Lynette, who wanted to be gay because she liked the idea, the protection of not wanting a man. I was completely, utterly shallow.

I had thought I was in control of my life, but all I was doing was running fast, devising one scheme after another that sounded like the kind of life that I thought I wanted.

One day about a week after Lynette's death, I came in from class and sat on the sofa. I did not change clothes. The sun was low in the sky. I did not turn on the television or make a drink. I simply sat. I did not mind the living room any more; I knew now that the ugliness of this furniture was not important. Where I lived no longer mattered. I now saw everything clearly. I sat on my sofa and the pieces fitted together like a painting, like the logic of a dream.

I saw myself leaving behind the women who had helped and perhaps loved me: Madeline, my sister, Mme Smith, even Naomi, for who are we without a model on which to create a self? I saw myself in France, walking to the market and the *Monoprix* with Meredith, leaving for London with Tomas. Pictures filled my mind: walking to my office, from Fulham to Knightsbridge, through Hyde Park, across Park Lane, into a Victorian façade, and my glass and chrome office. And later, from my white adobe house, across the interstate to Rosita's. Tomas and I had stopped to have lunch there, and then decided to stay. Rosita's, where I would sit with my *New York Times* each morning before opening the gallery. I saw myself walking up to the square for the first time after Tomas left me, and seeing Dewitt standing on the street.

He was alone. He was always alone. Where was his apprentice? Where was Linda? Linda. Linda Annette. Was her name *Linda Annette*?

I knew now why the name change had disturbed me. It

was not because I, too, had changed my name. I had thought that the name change was simply another strange coincidence that blurred the edges between Lynette and me. No, it was nothing so vague; Lynette had a reason to want me to stay with her, to change her life. It had been I that had altered hers so dramatically.

Dewitt had picked her up hitchhiking down the interstate; she had run away from home. He took her home and she had stayed. She took care of him; she cooked their meals and cleaned the studio. She was learning to throw pots. She read his books. *I was beginning to get my life together.*

And then what happened? Perhaps she got restless. She may have wanted to go to college. Dewitt was a perceptive man; he would have noticed her desire to learn more than she could from his stacks of books. I imagined them in that cold studio, Dewitt building shelves, and Lynette reading *Middlemarch, Emma.* He would have seen her transform from a seventeen-year-old runaway into a twenty-year-old, curious and ready for the world. He knew she would have to leave him soon. But Lynette had not been ready to be cast off. She had still needed him. She was still too shy to go to parties, to tend his booth at the arts and crafts fairs. She waited in the truck, or shopped for supplies in town, or returned to the studio.

And then, one night, Dewitt went off with another woman, a glamorous, successful woman. Lynette would have thought, *If he can have her, why would he want me?* She would have noticed his edginess the past few months. Her parents may have written to her to say, *If you come back now, you can either move with us to Australia or rent the house here. Or, we will sell it.* She would have had nowhere else to go. She would not have wanted to stay with a man who so obviously wanted her to leave.

I thought about all this, and still I did not know if it was true. Lynette had said, *How can women care about each other if they're stealing each other's men and hurting each other? I mean, really invading each other's lives?*

Was her name Linda Annette? I did not know. I did not know whether Lynette had run away to New Mexico or California. She had told me California, but she had told me hesitantly, and had never been specific about where she lived, or how. She could have lied, of course.

Then there was the patchwork quilt that lay on her bed. Her grandmother had made it. Dewitt had told me that she had been carrying a box when he picked her up; in it was her grandmother's patchwork quilt. Still, I did not know. Linda would be about twenty-three now. How old was Lynette? *I could not remember how old she was.* How could I have known so little about this poor girl? I would probably never know whether Linda and Lynette were the same. Unless, of course, I returned to see her mother, or wrote to Dewitt. I did not want to do these things.

Then I thought, *It does not matter whether she lied or not.* This came to me like a vision, liberating me from the need to know. Whether she lied or not would not change the fact that I had murdered her. I would never know whether Lynette had been the girl at that party, the girl who had taken the keys and driven the pick-up to Dewitt's studio and then to the Greyhound bus station. The girl whose life I had completely altered, disrupted. *I had started getting my life together when this guy I was living with dumped me.*

I would never know. But it did not matter, because I had done it to that girl, Linda. I would have done it to Lynette. I would have done it to anybody. I never thought about anybody else in the pursuit of my own selfish desires. *I think women should help each other.*

I looked around my living room. The light was fading. Lynette and I differed only by the accident of birth, by the unequal distribution of assets. I could take no responsibility for my successes; and I could not hate Lynette because of her failures. We had both left, changed our names. We had searched out a different life from Clearview; we had both taken lovers who, we thought, would give us something we wanted.

And our mothers did not love us. I thought of her mother looking at me placidly, and I could so easily see my own mother's face in hers: beyond pain, numb; a woman who had never loved. My mother had told me, coolly, *You didn't seem to need me.* She had wanted me to think *I* had injured *her.*

She had said that I had not needed her and in turn she had not loved me. But I had needed her; I had been a child. I had had to convince myself I did not need anybody. I accepted that I had to find a place for myself, alone and using my resources in a competitive, harsh world. Mother's voice came back to me from years before. *Don't come to me with your problems; you're big enough to figure it out yourself. Look at me. I don't go around whining.* Her detached expression, her obsession with my father, her utter indifference to her children said it all: *That's nice, dear.*

I had survived her indifference. I worked hard, and things happened to me, lucky things. Lynette was right. People like me always did get jobs. But I had used all my resources to deceive. I had even taken my talent for language and used it to lie. I had told Lynette, *Who knows where this will lead?*

Did it matter whether Lynette had lied or not? I decided to do one good thing. I decided to avenge her death.

The following day, I came home from campus and saw that Georgine had left a note asking me to call her. I threw the note away. But she must have seen my car, because minutes later she knocked on the door.

'Are you all right?'

'I'm fine.'

'You don't look fine.'

'I have an idea,' I said impulsively. Should I tell her? Would she help me?

'Kris, sit down. Sit down. You listen to me, honey. This was not your fault. Do you understand? Not your fault. Listen, I knew that girl. Sam knew her. She was nuts.'

I listened to this calmly. I knew that Georgine would say this; it meant nothing. It meant that she did not want me to get hurt. She would not help me.

Her voice said, *You should try to forget about this.* Her voice said, *It is all right to live with endless justifications, to not care about people, to lie to yourself.*

I thought, yes, I could lie, like my mother did. My mother knew that she had hurt us, and would never admit it. She had said, *You never needed me.* That was the lie that allowed her to go on living.

This was my plan. For the moment, I would do nothing. I would live as I always had. Later would come the changes. Later, I would cut my hair and throw out my clothes, the deceptive trappings of my life. My clothes, my hair, my jewellery, had hidden what was real. They were the opposite of risk, the antithesis of art. I had thought that good taste was important, but it was the pitiful compensation of a life bereft of creativity. Good taste was the terrible lie that I had lived with; I had tried to convince myself that my life was important.

The changes would come later. I had to wait. For the moment, I decided to do nothing; I would be a spy. I would hide in my clothes and hair and attractiveness for one last time. I was gay now; I was in the closet for the last time. *After this*, I thought, *I will live free.*

Mara's concerned face told me Georgine had called her. It was later that same day; Georgine had left an hour or so before.

'Hello,' I said, letting Mara in. She followed me into the kitchen. 'Want a cup of coffee? A drink?'

I looked at her. I hadn't felt this calm, this confident, in years. I was excited, full of energy, but in control. I knew exactly who I was and what I was doing.

She looked at me. 'No thanks.'

We sat down at the kitchen table. She watched me like a therapist, a doctor, a priest. I smiled a curt, superior smile. 'If you're worried about me, don't be. I'm fine. I've never felt better.'

She nodded. 'Are you, uh, planning to stay to teach this fall?'

'I don't know,' I said shortly. 'I haven't talked to Eleanor about it.' What a ridiculous question, I thought. I was humming with energy and confidence. What I would be doing was the furthest problem in my mind. I chewed my lip, thinking about the guns in the attic.

When I put the rifle above the fireplace away, I had not looked at the other guns carefully. Now I knew exactly what was there. The rifles and shotgun were not very practical. There were also three hand-guns. One was so heavy I could barely lift it. Just touching these weapons made my hands tremble. They were so powerful. Could I really do it? I thought about metal bursting through soft tissue. Why and how did it kill? How long did it take to die? Should I aim for the heart or the head?

There were no bullets. I would have to choose a gun and buy bullets for it. I did not know how to use a gun. I took the lightest hand-gun downstairs with me. But where would I practise? Where could I shoot a gun? I held it up and pointed it. I supposed that if I were close enough, it would not matter that I could not aim well.

'Kris, if you don't want to teach the rest of the summer, Georgine can talk to Eleanor about it.'

I looked at her. She thought that I wasn't able to teach. She thought that I was upset. 'Don't be ridiculous. Why would I want to do that?'

'Look, Kris, I'm going to tell you something that's confidential.'

I nodded impatiently.

'The Dean is going; it's not official yet. Georgine's being promoted to Assistant Dean, and will be Acting Dean until a replacement can be found.'

This was utterly unimportant to me; I could not understand why she was confiding in me this pleasant, but essentially trivial, news. 'That's nice.'

'Yes, she's sick of teaching, as you know. And, of course, it's more money. But listen, Kris, Georgine can arrange for you to take a leave from your classes. She can do almost anything now, before a Dean is appointed. You can still come back in the fall.'

'Why is the Dean leaving?' I was making conversation; I wondered when Mara would go.

'He's about to be sued for sexual harassment by five faculty.'

'Oh. Well, it's good then that he's leaving.'

Mara frowned at me. 'Kris, you are not well. This thing has hit you more than you admit.'

'Maybe that's a good thing.'

'Maybe. But you need some time to think about it.'

'I have thought about it.'

'Kris, that girl was slightly cracked. She was obsessed

with you. Georgine told me she was following you around in the halls. You can't imagine what an attractive woman like you must represent to a girl like that. It is not your fault that she went out and picked up that guy.'

'Well, she wouldn't have done it if it had not been for me.' I sighed impatiently. Why did I have to explain this to Mara? It had to be obvious to her. She had been the one to warn me about talking to the police.

'She would have found another excuse to do it. Can't you see that?'

I felt pale and brittle, with sharp patches of colour rising to my face. 'I was her excuse.' I wished now she would go. We would argue, and nothing would change my mind. 'You don't need to worry about me,' I said, as though she were a child. I thought of myself as an adult now. I did not need her charity. 'I'm sure you have enough to do with your battered women and Laotian refugees.'

'That is not a very kind thing to say.'

'Well, I'm sorry. I don't want or need your concern.'

'You make me sound like a monster. I'm not like that, like a social worker.'

'Oh, no?'

'No. I thought we were friends.'

'Sure, Mara. Of course we are,' I said. Since we weren't lovers, we were friends. It would be, of course, against her politics to dump a woman friend. Even if the friend were a murderer. 'If you want to be.'

'Why shouldn't I?'

I sighed again, annoyed. Did we have to lay it out on the table? 'I suppose that depends on where your loyalties are strongest.'

She looked at me. 'What are you talking about?'

'Mara, isn't it obvious? I fucked this girl and dumped her!

I *shit* on her.' I laughed. 'Don't you find it the least repulsive to watch one woman do that to another?'

She was silent for a moment. 'I see.'

Her face made me freeze. 'Don't tell me you didn't know.'

'Well, there was a rumour, but I thought it was exaggerated because of the murder.'

'But everything – that night we met, in that wine bar, you know, we were there together. We *sat* next to each other.'

'I guess I wasn't paying that much attention.'

'And this job? Why did you get this job for me if – '

'I didn't get that job for you. You got it. I just thought you might want it and I knew Eleanor was desperate. And anyway, I didn't know Lynette at all. She wasn't even enrolled in my course. She audited it sometimes. She tagged along that night.'

'She wasn't in your course?' I said slowly. Had I simply invented Mara's concern for Lynette?

'No. I'd seen her once or twice before. She didn't have enough credits to take it. I think she was a high-school drop-out. She had to take remedial courses.'

Well, that misunderstanding did not change anything. I said, 'Sorry, I thought you were sort of looking out after her – ' I stopped. 'But you must see now.'

'See what? That you slept with this girl and broke up with her and now you're determined to feel guilty about it?'

'Well, *yes*. Surely you must find this, well, abhorrent. Politically unacceptable.'

'Why should I? Because I'm a feminist? Look, Kris, you made a mistake. You may not have acted very well, but I suspect she didn't either. This is a terrible thing that's happened, and I can perfectly understand why you're suffering like this.

'But you must see that it will take time to come to terms with it. You mustn't start punishing yourself. I mean, if you had acted badly towards her and she were still here, you could apologize and talk about it, but she isn't. I mean, that's the whole thing. You have to live with this, to find a way to absolve yourself in some way.'

'So that I can feel better about it.'

'Oh, stop being so sorry for yourself. You weren't at the centre of that girl's life.'

'How can you be so callous? I thought you would be ethical; scrupulous, somehow.'

'I'm not callous; but I'm not a martyr either. Why do you want to set me up as some kind of model?'

'Because, for Christ's sake, Mara, you are *out*. And I'm not.'

'Out?' She stared at me. 'Kris, I'*m* not gay.'

I stared at her.

She smiled at me. 'Oh, I may look it, I suppose, but that's just because I'm not interested in men.'

I looked at her, saying nothing.

She laughed slightly. 'I guess if I lived a hundred years ago, I'd be one of those maiden ladies that taught school or painted china and lived alone or with another maiden lady in genteel poverty.' She thought about this 'Of course, if I lived a hundred years before that, I might have been burned as a witch.'

'I'm sorry I assumed that – '

. 'Oh, that's all right. I'm not offended. Occasionally, you know, somebody on campus gets it into her mind that I need to come out, or something. But, you know, I'm just not that interested in sex. I mean, with anybody. I've got my house and my job and my friends.'

'But you don't like men.'

'No. You know, for the same reasons a lot of women don't like them. It's impossible to be involved with a man without losing yourself. They take over; sex to them is a power game. It's impossible to love somebody when you are fundamentally unequal. They make more money, they put their interests first. Women want companionship; men want a housekeeper and caretaker. who needs it?'

'Yeah.'

We sat for a minute. I said, flatly, without emotion, 'How you live is – admirable. I haven't been able to live without men. Or women.'

'Oh, stop it. How can being what you simply *are* be admirable? Is being bisexual a crime?' She laughed. 'Well, it isn't any more, is it?'

I did not laugh. 'Because you don't lie. You are honest. And I have spent my entire life lying.'

'Well, if you go around feeling guilty about Lynette, it's just another lie. Kris, take some time off. Give yourself a break.'

'No. I am going to stop lying now.' I rose to let her know she could leave.

18

A week later I was standing in a place called The Atrium. An enormous white cage which reached from floor to ceiling, filled with greenery, a small waterfall, and four or five brilliantly feathered parrots, stood in the centre. Tables covered with backgammon boards extended outward from the cage, like the spokes of a wheel. I wedged myself closer to the bar and ordered a drink. I leaned against the heavy wood, holding my money. The bartender returned and handed me two drinks. It was only 6 o'clock, still happy hour. I took both drinks and weaved away from the bar to find a table.

I sipped one of my drinks, thinking about the next two or three hours of boredom. I had done this every night for the past week. Henry's Wine Bar, Maybelle's, Calloway's, Jumbalaya Joe's. I was prepared to visit every bar between Houston and the Gulf.

The Atrium's pianist was already drunk. He slurred his words. The din of the bar rose up like a cloud and echoed above me, far away. I watched the parrots, the men playing backgammon, money passing across tables, and from the waitresses to the bartenders. I wondered what it was like to be a waitress. They wore short black skirts and red tops, black high heels and red berets.

I noticed a waitress nod in my direction, but I was too tired to register the gesture. Five minutes later, a large man walked up to my table, holding two yellowish drinks, probably Screwdrivers. He wore black Levis, boots, a sky-blue cowboy shirt. He was balancing a black Stetson between his drinks. He said, 'Mind if I put these down?'

I slid my drinks over slightly.

He looked down at me gravely, with a polite nod, and said, 'I understand you're looking for me, ma'am.'

I looked at him. He sat down. 'I heard about the tragedy that happened to your little friend.'

'Tragedy?' I said idiotically.

'Your friend, ma'am. I understand she was killed.'

I stared at him and then at the Stetson. 'Yes, she was.'

'I'm sorry.'

I felt dazed and confused. I had been out every night, looking for anybody who looked familiar. Now he was here, the man with the Stetson. I suddenly felt frightened. I forgot what I had intended to do, what my plan was. This man was here, and I had to think of something to say. I felt the urge to make an excuse and run out. *Pull yourself together*, I told myself sharply. I concentrated on calling forth some charm, some electricity. I had to get this man to talk to me. But there was nothing inside me: his country-boy politeness left me cold.

'Was she a very good friend?'

'I suppose,' I said fatuously. He leaned towards me. He was tall, easily over six feet. I looked at his arms, his shoulders. He was as big as a refrigerator.

'My friend Darla over there – we've known each other since high school; she was telling me you were interested in meeting anybody who saw her that night.'

'Yes.' I had talked with the waitress when I came in. She knew of the murder. I told her that I was looking for anybody who knew Lynette, or had seen her that night at Maybelle's. I hoped to find a witness, I explained. The police seemed not to care about finding the murderer. I wanted to find out anything I could.

Now I thought, *Have I found a witness or the murderer?* Was he pretending to be a witness, an innocent witness? Had Lynette left Maybelle's with him?

'What's your name, ma'am?'

I stared at him, and without thinking said, 'Krystal.'

'Why do you want to talk to someone who saw your friend, Krystal?'

'I want to find out what happened.'

'Well, Krystal, I drove your friend home that night.' He was nearly finished with his first drink.

I swallowed, and tried to speak calmly. 'I see.' I watched him pick up his second drink with one large hand.

He said, 'Did you happen to see her that night, too?'

'Yes.'

'I thought so. I thought I'd seen you before. You were there, weren't you? At Maybelle's?'

'Yes.' Now it was out. He knew that I had seen him there. He would wonder whether I suspected him. But why had he admitted taking her home to me? I thought a moment, and said, 'Why didn't you go to the police if you saw her?'

'I drove back to Beauvue that night. I got a place out there, a couple of horses. You know. Didn't even hear about what happened till later. By the time I did, it was all over with. The only thing I'd do by telling the police would be getting them all over my backside.'

'Was she – ' I swallowed, trying to think of questions that I would ask an innocent man. 'Was she – drunk?'

'Oh, yes. Poor little thing couldn't hardly walk.'

I took a breath. 'Did you help her inside the house?'

'Sure did. Set her on her sofa there, and told her to go to sleep. No sense in making coffee in that condition. Sleep's the only cure.'

I suddenly felt very weak and frail. I wanted to go home and cry, to leave this man where he was. I was on dangerous

213

ground. It could have been him. He may have thought I saw them leave together, and knew that he could not deny it. He may have been the murderer, and was now trying to persuade me that he merely took her home. I could not push him too hard. I had to convince him that I believed his story. But I had to ask more. I said, very softly, 'What happened?'

He shrugged slightly. 'I left her on the sofa, passed out,' he said. 'I guess I should have left her at Maybelle's.' He downed his second drink. 'Get you another?'

I had not touched my drinks. but I nodded anyway, and he walked away. I thought about the gun at home. It lay on a bookshelf, hidden behind the liquor. I knew now how to shoot it, but I was suddenly afraid I would never be able to move fast enough. This man was so large he could encircle me with one arm.

Was it him? I had to know. I tried to think. If it were not, if he had just left her on the sofa, then who killed her? George had an alibi. It simply had to be this man. I exhorted myself to think of clever questions, ways to trick him into revealing himself. But my mind focused inexorably on my plan. I would get him to take me home. I would ask him to sit on the sofa while I made him a drink. I would pick up the gun, put my finger on the trigger. I would fire the second I turned around.

He came back and started talking about his horses. I tried to listen, but all I could do was watch his face move. I was deaf, looking at his lips. He was telling me about a mare about to foal, and about his house, which he had built himself. I realized that he was telling me that he would never give up all that, that he would do anything to preserve the life he had built up. He would do anything to hide the fact of this murder.

I knew I had to pretend that he was innocent. But I had to know more. I interrupted. 'Why?'

'Pardon?'

'Why – did it happen?'

'Oh, your friend. What was her name? Linda?'

'Lynette.'

'Right, Lynette. Some girls are just easy prey, I guess.' He added, 'Not like you; you're different.'

'Why – did you end up . . . taking her home?'

'Oh, she was acting silly, throwing herself around, if you know what I mean. I guess I realized she was asking for trouble. One of those self-destructive types.' He drank. 'Makes me wonder what you two were doing as friends. You're not like that at all.'

'No.'

'Look, you must be pretty sad about your friend. Do you really want me to tell you all this?'

'Yes, I want to know.'

'Well, I guess you oughta try to forget about it. It ain't going to bring her back.'

'No.'

'I'm getting hungry. Why don't we get something to eat?'

I took a deep breath. 'Yes, all right.' I felt my hands shake. 'If you like, you can come over and I'll cook us something.'

'No, no, I couldn't let you do that.' He looked at me intently.

Why had I ever thought I could play dangerous games · with a man and win? But now I had committed myself. I had to go through with it.

'All right, wherever you like.' I picked up my bag.

'Well, I know a little place down in Seagate.'

'Yes, all right. But I want to stop at my house first and change.'

'You look fine to me.'

'I have to stop at my house.'

'Sure, Krystal, we got plenty of time.'

He was in a white pick-up. Lynette's neighbour had seen white pick-up. I climbed in. An old tape-deck was bolted under the dash. He pushed in the tape. It was labelled *Women*. Bonnie Raitt began to sing, '*If you don't put yourself above me you can love me like a man.*'

I suddenly thought of Dewitt, of lowering myself on to him, of my terrible need at that moment to feel him touch my face and kiss the place on my neck that joins my shoulder. A picture of my bed in New Mexico came into. my mind with immediacy, and I saw myself straddling his thin body. How ugly sex was.

We pulled into University Place and I pointed out my house. He stopped in front and put the brake on. He did not turn off the engine. 'You don't seem too well, Krystal.'

'I'll be all right.'

'Maybe we should do this another time.'

'No, this is okay. Tonight's okay.'

'Look, is something wrong? I mean, is it all this talk about your friend that's made you feel kinda down?'

I stared at him. I tried to sound enticing. 'Why don't you come in?'

'Well, that's very kind of you, but I really think I ought to just call you some time.'

'You mean we could just forget about this.'

'That's not what I meant. I just think – ' He stopped. 'Krystal, do you mind if I ask you a personal question?'

'Why not?'

'You're not thinking that I – that I, you know, went to bed with your friend?'

I closed my eyes and then opened them. 'What?'

'I wouldn't want you to think that I go around picking up girls.'

I looked at him.

'You're a real nice lady, and I hope you don't feel that I

was trying anything funny with your friend. I'm not that kind of guy. Fact is, I wasn't interested in her at all, if you know what I mean. Poor kid, I don't go for girls with no self-respect.'

No, I thought, *you kill them instead.*

'I mean, I'd never want a real girlfriend like that.' *I'd never hurt a girl like you, Krystal.*

I suddenly felt nauseous. I knew I did not have the strength to go through with this, to pick up the gun, to point it and pull the trigger. 'A real girlfriend?'

'Yeah, you know, a girl who stood up to me.' *Who did not provoke me.*

My mouth suddenly felt dry and hot; I could barely speak. 'A girl who didn't ask for it?'

'What do you mean, ask for it?'

I had to get him inside the house, but I could not move. Everything was wrong; my plans were going awry.

'Why don't you come inside?'

He looked at me with some irritation. 'What do you mean, ask for it?'

I groped for the door handle and held on to the cold metal. I pushed it and the door clicked. It was open. 'Ask to be – hurt.'

'Krystal, what are you talking about?'

'You don't hurt – strong women.'

'Look, what is this?'

'When you went in, she must have seemed – vulnerable.'

'What do you mean? She was passed out.'

My face was so stiff, it felt as if it would crack. 'You didn't – ' I stopped. I remembered that she had been hit on the back of her heard and found on the floor in front of the television. 'Did she pass out as soon as you walked in the house?'

He looked at me with a curious, puzzled smile. 'Krystal, that girl couldn't walk. I *carried* her in.'

'You put her on the sofa?'

'Yeah.' He was wary now.' That's what I said. Hey, look, what's this about?'

'You didn't – when you left, she was – ' I was leaning against the door, the handle against my ribs. I held the word inside me for a few seconds. 'Alive?'

He looked at me for a full minute without speaking. I stared back at him. Then he turned angry, like men are supposed to: insulted, arrogant, contemptuous. His face changed colour; his eyes became small, and pointed and violent.

'You think I killed your friend?' He reached over and I drew back. 'What is this? Are you fucking crazy?' He reached past me and pushed the door open. I got out.

19

I watched the white pick-up drive off. Then I took out my keys. The sun was going down. I went inside, dropped my bag, poured myself a gin and tonic and put on a tape.

I went into the bedroom and changed into jeans. Then I took my drink into the bathroom. What was I doing? I had wanted to kill this man, a man who had not murdered Lynette. Would I have gone through with it? Would I have called the police afterwards and said, *I have murdered a man; please come*? Was I so stupid never to have thought about the aftermath of killing somebody? I pulled my hair back with a band and took off my make-up. Even in the harsh light, I looked young without make-up. I thought, *I am only twenty-nine*. Twenty-nine was not old.

I returned to the living room, sat down on the sofa, drank my gin and smoked a cigarette. What was I going to do now? I had gone through some kind of crisis, but what was on the other side? I could not think. I had to do something quiet and mindless. I got up and walked around. Finally, I decided to do some laundry.

· I went into the bedroom and sorted clothes. I filled the basket and walked out, locking the door. I walked down the concrete path towards the laundry room. It was dark now, and slightly cooler, although still humid.

The laundry room was unlocked, and I went in. As I put my basket down on a washing machine, a young man in shorts and an open shirt walked in. I nodded and said, 'hello.'

I put the clothes in the machine and added detergent. I

felt the boy looking at me, and although I was uncomfortable, I was too tired to listen to my female sixth sense, that instinct women develop for danger.

I put coins into the machine and turned it on. I looked up; he smile at me. I smiled back. 'See you later.' I walked out with my basket.

I opened my front door and went in. I made myself another gin and tonic. I opened the newspaper to see what was on television. I needed to watch something brainless to blot out the next two hours. Afterwards, I would get up and go to bed without having to think any more this day.

Fifteen minutes later, I heard a noise at the door. I opened it, and the boy from the laundry room was standing in front of me. 'Hi,' I said, surprised.

'Hi.' He stood, smiling. He was slight, blond. I wondered whether something had gone wrong with the machine. He said, 'Do you live here?'

'Yeah,' I said, without thinking.

'I saw you once.'

'Oh, really?' I was beginning to wonder what he wanted.

'Yeah, it was at Maybelle's.'

My mind cleared. Two things occurred to me in quick succession. The first was that when I had walked into the laundry room, it had been quiet. There were no machines going. And he was not carrying any laundry. Then I remembered him. He had been talking to Lynette before the man with the black Stetson. I remembered him walking angrily away, and Lynette, laughing a little, turning back to the bar to order another drink. Of course, I thought: the witness's conflicting descriptions. She had left with the man in the black Stetson. He had taken her home. This boy must have followed them. He must have waited until the white pickup had left. Then he had gone in. I was looking at the man who murdered Lynette.

All of this clustered and formed in my mind like the smell of fear, like the rustling of bushes on a dark street, like the telepathic moment between two opponents, when both know who has the edge, who will win; the minute space of time before the strong one goes in for the kill. I knew I had to be extremely careful not to think these thoughts, not to feel fear. I had to stay very calm, very relaxed, very unthreatening. I knew this. I forced my mind into blankness. I pretended I was in a science fiction movie, and I had to keep this alien from reading my thoughts.

'Oh, yeah,' I said amiably, my eyes opening with feigned interest. 'That's a pretty good place.' Had I fooled him?

'You don't dance.' It was a statement; he had seen me.

'No, I guess I never learned.' I felt my accent getting stronger.

'Your friend does. The blonde.'

'Oh, yeah, she's a good dancer. I guess I'm just too shy.' Did he believe me? 'Can you dance?'

'Na.'

'Have you ever tried?' I felt desperation creep into my voice.

'Na.'

'You'd probably be really good.'

'Na.'

'Yeah, sure. All you need is an good teacher.'

'Would you teach me?' A dare.

'Well, I would if I could.' I tried to laugh. 'You'd probably be better than me.' I was sure now the game was up; I would have to try to slam the door. I wanted to look down to see if his foot had crossed the threshold, but I knew not to take my eyes off his face.

'I saw you another time.'

I felt a spasm of fear. 'Oh, really?'

'Tonight. At The Atrium.'

'Oh.'

'That guy brought you home.'

'Yes.' I was nearly whispering.

'Is he your boyfriend?'

'No.' I added quickly, 'I'm – not his type.'

'Maybe we could go out some time.' Another dare, but softened a little.

I tried to put on a different smile. I was very frightened. I had had no practice at this game, putting myself below a man. I had never done this. I had never had to. 'Oh, I'd really like that.'

'I could pick you up.'

'Okay.' I was nearly certain it was all right now, but I was still afraid. 'When?'

'How about tomorrow?'

'Great. That'll give me time to wash my hair.' I tried very hard to look at him and smile gratefully. A few seconds passed, and I knew he was about to invite himself in. I suddenly pictured Lynette getting up from the sofa in a drunken haze to answer the door. I exclaimed, 'Oh! My laundry. Are you walking back to the laundry room? Will you walk with me? I'll just go get my keys.'

I turned my back to him. My keys lay on the hall table with the laundry basket: only two steps away, but those two steps were probably the longest I have ever taken. The relief I felt when I turned around and saw him still outside the door were enough to make me weep. If only I could get him outside, I told myself, I would be all right.

We walked out and down the path. I thought of and dismissed questions – about his job, where he lived – anything that might make him feel defensive. Then he said, 'You come from around here?'

'Yeah. I grew up down the street.' Lies came to my mind,

fruitful and multiplying. 'Sometimes I think about moving into the city. You ever think about that?'

'Na. I live in Harmony, on a boat. Always have.'

'Oh, we – my sister and I – used to go down to Harmony and look at the boats when we were kids.'

'Well, it ain't much, but I like it all right.' He looked at me. 'You ever been to college?'

'Oh, no. My sister went, but I was never good enough at school to go. Anyway, she always made me feel really stupid.'

He looked at me intently. 'Yeah, I know what you mean.'

We reached the laundry room and I began to pray to anything, anyone who might help me. *Please, please, make him go away.* I remembered once being in our back yard when I was about seven or eight and a copperhead slithered right past my foot. *Please, please, make it go away.*

'It was nice meeting you,' I said, turning to him at the door to the laundry room. His face glowered slightly at this. 'What time should we go?' I added quickly. 'How about seven?'

He said, 'What's your name?'

'Krystal.'

'You mind if I kiss you, Krystal?'

It took all my willpower to control myself. I felt shivers of revulsion run down my face and arms. I felt nearly nauseated. I imagined Jewish women raped by Nazis, black women by their white employers, girls by fathers. I knew this was a test and I had to pass it. I lowered my eyelashes coyly and said, 'If you would like to.'

He bent towards me and planted his open, wet mouth on mine. When he removed it, I fluttered my eyes at him coquettishly and resisted the urge to wipe his saliva off my face.

I turned towards the laundry room and said, sweetly, 'See you later.'

I walked in and slowly removed my wash from the machine. I felt him behind me, not moving. *Please, please, go away.* I turned around with my wet laundry and he was gone. I took the basket over to the drier and slowly, deliberately, placed every item in it. I closed the door and turned it on. Then I walked out of the room into the misty night. The path was empty.

I walked back, listening for movement in the grass, behind the crescent-shaped hedge. I knew if I ran he would be there, to grab me, drag me to my house, rape me, strangle me, kill me. I walked slowly up my front walk and turned around as I unlocked my door. Nobody was there.

I opened my door. Nobody was there. I locked the door and walked into every room. Nobody, nobody. I went into the bathroom and washed my face and hands and then brushed my teeth. I dried myself with a towel, and then sat down on the toilet and cried.

When I finished crying, I got up and dialled Georgine's number.

'Hi, there, honey,' said Georgine's wonderful, predictable voice.

'Georgine,' I said, and started crying again.

'Kris, what's the matter?'

'Georgine – ' I began again, and again broke into sobs.

'You stay right there. I'll be over in two shakes.' She hung up.

I sat on the sofa, frozen, watching the telephone, the door, I got the gun from behind the liquor and held it between my knees, barrel pointing outwards. Georgine would come and I would be all right. I would not be alone.

Georgine insisted that we call the police. She picked up the phone, saying, 'Honey, are you crazy? That man killed that girl and he almost killed you.'

'Georgine. What are you going to say? That he came over and asked me out on a date and that I just happen to have the feeling that he's the one?'

'He as good as told you he did it. He said he was there. You saw him. He's a psycho.' She moved the receiver to her mouth. 'This is Dr Georgine Brightman. I want a patrol car out here right now. Yes, it's an emergency. What do you think *right now* means?' She gave my address.

'And don't you send some rookie,' she added. 'There is some crazy man going around threatening women and he was just here scaring the daylights out of my friend, and we have good reason to believe that he was involved with the death of a woman we know. He just left here.'

She listened briefly and hung up.

We left my apartment at 1 in the morning. The two policemen agreed that I should sleep elsewhere and walked us to Georgine's house. Georgine and I stayed up another hour, waiting for the call the police had promised us to tell us that he had been picked up. They did not call, and we finally decided to go to bed. Georgine lent me a nightgown and we slept together in her double bed, each curled up, back to back.

He was picked up the next day. The police told us that he was suspected of killing two other women besides Lynette. His *modus operandi* was to approach a woman in a bar. He chose confident outgoing women. If she snubbed him, he followed her home and murdered her. He did not murder women who did not reject him, who were kind to him. He admitted all this.

This was why he did not kill me: I had not rejected him. My instincts had saved me. He had killed Lynette because she had acted superior to him. He had killed her because she had been trying to act like me.

20

I moved out of the University Place house and into Alicia's until I could find an apartment of my own. The night I arrived with my bags, we picked up boxes of Chinese food, a six-pack and two videos.

Between *Bringing Up Baby* and *Arsenic and Old Lace*, I said, without looking at Alicia, 'You know, Alicia, I've never thanked you for, you know, being here, staying in touch.'

She was rewinding the videotape. 'Yeah, it's okay. Anyway, you're the one who's stayed in touch.' She pointed to the postcards.

I knew I could leave it at that. But I said, 'I mean, you mean a lot to me.'

'Yeah, I know, Krystal.'

'I hope we'll' – I scraped the last of the chicken-fried rice on to my plate – 'see each other more now.'

'Well, it would be nice. You know, we don't really have anybody else.'

'Yeah,' I said. 'I know.'

After *Arsenic and Old Lace*, we opened a bottle of port and · emptied our ashtrays. I was drunk, but I didn't want to go to bed.

'Shit, I wish we had another video,' Alicia said, picking up a *Cosmo* and throwing me a *Vogue*.

We did not tell Mother. 'Look, Krystal, Mother's probably figured out you aren't completely straight. I mean, God, Krys, did you really think it wasn't obvious?' I blushed slightly at this. Alicia went on, 'But she's not going to like having it shoved in her face. And, I mean, you can't just say that this guy almost murdered you without telling her about Linda.'

'Yeah, you're right.' I felt relief; it would have been a mistake. I would have expected too much from Mother by telling her.

I would not get what I wanted from Mother, but I could find it elsewhere. I would learn to love: my sister, Georgine, Mara. Georgine was going to marry Jack; she would need good friends like me, like Mara. Washington State had come back; we had gone out for a drink. I had friends; I would eventually have a lover. I wondered, would it be a man or a woman?

This was my life now: not a single-minded path, but a life of people, complications, a tangle of commitments. Eleanor had offered me a job, probably as a result of a memo from Georgine, who was now Acting Dean. I would do a Ph.D at the main campus in town, which had better facilities, and commute to Clearview to teach. The Ph.D would take three or four years. I would find an apartment near my sister. I would try to be friends with my mother. Eventually I might be able to move to the ivy-covered private college of my fantasy.

I had draped my life with the trappings of culture and good taste, and then wanted to punish myself for being a shallow woman of no substance. But, of course, there was nothing wrong with caring about aesthetics, with liking the old and enduring. That in itself had not been my mistake. Desires and tastes are always exclusive; you always like one thing in preference to another.

That is the terrible thing about love: it excludes others; it says that one person is more important than the others. And yet, I could do this, I could love, I could say that I now loved Alicia, because I could also say that I would try not to hurt anybody else. This was what I could have done for Lynette: I could not have loved her, but I could have decided not to hurt her.

I did not have to love women collectively. I did not have to cut my hair and throw out my clothes. I did not have to love women I hated, like Charlene. But I could decide not to hurt them. And to throw away opportunities simply because somebody else did not have them, to avoid putting myself above other women, was a kind of suicide. I had talents, I needed to strive. I would also remember that luck plays a big part in success.

I had wanted my life to be simple; it would not be. Life was full of ambiguities; I had to believe in myself and yet acknowledge the help of friends, of my sister, of other women; I loved women and yet I would still apply rigorous standards to them.

Now my life would be full of pain. I had been afraid of the awful pain of loving. It was easier to be married to a man I did not love, easier to sleep with girls for fun. It is hard to live with the love of women. There is a constant fear of loss, because the only thing that holds you together is love.

I could now live on the edge, without stability, predictability, pretence. Marriage lulled me into a sense of safety, a feeling that things last for ever. Now death would be at ·every corner.

I sat in Alicia's apartment, surrounded by the hundreds of objects she had collected – the remnants of her past; I had cast mine off. I would be moving into an empty apartment soon with two suitcases and a tape-player. I had nothing. But I could still re-create things: I could sew curtains, buy books, study, write papers. I could start again. Here was life, and Alicia, solid and alive.

Alicia flipped the pages of her magazine. Then she looked

up and saw me scanning the room. She said, 'God, I have so much junk; it depresses me. It's all I've got to show for myself.'

'Let me have the stuff you don't want,' I replied. 'I'm going to need it.'